HOT LEAD!

Lance heard the bullet thud into the tie rail at his rear. His hand stabbed toward the holster, came up in a swift, eye-defying arc. Lead started to pour from the six-shooter muzzle the instant it left the holster. A leaden slug threw up dust at Kilby's feet. Lance's aim lifted higher. Kilby fired again. Lance thumbed his hammer once, twice, three times.

Kilby was flung violently sideways by the impact of the heavy slugs. For a brief moment he swayed uncertainly; then his right leg buckled, and he pitched to the roadway. For a short interval he struggled to regain the weapon that had fallen from his hand, then, as Lance closed in and kicked the underarm gun out of reach, Kilby shivered and slumped in the dust.

Behind him came Chiricahua Herrick's voice, violent with hate. "Damn you, Tolliver! You can't do this to a friend of mine. Now, by God! We'll see how you like the taste of hot lead!"

THE BATTLE AT THREE-CROSS

THREE-CROSS

William Colt MacDonald

LEISURE BOOKS NEW YORK CITY

A LEISURE BOOK®

June 2008

Published by special arrangement with Golden West Literary Agency.

Dorchester Publishing Co., Inc.
200 Madison Avenue
New York, NY 10016

ISBN 10: 0-8439-6100-7
ISBN 13: 978-0-8439-6100-3

Printed in the United States of America.

10 9 8 7 6 5 4 3 2 1

Visit us on the web at www.dorchesterpub.com.

THE BATTLE AT THREE-CROSS

I
Two-Handed Mystery

There were several things about the dead man that interested Tolliver, but mostly it was the cold, stiffened hands that drew his greatest concentration of attention. The right hand, even to the fingernails, had been painted a brownish black as far as the wrist. The left was clutched tightly—almost fiercely, as though determined to retain the object at all costs—around an article of desert plant life known in parts of the Southwest as the "mezcal button." No doubt about its being a mezcal button; Tolliver could see the thick, carrot-like root with bits of sandy earth still clinging to it protruding from the firmly clenched dead hand. Even a bit of the bluish-green flattened top was visible between the thumb and forefinger.

Tolliver had been in the saddle from early morning, having crossed the Mexican border to return to the States about two o'clock that afternoon. He was a lean, rangy man with good features and gray eyes. A dusty sombrero that had once been fawn colored covered his unruly reddish hair. His denim overalls were clean, though somewhat faded, with wide cuffs just above the ankles of his high-heeled cowman boots. His woolen shirt fitted smoothly across wide shoulders, and there was a blue bandanna knotted at his throat. A Colt forty-five gun was slung at Tolliver's right hip. He wasn't more than twenty-seven or -eight.

After crossing the border that afternoon Tolliver had headed his roan pony in the direction of Pozo Verde which wasn't more than six or eight miles from the Mexican line. He was still some three miles or so distant from the town, riding along an ancient, rock-littered, sandy dry wash, when he had come upon the body of the dead man, sprawled on its left side, the left arm cramped beneath the body, one leg slightly drawn up. Tolliver had immediately checked his horse, dismounted a short distance away and approached the still form to make a closer survey.

There was an ugly black hole just beneath the dead man's right cheekbone. Dried blood streaked the man's face and had run up into the iron-gray hair. There was no sign of his hat about. Flies buzzed in the afternoon heat. Overhead a buzzard wheeled in a wide circle, dropping lower, then at a movement from Tolliver again lifted toward the higher reaches of the cloudless sky. Tolliver's normally firm lips tightened still more as he studied intently the features of the corpse. After a moment he drew a clean bandanna from a pocket and spread it over the dead face.

Stooping carefully close to the dead man, Tolliver pried open the rigid fingers of the left hand. It was considerable of a job getting possession of the mezcal button, so tightly were the cold fingers clenched about the spongy top of the plant, but Tolliver finally straightened up with the mezcal button in his hand. Root and all, it wasn't more than four inches long. The top of the plant was circular, about an inch thick and two inches across, with tiny lines, or indentations, running from the top center to the earth line at the sides. Spaced at regular intervals on the segments formed by these lines were tiny woollike tufts. A pinkish cast shoved through the bluish-green surface of the plant.

Tolliver frowned as he studied the object in his hand, looked again at the dead man before thrusting the mezcal button inside his shirt. "Hmmm!" he muttered. "I wonder what *he* was doing with dry whisky." There didn't seem to be any immediate reply to that question. The dead man's six-shooter was still in its holster Tolliver noticed next. That made the business look like murder.

There were two buzzards soaring overhead by this time, their wheeling, dipping gyrations forming black patterns against the turquoise sky. To the west rose the high, serrated peaks of the Saddlestring Mountains, their ravines and hollows etched clearly in brilliant desert light. Here in the dry wash the way was littered with boulders of all sizes and shapes. The near-by slopes were covered with brush at some spots, sandy, gravelly soil at others. Here and there among the brush were clumps of cholla and prickly pear. A few yuccas with the stalks of last spring's blossoms showing brown and dry dotted the landscape.

Tolliver spoke his thoughts half aloud: "I'd judge he was killed last night sometime. Now, I wonder . . ."

Without waiting to complete the words, Tolliver stepped back from the corpse and commenced to circle around, scrutinizing closely the earth as he moved. There were prints to be seen in the sandy bed of the dry wash, prints showing that three riders had arrived at this spot—at least there were the prints of three horses. The sandy soil was too loose to leave definite impressions though to a keen, understanding eye like Tolliver's certain details were clear. Back at the body again, Tolliver found blurry footprints.

"They came out here," Tolliver muttered, "from the direction of Pozo Verde. When they left they returned the same way. One horse left considerably later than the others, though. Why?"

He knelt near the corpse, closely studying the dead man's form—woolen shirt, denim overalls, boots and spurs. His gaze returned to that black-painted hand again and again. He stooped close and sniffed the atmosphere in the vicinity of the hand. After a time he went back to the high-heeled boots once more. Several minutes slipped past with Tolliver lost in deep concentration.

So intense were his meditative speculations that the riders were almost upon him before he realized it. Then as his ear caught the thudding of running hoofs and creaking of saddle leather Tolliver straightened up to await the arrival of whoever was coming. A big gray horse with a rider wearing a law officer's star was first to pull to a halt on the edge of the dry wash. Then, in quick succession, five other riders drew alongside the rider with the sheriff's star. A look of surprise swept across six faces as they glanced down into the wash and saw Tolliver and the dead man. Almost immediately the six faces went hard. Certain hands moved toward guns. No one spoke for a moment.

Tolliver broke the silence. "Mister Sheriff, it looks like you'd arrived at a good time."

The big man with the sheriff's star grunted, "Maybe I didn't arrive soon enough." He was middle aged, grizzled, sharp eyed, with a close-cropped gray mustache. He pushed back the big black sombrero from his forehead and repeated meaningly, "Maybe I didn't arrive soon enough. That man dead?"

"That's my opinion," Tolliver said easily. "Maybe you'd better examine him yourself."

"Exactly what I'm aimin' to do," the sheriff said, tight lipped.

The other men were talking now, all offering advice to the sheriff. He spoke sharply over one shoulder without removing his eyes from Tolliver and told them to shut up.

Tolliver said, "If you and your riders are coming down into this wash it might be a good idea to come on foot and move careful. You wouldn't want to mess up the sign."

"That's good advice"—the sheriff nodded—"though I don't know as I need it."

He and the others dismounted and started down into the wash.

A new voice broke in. "I don't reckon we're going to waste time looking for sign. I guess we've got our man."

The sheriff nodded. "You might be right, Chiricahua."

Tolliver didn't say anything, though he didn't like the manner in which things were shaping up. He glanced at the man named Chiricahua and saw a well-built individual with a swarthy, hawk-like face and beady eyes. A beaded hatband encircled Chiricahua's flat-topped sombrero, and he wore tight Oregon breeches. His lips were thin and cruel. A braided horsehair quirt dangled from his left wrist. The six-shooter at his hip looked as though it had received plenty of use. The remaining men, all dressed in cowboy togs, were an unprepossessing lot. All were armed.

Tolliver stepped back as the men approached to gather about the still form on the rock-littered floor of the wash. The sheriff lifted the bandanna from the face of the corpse, then after a moment replaced it and moved back. He seemed to be the only one of the group with sense enough to step carefully so as not to disturb any "sign" that might be present and voiced a warning to the others to walk prudently. "Mind what I'm telling you," he added.

"Cripes!" one of the men said. "This wash is too sandy to leave much sign anyway. See?" He scuffed one booted toe across the loose, sandy soil. "Sheriff, this won't hardly hold any sign. Hell! There ain't no use trying to read tracks——"

"I'm the best judge of that," the peace officer said shortly.

Tolliver put in, "Sheriff, your man has already messed up some sign. Suppose I tell you what I've found out . . ."

"What you already made up, you mean," sneered the man who had scraped his foot through the sand. "It don't go down, feller. I reckon we don't need to search any farther for the killer."

Tolliver ignored the man and continued to the sheriff, "I figure the killing occurred sometime last night. Three horses came out from the direction of Pozo Verde; three returned that way. There were some boot prints around the body, but nothing much could be made of 'em. However——"

"Exactly the point I'm making," said the man who had messed up the boot prints. "Sheriff, we've got our man. The two of 'em probably had a fight, and this hombre gunned him out. . . ."

"Kilby," the sheriff interrupted sarcastically, "I've made to run Sartoris County a long spell now without any help from you. When I need any assistance or advice I'll let you know."

The man named Kilby reddened and fell silent.

"Hey," Chiricahua discovered, "look at Bowman's hand. It's painted black!"

The sheriff grunted. "I already noted that. Don't understand it no more than you do." He wheeled abruptly on Tolliver. "I figure you'll explain it."

Tolliver shook his head. "I don't know any more about that painted hand of Bowman's—if that's the dead man's name—than you do."

"If I'm convinced I ain't saying so," the sheriff snapped. "You might be speaking truth; again, you might not. Speaking of names, what's yours?" He came a step nearer Tolliver.

"Tolliver—Lance Tolliver."

"So?" the sheriff jerked out. His eyes hardened a trifle. "I suppose Lance stands for Lancelot."

There was some laughter from the other men. Tolliver's tanned features flushed a trifle. "You're supposing correct," he said quietly.

"Cowman, I take it," the sheriff snapped.

"You're right again."

The law officer said dryly, "I usually am. Where you heading for?"

"Pozo Verde."

"Why?"

"Figured to get a job with some cow outfit."

The sheriff smiled thinly. "I reckon you might as well postpone that for a spell. What did you kill Frank Bowman for?"

"Now, look here, Sheriff," Tolliver exclaimed, "if you think I had anything to do with this killing you're mistaken——"

"What say we string the coyote up?" Kilby interrupted.

The sheriff nodded. "Maybe that's a suggestion, but it will have to be done legal. Kilby, I told you once to keep out of my affairs. If you want to be useful you might remove this Tolliver's—if that's his name—belt and gun."

Kilby jerked his own six-shooter and approached Tolliver. "Stick 'em high, hombre," he growled. "I'm relieving you of your hardware."

There was no use resisting. Fighting down the indignant words that rose to his lips, Tolliver remained silent. He didn't put his arms in the air, merely held them well out from his sides, while Kilby unbuckled his cartridge belt, then, at the sheriff's order, buckled it again and hung it over the sheriff's shoulder.

The sheriff's eyes were boring into Tolliver's. "Where you been all day?" the sheriff demanded.

"On the trail, heading for Pozo Verde," Tolliver replied. "If you want the whole story, I've been down in Mexico and——"

"What were you doing in Mexico?" the sheriff snapped.

"Just riding around, looking at country I've never seen before."

"Humph!" The sheriff's short grunt sounded skeptical. "I'd bet dollars to doughnuts you won't be able to prove that."

The sheriff's manner was commencing to get under Tolliver's skin. "Maybe I'll do more than that when the right time comes," he asserted coldly.

"Hah!" the sheriff jerked out. "Tough hombre, eh? I reckon we'll have to take that out of you."

"You'll live to regret it if you try to take anything out of me," Lance Tolliver said, steady voiced. "I've told you my business, given you my name. That's more than you've done."

The sheriff laughed sarcastically. "Asking for an introduction, are you? Well, Mister Tough Hombre, if you must know, I'm Ethan Lockwood, Sheriff of Sartoris County. These fellers with me are known as Chiricahua Herrick, George Kilby, Bert Ridge, Larry Johnson and Luke Ordway. Don't expect 'em to shake hands with you. They don't like murderers——"

"I tell you I didn't kill Bowman——" Tolliver protested.

"Don't lie to me," Lockwood said savagely. "I want the truth. What was the idea? Did Bowman have some money you wanted? Come across. What was the quarrel between you two?"

"Hey, Sheriff," Kilby suggested, "supposin' I search him?"

"I'll 'tend to that myself, later." Lockwood scowled. "And I'll do all the talking, too, so keep shut. One way or t'other we're going to make this Lance Tolliver tell why he killed Frank Bowman. C'mon, feller—speak up!"

Lance smiled coldly. "I thought you were going to do *all* the talking, Sheriff."

Lockwood's features crimsoned. "Now don't get too smart for your own good, Tolliver," he advised ominously.

"A six-gun barrel bent over his conk," Chiricahua

Herrick growled, "might act as a primer on his talk. What say, Sheriff?"

Lockwood shook his head. "If there's to be any gun whuppings handed out, I'll do it myself. I just reckon we'll take this murderin' sidewinder into my jail and prefer the usual charges——"

"You're not arresting me," Lance snapped.

"Suit yourself," Lockwood said coldly. "Put up a fight if you like and see what happens to you. Maybe that would be best. I always like to save my taxpayers the cost of a trial when it can be done. Now, are you coming gentle or aren't you?"

Lance showed pale under his tan. His gaze shifted quickly about the half-ring of men confronting him. Three of them already had their hands on gun butts. The sheriff eyed him sardonically.

Lance relaxed. "All right, I'll come without a fuss," he said quietly, "but I'm protesting this arrest——"

"Protest, and be damned to you," Lockwood sneered. "There ain't been a killing in my county in six months, and I don't aim to have any murderer escape me now. You'll learn I have a rep for bringing criminals to justice and——"

Lance Tolliver interrupted, "If we're headed for your billy-be-blasted jail, let's go. I'm not honing to stand here and listen to a tinhorn political speech any longer than possible."

"Still feeling hard, eh?" Lockwood snorted. "Once I get you in Pozo Verde you'll get over that. That roan gelding over there yours?"

"That's my horse." Tolliver nodded.

"Get on it and don't give me any of your lip," Lockwood commanded. "Chiricahua, get a piggin' string and tie his hands to the saddle horn. You,

Ordway, you stay here with the body until the coroner can come out and view it. I'll tell Doc Drummond as soon as we hit town. And don't touch that body—not none. I want it left just the way it is until Doc gets here."

Tolliver was roped into his saddle, then his pony was led up out of the wash.

With Sheriff Lockwood on one side and Chiricahua Herrick on the other, the start was made for Pozo Verde, Tolliver riding between the two. Kilby, Ridge and Johnson fell in at the rear, leaving the man named Ordway to stay with the dead body until the arrival of the coroner. Kilby filled the time with a loud mouthing of threats regarding what was to happen to Tolliver until even the sheriff could stand it no longer. In no gentle voice he ordered Kilby to "pronto quit that runnin' off at the head before somebody slaps down your ears." Kilby flushed and kept quiet from then on.

Tolliver remained silent during the ride to Pozo Verde though his mind was rife with speculation. Chiricahua Herrick on a couple of occasions insisted on Tolliver making a statement regarding his reasons for killing Bowman, but the prisoner just smiled coldly without answering.

"Lay off, Chiricahua," Lockwood said finally. "Once I've got this hombre in a cell I'll get the truth or know the reason why. You just leave it to me."

By this time the sun was picking out crimson high lights on the distant peaks of the Saddlestring Mountains and the air had commenced to cool a trifle. Before long the riders reached a wagon-rutted trail running across the campo and ten minutes later, topping a low ridge of ground, they spied the roofs of Pozo Verde. Following the trail, they soon commenced to see blocky adobe houses on either side. The houses became more numerous. The smoke from mesquite fires was drifting lazily in the air, and here and there lights shone from windows.

Tolliver saw, when they reached it, that Pozo Verde was quite a sizable town. A double row of hitch racks before which stood a scattering of ponies and wagons stretched the length of Main Street, along which the riders were guiding their ponies. Yellow squares of light from store windows made rectangular patches on the dusty roadway; already it was too dark for passing pedestrians to notice that Tolliver was tied to his saddle. On either side were buildings with high false fronts. There were saloons, restaurants, a savings bank and a two-story brick hotel.

They had already crossed two intersections—Las Vegas Street and Laredo Street—and were approaching a third—Yuma Street. At the southwest corner of Yuma and Main stood a long, low building of rock and adobe construction before which swung a board sign bearing the words: "Sheriff's Office & County Jail." There was no light in the office.

"Dang it," Lockwood grunted, "I suppose that deputy of mine has gone to his supper already." He signaled the horses to a stop before the hitch rail. "Untie this gent, Chiricahua. He's arrived at his steel-barred apartment."

Chiricahua untied the rope that bound Tolliver's wrists, then whipped out his gun. "Get down off'n that horse, hombre, and move right cautious. I'll plug you if you try a getaway!"

Lance slid down from his saddle. "How about taking care of my horse?" he commenced. "He's covered a lot of——"

Kilby sneered. "You ain't goin' to have no more need of a horse——"

"Shut up, Kilby," Lockwood growled. "I'll see your horse is watered and fed, Tolliver. Now you get on there!"

The door to the sheriff's office was open. Lance "got on there," with the barrel of Chiricahua's gun boring into his backbone.

II
Evidence

There wasn't any light in the cell. Lance heard the steel-barred door swing behind him, then the retreating steps down the corridor between the double row of cells. Kilby was talking again, saying something about hoping he'd have a chance to have a hand on the rope when they hung Tolliver. The door to the sheriff's office slammed shut. A moment later the door to the street closed loudly. The voices died away, leaving Lance to his own thoughts.

He fumbled around in the darkness, found a wooden bunk in which was a burlap sack filled with straw and sat down to roll a cigarette. He could thank heaven they hadn't searched him nor taken away his tobacco and matches anyway. He struck a match, dragged deeply on the brown-paper cigarette, then held the match up and glanced around. The cell had one barred window in its outer wall. Lance saw that much and little more before the match flickered out.

"This," he told himself, "is a hell of a note."

Not that he was unduly worried about the situation. His mind dwelled more on the dead man he had found that afternoon. And there was that black-painted hand. And the mezcal button. The plant still reposed inside Lance's shirt.

"There's something damnably queer about the whole setup," he muttered.

His cigarette had burned nearly to the end when he heard footsteps entering the office from the street. It suddenly occurred to Lance this was the first sound he'd heard since the sheriff and the other men had departed. It must be that all the other cells in the jail were empty. The door between the sheriff's office and the jail opened now. Light shone along the corridor between cells, and a long shadow appeared on the floor.

Lance caught the gleam of the deputy sheriff's badge first, then he saw its wearer standing before the cell door holding in one hand an oil lamp and in the other a platter of food. The food was placed on the floor while the cell door was unlocked. Picking up the platter, the deputy kicked open the door and stepped inside. He handed the platter to Lance, set the lamp on the floor and turned back toward the corridor with the explanation that he had to go back for the coffee.

Lance considered the matter while the deputy was gone. The man hadn't bothered to close the cell door. Careless or—something else? Prisoners had been known to be allowed to escape just so they could be shot down when they emerged into the open. Lance decided not to take any chances.

The deputy reappeared in a few moments bearing a pail of steaming coffee. Lance felt better as he commenced to eat the potatoes and roast beef and biscuits on the platter. Apparently the deputy hadn't intended him to escape.

"I understand your name is Tolliver," the deputy said. "I'm Oscar Perkins."

"Glad to know you," Tolliver said gravely. "This chow is sure welcome."

"I figured it might be." Perkins nodded.

There was something comical about the man. He had large, bony wrists that hung well below his shirt sleeves. His black sombrero's brim was sadly tattered along one side. The skinny legs in corduroy trousers appeared to be badly warped. He had sleepy, indolent eyes, and a mild manner of speech. Looking at Oscar Perkins Lance Tolliver was reminded of nothing so much as a tall, skinny, blond scarecrow. Even the gun belt at the deputy's hips looked as though it might slip down around his knees at any instant.

Perkins produced a small paper sack from a hip pocket. "Would you like a lemon drop?"

"A what?" After the day's experiences, Lance could scarcely believe his ears. It sounded too mild to be true.

"A lemon drop." Perkins thrust the bag toward Tolliver.

"Not right now, thanks. I'll finish my supper first."

"Uh-huh. Lemon drops is right good for indigestion." Perkins seated himself across the cell with his back resting against the wall. He shoved a couple of lemon drops into his mouth and made loud sucking noises while he watched Tolliver eat. "Fact is," he added after a time, "lemon drops is good for nigh any ailment. They offset the acidity in one's stomach."

Tolliver gulped. "Did I hear you right?" he ventured.

"Reckon you did. Anyway, that's what a sawbones

in Kansas City told me one time. I always remembered just how he said it. Sounds genteel like, don't it?"

Lance swallowed some more coffee. "Sort of," he admitted. He changed the subject. "Seems to me like I'm the only prisoner in your jail."

"Y'are. Every crime wave in this town has been washed out for a long spell. Folks don't start things with Ethan Lockwood enforcing the law like he does. You're the first prisoner we had to entertain in a year of Sundays, seems like." He crunched a lemon drop between his teeth and went on, "That's just the trouble. With crime at a minimum, the taxpayers can't see why a deputy is needed here. I reckon they figure Ethan can handle it all—and I reckon he can. Eventually I'm going to commence to begin looking around for another job. Say, you don't look like a murderer."

"Much obliged," Lance said dryly. "Same to you. Did the sheriff tell you I was a murderer?"

Deputy Perkins shook his head. "Not for certain. As a matter of fact, after he told me to come down here and feed you—he found me in the general store getting some lemon drops—he tipped me off I was to treat you like a guest. Didn't think I heard him right at first. First time I ever knew him to act that-a-way. Y'ain't got anything on him, have you?"

"Not yet," Lance commenced grimly "But I hope——"

The door between the sheriff's office and the jail corridor opened. The deputy said, "Here comes Ethan now." He scrambled to his feet, still holding the bag of lemon drops.

Lance glanced at the open cell door and wondered

what the sheriff would have to say regarding that oversight. Apparently Lockwood was accustomed to such happenings. He strode into the cell, saying, "Oscar, there's a lot of noise coming out of the Red Steer Saloon."

"There won't be long." The deputy nodded. "I'll go down and see can I quieten 'em a mite. See you later, Tolliver." He popped a lemon drop into his mouth, thrust the paper sack into a hip pocket and sauntered leisurely out along the corridor.

"And how he'll quiet 'em," Lockwood chuckled. Lance had left his seat on the bunk now. The sheriff came nearer, one hand outthrust. "Reckon I owe you an apology, Tolliver."

Lance took the hand but said cautiously, "Thanks. You must have discovered I didn't have anything to do with the murder."

Lockwood laughed. "I knew that right along. You see, Tolliver, I had a letter from your outfit a couple of days back telling me to be on the lookout for you and give you all assistance possible. The instant you told me your name today I realized who you were. Didn't know just what you were after but figured it might be as well to put on an act for the benefit of Chiricahua Herrick and those others."

Relief flooded through Tolliver. He grinned a bit wryly. "You're one good actor, Sheriff. You had me feeling I was in a tight for a spell. It all came as a bit of a surprise, particularly as I'd been given to understand that Sartoris County had an honest peace officer on the job."

They sat down together on the bunk and rolled cigarettes. "Never suspected you for a moment, of course," Lockwood was saying. "But I'm not so sure that some of that gang that rode out with me today don't know more about that murder than they were letting on. Bowman's horse came wandering back to town about noon and——"

"That explains," Tolliver said, "how one of the three horses left after the others. I read that much from the sign."

Lockwood nodded. "Herrick, Kilby and a couple of others came running to me with the news that their pal, Bowman, was missing. We followed the hoofprints back toward that dry wash where we met you."

"I figured something of the kind might have brought you out," Lance said, "providing you were on the square. At the same time I wasn't sure but what you and your riders might be looking for somebody to frame."

"Not *my* riders," the sheriff denied strenuously. "I don't ride with those hombres unless I can't help myself. It smelled fishy to me when they kept calling Bowman their pal. So far as I know Bowman was a right decent sort, and I don't remember seeing him mix with Herrick and his crew to any extent."

"What was Bowman doing here?" Lance asked.

"Not much of anything," Lockwood replied, "until recently. Last week or so he's been acting as a guide to a professor who's been riding the near-by hills."

"Guide, eh?" Lance frowned. "Wonder what was back of that play. Confidentially, Frank Bowman was one of our best operatives."

"T'hell you say!" Lockwood's jaw dropped. "It must have been considerable of a shock finding him dead that-a-way."

"Worse than that," Lance said grimly. "All I ask is to meet the man who did it. Who is this professor you mentioned?"

"Name's Ulysses Z. Jones. Claims to be working out of the Jonesian Institute of Washington, D.C. Ever hear of him?"

Lance shook his head. "What's his game?"

"Cactus. He rides——"

"Cactus?"

Lockwood shrugged his shoulders. "I'm just telling you what he claims. It sounds crazy to me, but he says he's making a study of the flora—I think that was his word—of the Southwest. He's staying at the hotel. His niece is with him acting as secretary. Her name is Gregory——"

"One minute. Is this Professor Jones a big man, dark, around thirty or thirty-five?"

"Nothing like that at all. He's——"

"Never mind. I'll see him eventually." Lance's frown deepened as he drew meditatively on his cigarette. "I can't understand Bowman acting as his guide unless he ties into the situation——"

"Do you mind telling me what, or who, you're looking for?"

"Anybody by the name of Matt Foster in town?"

Lockwood considered, then shook his head. "Not that I know of. The name isn't familiar."

"Probably he'd change his name anyway. I'll give you more of the story later, Sheriff. Meanwhile, what of those hombres who were with you this afternoon? Who are they? What do they do?"

"Chiricahua Herrick is the leader of that gang. Frankly, I don't know what they do. They've been hanging around Pozo Verde for quite a spell now—that is, Herrick, Kilby, Johnson and Ridge have. Those four are right thick. Ordway is a local man. Never amounted to much. Lately he's been tagging after Herrick and the others. If he's considered one of their gang I don't know it. Fact is, I'd like to know more about that crew myself but I haven't anything to go on. They don't break any laws that I know of. I haven't any legal excuse for bopping down on 'em."

Lance smiled. "I understood from your deputy that you ruled with an iron hand here and that there wasn't any crime."

"You can give Oscar the credit for that."

Lance showed his surprise. "You mean that—that——?"

"Yeah," Lockwood chuckled, "that sleepy-looking, lemon drop-devouring, lengthy bag of bones that brought you your supper. But don't you make any mistake about Oscar Perkins. He's the one who keeps this town on the straight-and-narrow path."

Lance said skeptically, "I'd sure like to know how he does it. Has he got a rep for a fast draw or something?"

"That ain't been put to the test yet." Lockwood laughed. "Ain't been necessary. Oscar just hits 'em!"

"Oscar just what?" Lance's eyes bugged out.

"Hits 'em. When a hombre starts misbehaving Oscar cracks him over the head with his gun barrel. If the fellow shows signs of coming back for more Oscar lets him have it with his fist. That always settles it. Talk about a mule's kick!"

Lance grinned. "Maybe the lemon drops have something to do with it. I can't think of anything else to explain it."

"Oscar has fooled a heap of folks. Now, me, I used to slam the hell raisers in my cooler. They didn't mind that so much in the long run, and my jail was always full. Howsomever, this town has discovered it would rather behave than be hit by Oscar. Consequently, Pozo Verde has tamed down a heap. So much so, in fact, that the taxpayers are commencing to say it isn't necessary to maintain two peace officers here."

"Bowman's murder may cause them to change their minds."

"I wouldn't be surprised. By the way, Tolliver, what do you make of Bowman's hand being painted black?"

Lance shook his head. "It's a mystery to me. Here's something else that's got my brain going in circles." He drew the mezcal button from inside his shirt. "I found this clutched in Bowman's left hand before you got there. Know what it is?"

Lockwood took the plant, said immediately, "Hell, yes! This is a peyote. I've heard it called 'sacred mushroom,' 'piote bean,' 'hikuli'——"

"And 'mezcal button,'" Lance interrupted. "Also 'dry whisky.'"

"I've heard it called a lot of other names by people who tried to keep it away from the Indians." Lockwood frowned. "But it seems to be as hard to stamp out as the marijuana habit."

"The question is"—Lance frowned—"what was Bowman doing with it? What did it have to do with his death—if anything?"

"In the first place," Lockwood said slowly, "I wonder where it came from. I can't say I ever noticed peyotes growing around here. When I was in Texas I used to run across 'em right often. There's a lot of peyote growing down in Mexico too. You say you found this in Bowman's hand?"

Lance nodded. "He was hanging onto it like he never meant to let go too. Cripes! I've got to get out of here and find out what it's all about."

"You're free to go any time," Lockwood said.

"I did figure it might be a good idea for you to stay overnight, though, until we can cook up an alibi—that is, if you don't mind. After that act I put on to impress Chiricahua Herrick and his gang——"

"I understand. I'm glad you acted as you did. I figure Bowman was killed sometime last night. If so, I'm alibied. About the time he was killed I was asleep in a little fonda in Tipata over across the line——"

"I know Tipata—and Moreles who runs the fonda over there. I'll let on like I've sent someone to check up on you. If Bowman was taken out there and killed last night——"

"He wasn't killed out there," Lance interrupted. "He was taken out there after he'd been shot."

"You got proof of that?" the sheriff said quickly.

"It's what the evidence showed me," Lance replied. "When his body is brought in you look careful at the blood——"

"His body was brought to Pozo Verde quite a spell ago. It's over to Doc Drummond's place. Doc's going to hold the inquest tonight."

"As I see it, two riders took Bowman out there after he was shot. I don't know why. They left him there dead and returned to Pozo Verde. Hours later, Bowman's horse wandered back to town——"

"But you said he was shot before being taken out there. How could he ride his horse——?"

The sheriff paused, frowning. Oscar Perkins stood at the doorway of the cell. "Doc Drummond's ready to start the inquest now, Ethan," Oscar announced, sucking on a lemon drop. "You said you wanted to be there."

"I sure do." The sheriff rose from his seat on the bunk.

"I'd like to hear it myself," Oscar said. "At the same time, if Tolliver wants me to remain and keep him company——"

"You go along, Oscar," Lance said. "Both of you keep your ears open. You look at that blood careful, Sheriff. Maybe you'll get what I'm driving at."

"I'll do that. And I'll bring you word of the findings just as soon as a decision is reached."

The sheriff and his deputy closed the cell door without locking it and made their way out of the building. Lance waited a long time for their return but when they didn't put in an appearance he extinguished the lamplight and curled up on the bunk to get some sleep.

III
The Cactus Man

Early-morning sunlight was streaming through Lance's cell window when he awoke. Oscar Perkins was standing in the cell. Lance had slept the night through without interruption. He shoved his sombrero onto his head and got to his feet.

"Inquest kept going dang nigh all night," Oscar was saying. "When a verdict finally was reached it was so late that Sheriff Ethan figured you might as well get your whole sleep in. Just as soon as you wash up there's some breakfast waiting for you in Ethan's office. He'd like to talk to you."

"I'll be right with you," Lance said. "Much obliged."

"Don't mention it," Oscar said politely, and withdrew.

Five minutes later Lance was sitting down to a tray of breakfast on Lockwood's desk. Lockwood leaned back in his office chair and talked while Lance consumed food. Oscar slouched back on another chair and made inroads on his sack of lemon drops.

"We had quite a session," the sheriff was saying. "Chiricahua Herrick and his crowd were there, along with a lot of other folks. Chiricahua insisted the murderer was already caught, meaning you, and the jury was some impressed. There were a lot of squabbles and arguments, Chiricahua insisting that the jury bring in a verdict against you. I stalled things along by telling them I had sent a man over to Tipata to check on your alibi. 'Bout two this morning I strolled down here to the office, stalled around a spell and then went back to the inquest with the word that my messenger had returned from Tipata and that your alibi was airtight——"

"And they took your word for that?" Lance asked.

"My word was good with everybody except Chiricahua and his crowd. They wanted to talk to my messenger personal and they asked a lot of other questions. Howsomever, I represent the law here, and they didn't get no place. Doc Drummond gave his jury a talk. The jury retired for a spell and finally returned a verdict that Bowman had met his death at approximately midnight, night before last, at the hands of some person unknown. Doc had probed out the slug, of course. It was some battered but looked like a forty-five. It had entered below the right cheekbone and ranged up at quite a sharp angle. Doc says he thinks Bowman may have lived quite a spell after the bullet struck, though he'd be unconscious, of course."

"Ranged up at a sharp angle," Lance repeated slowly. "Bowman was a fairly tall man. He may have been shot by a shorter one or he may have been on his horse, and the killer on foot."

Lockwood said, "You're positive he wasn't killed where you found the body?"

"Positive. Did you examine the blood on Bowman's face?"

"Yes, I did," the sheriff replied, frowning. "There was a streak of dried blood that had run across his nose. Another streak had run up across his forehead and into his hair——"

"There's the point," Lance quickly pointed out. "Blood doesn't run up. See what I'm getting at? Bowman was shot, then the murderer threw the body across the saddle of Bowman's horse and traveled out there where the body was left in the dry wash——"

"And if Bowman's head hung down over the saddle"—Oscar had straightened in his chair—"the blood running from the wound would course down across his forehead and into the hair. That's the way it looked——"

"Oscar, you're smart," Lockwood said.

"Lance is the smart one," Oscar said indolently. "I just recognized what was pointed out to me."

"And when they took the body out to that dry wash," Lance continued, "they may have put Bowman down on his side. That would account for blood running in the other direction, though there wasn't so much of it by that time. Maybe he was just left out there on his horse and fell off after a time. That part's not so important. But I think I've proved that Frank Bowman's shooting didn't take place in that dry wash."

"By cripes!" Lockwood exclaimed, "you certainly have." He paused, then: "That still doesn't explain what he was doing with that mezcal button."

"No, it doesn't," Lance admitted. "But I picked up a couple of other clues out in that dry wash before you arrived, Sheriff, that I haven't mentioned before. I call them clues—maybe they don't mean a thing." He ceased talking to produce a small notebook from between the pages of which he extracted a tiny splinter of pine wood and a few threads of dark woolen cloth.

"What are those?" asked the sheriff.

"This bit of pine splinter was sticking to Bowman's sleeve on the arm that held the mezcal button. Those twisted wool threads I picked off his right spur. Apparently his spur had caught in a piece of cloth at some time or other."

"What do they tell you?" Lockwood asked.

"Not a great deal," Lance confessed. "They're not objects that would ordinarily be found in a dry wash, of course. Particularly these threads of wool I picked from Bowman's spur. A man couldn't walk far without losing those threads, so I figure he must have picked 'em up about the time he was shot."

Oscar Perkins put in, "There wasn't any chance that Bowman did a little peyote chewing, was there?" He paused, then added, "Ethan was telling me about finding that mezcal button."

"Not a chance," Lance said definitely. "In the first place, that button hadn't been dried. In the second place, I knew Frank Bowman. He was in the organization long before I joined and he had a right good reputation. No, we'll have to leave that peyote-eating habit to certain of the Indian tribes and their ceremonies. You haven't heard anything of the kind around here, have you?"

Lockwood shook his head. "The Indians hereabouts gave up that sort of thing long ago—if they ever did anything like that." The sheriff paused, then, "There's a small tribe of Yaquente Indians down below the border that might go in for peyote eating. Come to think of it, I've heard they do."

Lance nodded. "I've heard of the Yaquentes. Pretty fierce fighters at one time, though they've made peace with the Mexican Government——"

"A sort of armed peace." Lockwood nodded. "The

Mexican Government never did entirely subjugate them. Howsomever, those Yaquentes I mentioned haven't kicked up any trouble in years. Small bunches of 'em come to Pozo Verde now and then. They seem civilized enough."

"Maybe they dropped peyotes in favor of lemon drops," Oscar drawled.

"Come to think of it," Lockwood put in, "some Indian tribal ceremonies call for painting parts of the body. Do you suppose there'd be any connection between that and Bowman's hand being painted black——?"

"Jeepers!" Oscar exclaimed. "That's an idea."

Lance shook his head. "I don't think so, Sheriff. That wasn't regular paint on Bowman's hand. I examined it right close—even smelled it. It had a sort of creosote odor."

"Creosote?" Oscar pricked up his ears. "Wait— where did I hear about creosote? Oh, yeah, I remember. There was a section gang working down near the T.N. & A.S. depot, replacing a couple of railroad ties. They painted the new ties with creosote. When the gang left they forgot a bucket with some creosote in it, standing on the depot platform. Night before last somebody tipped the bucket over. Old Johnny Quinn, the station agent, was madder 'n a wet hen. Seems like he stepped into the creosote that had been spilled and then tracked it into his office. He'd just mopped the office the day before. You know what an old woman Johnny is, Ethan."

"When did this happen?" Lance said quickly. "The same night Bowman was shot?"

Oscar nodded. "Yeah, night before last. Yesterday was one tough day for old Johnny Quinn. On top of being peeved about that spilled creosote, Johnny claimed somebody had broke into his office and stole his bills of lading for what freight came in day before yesterday. He probably lost 'em and had to blame somebody. You 'member, Ethan, I mentioned it to you?"

The sheriff said he remembered. "Johnny Quinn is always finding fault with something. S'far as concerns his office being broke into, all's he had to base that on was the fact his window was open when he come to work. Nothing else was missing except his bills of lading. It's my opinion he forgot to close his window the night before, and his bills blew away."

Lance had finished his breakfast by this time. He rolled and lighted a cigarette, rose and donned his sombrero. "I reckon I'll walk over to the railroad station and see where that creosote was spilled. Can't tell, I might pick up something."

"Want I should go with you?" Lockwood said.

"Not unless you feel like it. If you're busy——"

The sheriff made a wry face. "I ain't made out my expense report for last month yet and I've got to get to it. Take Oscar along with you. By the way, that's your gun and belt hanging on that hook across the room. Might be a good idea to put 'em on."

"I'll feel more comfortable anyway." Lance smiled.

A few moments later Lance and Oscar were walking east along Main Street. They passed shops and stores of various commercial enterprises, nearly all of which had built-out wooden awnings over the plank sidewalk to protect pedestrians from the broiling sun baking the dusty roadway. Oscar nodded or spoke to several townspeople he met. He and Lance were just passing Lem Parker's General Store when a man in riding breeches and knee-laced boots emerged from the doorway.

"Hi yuh, Professor?" Oscar said.

An irritated, vague look disappeared from the man's eyes as they focused on the deputy. "Ah!" He smiled suddenly. "It's my lemon-drop friend. How's everything this morning? I've just been trying to get a trowel in the general store. It seems they don't stock such implements."

"Try Herb Rumler's General Store," Oscar suggested. "He carries a line of such tools, rakes, and so on to accommodate some of the ladies in town who go in for raisin' garden sass and such. By the way, shake hands with my friend, Lance Tolliver—Professor Jones. It was Lance who found Frank Bowman's body."

Professor Ulysses Z. Jones was probably forty-five or fifty years old, with thick, gray-streaked, dark hair. He was of medium height with a bony frame and an energetic bearing. His face was thin, accenting the contours of rather high cheekbones, although healthily tanned. He was smoothly shaven. His gray eyes had a manner of suddenly taking on a vague expression, as though the man were chary of revealing innermost thoughts, though at times they could be unusually keen. Almost instantly Lance gained the impression that Professor Jones's mind concealed far more knowledge than was put into words. Despite the heat of the southwest sun Jones wore a necktie and loose-fitting tweed jacket. His hat was a soft gray felt with a fairly wide brim. There was something trim, neat, compact about the man, and he displayed a sort of nervous, driving energy in every movement.

Jones was commenting on the Bowman killing: ". . . I was most distressed . . . very sad affair . . . I like Bowman . . . excellent chap. Great shock to you . . . presume . . . Tolliver. Acquainted . . . by any chance?"

"We had mutual friends," Lance evaded. "I felt as though I knew him."

"Sincerely hope . . . authorities . . . bring murderer to swift justice."

"I understood," Lance commented, "that Bowman was working for you. Would you have any idea of what he was doing the night he was killed?"

"Not the slightest," Jones replied instantly. "I had hired him to guide me through the hills near by. He knew this country. Later we planned going down into a section of Mexico with which he claimed to be thoroughly familiar. I'll miss him no end."

Lance said, "Oscar tells me you're on some sort of expedition for the Jonesian Institute."

"Right, right, quite right." Jones spoke jerkily. "Our board of directors decided I was the man to go. You see, we're planning a rare plant garden—all under glass, of course—you understand, cacti deserves its place—will be one of our largest exhibits, in fact. I'm looking for rare specimens—studying distribution—type locality—that sort of thing—really a splendid vacation for me."

Oscar bit suddenly down on a lemon drop. His eyes bulged. "Do you mean to say you're going to grow cactus in a garden? What's the good of that? It grows wild all over around here."

Jones laughed shortly. "That's one thing I've discovered people hereabouts don't realize—that they've one of the most striking cacti displays in the Western Hemisphere, right at their doorsteps, you might say. Not appreciated as it should be, not at all. The value of a garden such as we plan will be great to collectors— they can study firsthand specimens many of them will never have an opportunity to see otherwise."

Oscar's jaw dropped. "Collectors?"

"Certainly." Jones sounded a bit irritated. "People collect books, stamps, coins—why not cacti? All over the world there is a rapidly growing interest in cacti."

Oscar seemed stunned by the thought. He crammed a lemon drop into his mouth. To keep the conversation going Lance said, "I suppose Europe and Asia have different forms of cactus like in the United States?"

"Not at all, not at all. There are no cacti at all in the Eastern Hemisphere—that is, native cacti. Africa, of course, has its own form of succulents, but the Western Hemisphere is the only place—true cacti—to be found. Anything in Europe or Asia—matter of propagation—transplanting."

"These collectors"—Oscar had somewhat recovered from his surprise—"where do they get their cactus?"

"Cactus nurseries and companies, of course. It's a growing business. Out in California one company has been in business since the early seventies—just furnishing—Eastern trade."

Oscar burst into laughter. "Haw-haw! First time I ever heard of a cactus needin' a nursery."

Jones turned half impatiently away. Struck by a sudden impulse, Lance withdrew from his shirt the mezcal button. "You seem right well posted on cactus, Professor. Maybe you can tell me what sort of plant this is?"

Jones stiffened suddenly at sight of the plant. A warm glow entered his eyes. "Why, bless me! A *Lophophora williamsii!* Wherever did you find this? I've seen none on the hills hereabouts. Its distribution generally is from central Mexico to southern Texas. Where did——?"

"What did you call it?" Oscar looked narrowly at Jones. "Loafer-for-William? Is that what you said?"

Lance smiled. "We generally call it a peyote or mezcal button."

"True, true," Jones jerked out. He had the plant in his hand now, examining it. "I've heard those names. It's one of many forms—known as 'dumpling cacti.' I say, have you ever——?"

"Dumpling cactus?" from Oscar. "There's no spines on that——"

"Several species—cacti—practically no spines." He turned impatiently back to Lance. "I've heard— Indians of certain tribes—eat these. Some sort of narcotic effect—delusions of grandeur—fantastic, colorful visions—trances—all that sort of thing. Is it true, do you know?"

"I've never tried eating 'em myself." Lance smiled. "But I know it's done. Those peyotes are first cut in sections and dried, of course, before being eaten. The whole practice has been pretty well stamped out nowadays. It's forbidden, you know."

"It is possible then." Jones was intensely interested. "I understood that a Doctor—Doctor—the name escapes me at present—had isolated certain alkaloids—analysis of this genus. You say you didn't find it in this region?"

"I found it," Lance said cautiously, "but not growing. I don't know just where it came from."

"May I?—I'd like to have this specimen—interested in studying it—if you don't mind——"

"Sure, take it along." Lance scarcely knew what else to say at the moment. He decided right then, however, to see more of the professor.

Jones was shaking hands again. "Delighted if you'd come to my hotel—meet my niece—tell me more of the Indians who make—practice—becoming intoxicated—on peyote—pleasure—assure you." He shook hands again and departed, walking swiftly along Main Street.

Oscar heaved a long sigh. "There goes your Loafer-for-William," he chuckled. "Me, I can't figure whether the professor is a nut or just plain cuckoo. Imagine, trying to make us believe folks grow cactus gardens."

"Don't jump to any hasty conclusions, Oscar," Lance advised thoughtfully. "He may be a nut, but I figure there's more to Jones than shows on the surface."

They had progressed along Main Street and were just turning the corner at Laredo Street when an angry shout reached them from across the roadway. George Kilby had emerged from the doorway of a building which bore the sign of the Pozo Verde Saloon.

"I may get balled up on cactus," Oscar said with some satisfaction, "but here comes something I do understand. Kilby looks like he's heading for trouble, and we're in his path!"

IV
Lance Hits Hard

It was evident to Lance and Oscar that Kilby had been imbibing rather heavily at the bar of the Pozo Verde Saloon. The man approached them from across the street, walking with a decided lurch. His eyes were bloodshot and angry, and liquor, or some liquid, had been spilled down the left leg of the brand-new overalls he was wearing.

He was halfway across the roadway when another torrent of angry words spilled from his lips, ending with, "Travelin' with murderers now, eh, Deputy Perkins?"

Oscar muttered, "I'm sure going to have to bend a gun barrel across that hombre's Stetson. I wonder how much he can stand."

"Wait, let me handle this," Lance said quickly. "It's me his words are aimed at."

Oscar shrugged. "Go to it, but watch yourself."

Kilby's step was a trifle uncertain as he confronted Lance. "Pretty lucky, you are, Mr Lancelot Tolliver. Only for the law being on your side we'd have the sidewinder who bumped off my good old pal, Bowman."

"I figure you're wrong, Kilby," Lance replied

quietly. "Look, you've had a couple of drinks too many. Why don't you go away and sleep it off?"

"Tryin' to get rid of me, eh?" Kilby sneered. "Well, it don't work. We're going to put the bee on you yet. We'll bust that alibi of yours wide open. You know what? Chiricahua, hisself, has gone ridin' down to Tipata. He's goin' to find out if you stayed there that night or not. I say not, but Chiricahua is checking you up. We was both going, only——"

"Only," Oscar drawled, "it looks to me like you was too drunk to ride at leaving time. Well, Cherry-Cow Herrick will find out that Lance's alibi holds water— which same you'd be better off if that's all you held."

Kilby teetered gravely back and forth a moment, owlishly eying the deputy. He lifted one admonishing finger. "Now I ain't got no—hic!—quarrel with you, Oscar. It's this Tolliver hombre I'm aimin' to——"

"Forget it, Kilby." Lance laughed good-naturedly. "Go get yourself some sleep." He talked to the man as one would to a child. "Look, you've spilt some whisky on your nice new overalls. You'd better go wash them——"

"What do you know about my overalls?" Kilby's eyes had narrowed. For some reason Lance's words appeared to have a somewhat sobering effect on the man. He straightened up and came a step nearer, curses tumbling from his thick lips.

"Cut it out, Kilby," Lance said sternly.

Kilby rushed on, heedless of the warning. He called Lance a name no fighting man will take. Lance didn't want to hit him, but there seemed nothing else to do. His fist shot out—not too hard—and Kilby went stumbling awkwardly off the sidewalk to sprawl on his back in the dust.

That completely sobered the man without knocking any sense into his head. He came struggling up from the roadway, one hand clawing at his gun butt.

Lance took two quick steps forward. His left fist sunk to the wrist in Kilby's middle; his right crashed against the side of Kilby's jaw. An explosive grunt was expelled from Kilby's lips, and he commenced to sag. For a moment he stood bent over, arms dangling limply at his sides. Then slowly he sank to his knees and rolled on his back. His eyes were closed, and he was dead to the world.

"The old one-two," Oscar said approvingly, calmly stuffing a lemon drop into his mouth. "Very nice. I don't think I could've done better myself."

A crowd had commenced to gather. Lance said, "C'mon, let's get out of here." Oscar told a couple of men in the crowd to get Kilby's unconscious form off the street, then followed Lance down Laredo Street in the direction of the railroad station.

"Dammit!" Lance growled when Oscar had caught up. "There wasn't any other way out of it, but I do hate to hit a hombre that's been drinking heavy."

"Mebbe so," Oscar said judiciously, "but they go out quicker in that condition. Now if you'd just get a mite more snap into your wrist as you hit——"

"Let's forget it," Lance cut in.

"You're upset." Oscar thrust a paper sack toward Lance. "Here, have a lemon drop. It'll soothe your nerves."

Without realizing what he was doing, Lance thrust a lemon drop into his mouth.

"Ah, another convert," Oscar chuckled. "You'll be an addict in no time."

Lance started to smile, then laughed. "Like I say, I

hate to hit a drunk, but I was thinking about something else. It seemed to make Kilby madder 'n ever when I mentioned his new overalls. Danged if I understand why. I was speaking as friendly as possible."

"Drunks are sensitive on queer points sometimes," Oscar drawled. "I've known 'em to fight at the drop of the hat at the mention of a new one.

"New what?" Lance asked absent-mindedly.

"Hat. Don't you know what we're talking about?"

"I was thinking about overalls."

"I certainly pick intelligent company this mornin'," Oscar commented. "One talks about spiny plant life and t'other about everyday clothing. Forget it. Here's the depot."

They had reached the T.N. & A.S. railroad tracks that paralleled Main Street a block back. Beyond the tracks were scattered a line of Mexican adobe houses, strung along a rather crooked roadway. Between the tracks and the single line of buildings fronting Main were heaps of old rubbish, tin cans, littered papers. Oscar led the way toward the railroad station, a small frame building, painted red, with the T.N. & A.S. sign erected on its roof. The station stood about five feet above the earth on a platform constructed of heavy planks.

Oscar led the way up the short flight of steps to the platform. From inside the station came the clattering taps of a telegraphic instrument. Abruptly the sound ceased, and a fuzzy little old man appeared in the doorway.

"No, Oscar Perkins, I don't want no lemon drops," he stated in a cantankerous voice before Oscar had had an opportunity to say a word. He wore faded overalls with bib attached, and on his scanty gray hair was a stiff-peaked cap bearing the letters: "T.N. & A.S.R.R." Spectacles rested on his sharp nose.

"Ain't asked you to have one," Oscar stated calmly. "Johnny Quinn, shake hands with my friend, Lance Tolliver. You know"—to Lance—"Johnny just about runs the T.N. and A.S. He's the combination station agent, freight agent, telegraph operator, swamper, train dispatcher——"

"There's more truth 'n poetry in them remarks," Johnny Quinn squeaked. He gave Lance a limp hand, then turned back to Oscar. "What ye want?"

"Don't want nothing," Oscar said quietly. "Lance is new to town, and I was just showing him the sights. We didn't want to overlook your depot."

"I can 'preciate thet." Johnny Quinn nodded. He seemed more friendly now. "Ye'd be surprised now to l'arn just how much freight was put off at this little depot. By the way, Oscar, ye didn't catch them thieves whut took my bills, did ye?"

"Sheriff Lockwood is running down a hot clue on that right now," Oscar said without batting an eye.

Lance said, "Oscar was saying you found your window open yesterday morning and certain of your papers missing."

"Valyble papers they was, Mister Tolliver. I been a-maintainin' right along we should have a night man on duty in the depot, but them brass hats back East won't pay me no 'tention. Someday I'll up and quit 'em, then they'll see whut's whut! And we should have better law enforcement in this town, too, whut with hoodlums spillin' cre'sote all over my platform— right after I'd mopped the office, too—and it got tracked inside."

"Where was the creosote spilled?" Lance asked.

Old Quinn led the way to a place near the edge of the platform where a dark brownish-black stain had seeped into the heavy planks. "Lucky they wa'n't much cre'sote in thet bucket. It 'd made a fine mess! I'm a-keepin' thet bucket and next time when them section hands come back and ask for it I aim to give 'em Hail Columbia! Bein' wasteful with company property is bad enough, but—and another thing"—Johnny Quinn was warming to his subject now—"if them hoodlums whut tipped over the cre'sote come back a-whinin' for their cold chisel I ain't a-goin' to give it to 'em——"

"Was a cold chisel left here?" Lance asked.

Old Johnny nodded indignantly. "It's my opee-nion," he said confidentially, "thet they figgered to pry open some of the boxes of freight and steal some-thin'. Yes sirree! But I reckon nothin' was left for 'em. Folks usually come here and collect whut freight's due, and I ain't had no complaints ner an inquiry 'bout anythin' that didn't come when it should."

"You mean," Lance asked, "that folks just come and collect their freight when it arrives without sign-ing for it?"

"Sartain, I know everybody here. I bring 'em the bills at the end of the month, and they sign 'em then. Only, this time I'll be minus them bills thet was stole."

"Can't you check up and get duplicate bills?" Lance asked.

Quinn nodded. "It 'll take a mite of time, though. I figure to get at thet right soon."

"I take it," Lance said, "that the same folks get freight shipped in right along."

"Same folks," Johnny said. "Cases of liquor for the saloons, canned goods for the general stores, small boxes for the barber shops and so on. Folks jest come down and pick up their stuff when it's put off'n the train. Anything unusual is put off, I notice it, ye betcha!" He paused, then his mouth sagged a trifle. "Come to think on it," he said slowly, "there was one box I never noticed before. From a company strange to me. Now I wonder who got thet?" He removed his cap and scratched his scanty hair in perplexity. "Shucks! Reckon it don't make no difference. Whoever it b'longed to picked 'er up, or I'd had a complaint. Thet's the trouble, with my bills missin'——Whut'd ye find, Mister Tolliver?"

Lance had suddenly stooped and retrieved from between two planks, clogged with dirt, a small pine splinter. There were two or three other splinters near by. Lance said, "Only this," and held up the splinter to the old man's view, after which he calmly commenced picking his teeth with it.

"Oh," Johnny grunted, "I thought ye'd found somethin' valyble."

Lance laughed. "It might be to some people. You were talking about a box of freight that looked strange to you, Mr Quinn. What kind of a box was it?"

"Jest an ordinary pine box," Quinn sniffed, "like freight is usual shipped in. Whut did ye expect?"

"I mean," Lance said easily, "how big was it?"

"Oh, I dunno." Quinn was vague in his ideas. "'Bout so big, I reckon." With his skinny arms he measured the size of the missing box in the air. Lance judged the box to have been approximately one by one by two feet in size.

"Pretty heavy?" Lance asked next.

"Not turrible," Quinn said, frowning. "I just

remember puttin' it on my truck with some other boxes and wheelin' 'em over to stack ag'in' the depot wall. Hefty enough though."

"You don't remember who it was for?"

"Consarn it," Quinn said angrily. "Ain't I told ye I don't know? Now ye've got me thinkin' on thet ye've spoiled my hull day." His frown deepened. "I jest remember seein' the label pasted on the box, tellin' who it was from and where it was a-goin'. Folks was all around me, already pickin' up their shipments. Thet address was writ in pen an' ink. I didn't have no time to stop and decipher writin'——"

"Was the whole address label in writing?" Lance asked.

"No, I rec'lect that was in print, like most labels."

"Think hard," Lance urged. "Where was it from?"

"Tarnation an' damnity!" Johnny Quinn squealed angrily. "Ain't I a-thinkin'? I'm concentratin' like all get out and——" He paused suddenly, then, "Wait, wait—thet box had been shipped from—— Cracky! I can see thet label plain's day, only I don't remember——It was shipped from—from—some sort of Southwest Something Company. I wish I could think of that middle word. All's I can think of is cactus. Wouldn't that be the consarnedest idea? Southwest Cactus Company. Hee-hee! Like if there was a company org'nized to sell something that grows wild all over——"

"Cactus?" Lance said quickly, breaking in on the oldster's gleeful cackling.

Quinn paused from lack of breath. "I do get th' most redickerlous idees sometimes," he panted. "No, it sartainly couldn't have been cactus. Must have been somethin' else."

"Do you remember where it came from?" Lance queried.

Quinn concentrated. "Texas," he said at last—"El Paso, Texas. Nope, I'm wrong! It was some place in New Mexico. Or was it Texas? Come to think on it, seems like I rec'lect readin' Colorady on thet box." He removed the cap and scratched his head some more. The harder he concentrated the angrier he became. Suddenly he exploded heatedly, "I don't know why it should make any business of yours where my freight comes from. You come around here askin' questions like a brass hat and a-wastin' of my time. Valyble railroad company time! If ye're figgerin' to ship anythin' or if ye expect freight to arrive I'll be pleased to take care of ye. Otherwise, I'm too busy for more lallygaggin'!"

He spun angrily about, entered his office. At once the telegraph instrument commenced rattling at a furious rate.

Lance looked at Oscar. Oscar looked at Lance. "I reckon we might as well leave." Oscar sighed. "I know that old coot, and he won't talk to us no more today. But, Lance, do you reckon a box did come from the Southwest Cactus Company—if there is such a company? And how does it all fit in? What's the creosote got to do with it? That's the first I've heard of a cold chisel too. And that pine splinter you picked up——"

"Whoa!" Lance laughed. "Maybe we got more out of that conversation than you figure." They slowly descended the steps to the cinder-packed earth around the platform. Lance surveyed the ground for "sign," but it was too tracked up to furnish any fresh information. Oscar remained silent while they walked slowly back toward the center of town.

Finally Lance spoke. "I'm going to do a little supposing and speculating and see if I can reconstruct a picture of what happened to Frank Bowman. I may be miles off in my guess, but here's the way I see it. As you know, Bowman was here as one of our operatives—I'll explain why at another time. Anyway, we'll say he hit on some sort of clue here. I don't know just what, but it was hot. I've a hunch it was connected with peyotes——"

"Basing that on the fact he had one in his hand when you found him?"

"Exactly. We'll say Bowman was watching a certain man. Now, mezcal buttons don't grow hereabouts, so this certain man had a supply of the plants shipped here from some cactus company. Let's suppose Bowman saw that box of cactus plants and got suspicious, though he wouldn't know for sure there were peyotes inside. He watched, and no one called for it. Maybe the guilty man knew Bowman was watching the box. When no one called for the box Bowman decided to open it and learn what it contained. With a cold chisel he pried off the top of the box——"

"There's the cold chisel Johnny Quinn found!"

Lance nodded. "We'll say the box top splintered when it was forced off. I saw splinters on the station platform, remember, and picked one up. With the box open, Bowman stuck his hand inside and got a peyote. A loose splinter at the edge of the box stuck in Bowman's shirt sleeve."

"Could be, could be!" Oscar had lost his indolent manner.

Lance continued, "Now Bowman has his peyote evidence. He knows who the box is shipped to. But that person or some of his gang are watching Bowman. They see him break into the box. Remember this is around midnight; it's dark. Bowman doesn't see his assailant approach. Just as Bowman straightens up from the box someone comes running toward the platform. It's too late for Bowman to pull his gun. The killer's bullet strikes at a sharp angle—proving the killer was on the earth below the platform. He may even have been hiding under the platform. Bowman falls, and as he goes down his right hand strikes that bucket of creosote standing near, tipping it over. The creosote floods out over Bowman's hand, accidentally painting it black."

"Lance, you're sure knocking the mystery out of this."

"When a man hasn't the facts," Lance said grimly, "he has to work his imagination overtime. . . . Let's get on. Somebody takes away the box of peyotes. Somebody gets through Johnny Quinn's office window and steals the bill of lading so the shipment of cactus can't be traced to the guilty man—right off at least. Now, remember, it was Doctor Drummond's opinion that Bowman, while unconscious, didn't die at once. Something had to be done with the body. The killer didn't dare risk firing more shots for fear of attracting attention. And he didn't dare leave the body there for fear it might be found and Bowman, regaining consciousness, make some sort of dying statement——"

"So they took the body out to that wash where you found it."

Lance said, "That's my idea. They threw the body across the saddle of Bowman's horse and lit out pronto. I figure it took two to lift him to the saddle, one at the shoulders, one at the feet. Maybe Bowman's spur rowel caught on one man's shirt. That accounts for the woolly threads I found on Bowman's spur. Remember, this is largely guesswork."

"Damn good guesswork," Oscar said admiringly.

"Meanwhile," Lance continued, "in the darkness the killers had failed to notice that Bowman clutched that mezcal button in his hand. Bowman was a man of great determination, strong will. Probably his last conscious thought was to hang onto that bit of evidence at any cost. So he was still gripping that button when they dumped him off his horse out in that dry wash. As he died and grew cold his fingers stiffened rigidly about the plant—and didn't release it until I took it from his hand."

"Cripes A'mighty, Lance! You've hit it!"

"Don't be too certain, Oscar. I may be striking far wide of the mark. But who do you suppose might be having a box shipped from a cactus company?"

"I just see one man," Oscar said promptly. "Professor Ulysses Z. Jones."

"I may be mistaken," Lance said slowly, "but I sure aim to further my acquaintance with the professor."

"He was plumb eager to get that mezcal button you had."

"He won't be so eager to get another one," Lance stated grimly, "if I'm right in my suspicions!"

V
War Talk!

It was nearly noon by the time Oscar and Lance arrived back at the sheriff's office to find Lockwood still working on his monthly accounts. The sheriff glanced up as they entered, then resumed work on the printed forms before him. "Well, sleuths," he grunted, entering some figures in lead pencil, "did you get to the bottom of our crime problem?"

"We mebbe didn't get to the bottom of it," Oscar stated, "but Lance sure constructed a picture that brings us nearer the top, I'm thinking."

Lockwood looked quizzically at Lance. "Think you found anything definite?"

Lance nodded. "Yes, I do, Ethan. Here's the way it looks to me. . . ." From that point on he told the story of what he and Oscar had discovered. When he had finished:

"By grab!" Lockwood exclaimed. "I think you've hit it."

"So far, so good," Lance pointed out, "but I still don't know who the murderer is nor what Bowman found here that had to do with mezcal buttons. That's not the case he was on—what I mean is, I don't see what mezcal buttons have to do with the case. But it's all tied in—somehow."

"Do you feel like telling us just what brought you and Bowman here?" Lockwood asked.

"I'll give you the story," Lance consented. "This information is to be held confidential, of course. I'm after a man named Matt Foster. Something over a year ago Foster and a gang of four accomplices stuck up a United States messenger who was delivering thirty thousand dollars, in bills, to a bank in Kansas City. The messenger and two guards were killed, but one of Foster's men was wounded and captured in the fight that took place. Through information from this captured bandit we managed to run down and capture all but Foster himself. Foster got away scot free. Not only that—he had all the money. The gang hadn't had an opportunity to divide the spoils. Luckily, the numbers of the stolen bills were on record and a warning sent out. The first bill showed up in New Orleans. My Denver office sent me to New Orleans to trace it down. From there the chase took me to Tampico, in Mexico, then up to Chihuahua City. I worked out of Chihuahua City a spell, trying to find something. No luck. I returned to Chihuahua after a month and found a letter for me saying some of the stolen money had showed up in Pozo Verde and that Frank Bowman had already been sent here. I was ordered to come here also."

"And on your way here," Oscar put in, "you found Bowman's body."

Lance nodded. "Now you know about as much as I do."

Lockwood asked, "Who in Pozo Verde reported the bills?"

"A traveling salesman passed them in Saddleville. He claimed that he'd got them from your local bank. The cashier here said he thought he remembered the bills but he'd never seen a list of the recorded numbers, so he couldn't be sure. The president of the Pozo Verde bank insisted his cashier was mistaken. Anyway, Bowman was sent on to investigate. Incidentally, the traveling salesman was released; he proved to be an honest man."

Lockwood looked thoughtful. "I wouldn't say our local banker was particularly bright. On the other hand, Elmer Manley, the cashier, is quite a smart boy."

Oscar said, "I suppose the bank would have a list of the numbers."

"Every bank in the country has them," Lance replied.

"Do you happen to have a description of Matt Foster?" Lockwood asked. "Or any idea what he looks like?"

"We have a description from his pards we captured," Lance replied, "but it's the sort of description that fits any number of men. One of the captured gang had a photograph on him that helps some, but not much. Before they pulled that Kansas City job they'd been operating up in Wyoming. They held up a small bank there. Later, when they got down as far as Nebraska, they went on a wild party with the stolen money and ended up in a photo gallery where they had a group picture taken. Trouble is, Matt Foster was at the back of the group and he was wearing a heavy crop of whiskers——"

"And he's probably clean shaven now, eh?" Lockwood said.

"That's the way I figure." Lance drew out of one pocket a small photograph of five men seated in the typical photographer's gallery of the time, replete with palms, wicker furniture and a painted background. The five men all wore derby hats; their clothing looked new; wide watch chains stretched across each fancy vest. Apparently they had gone on a wild buying spree with their ill-gotten gains. Four of the men wore heavy mustaches; the fifth, only his head showing in the background, had a thick, dark beard that nearly covered his face.

Lance pointed out the bearded man. "That's Matt Foster. He doesn't look familiar to you, I suppose?"

The sheriff shook his head. "Never saw him so far as I know. With only his head showing that way and with that beard you haven't much to go on. I figure this Matt Foster had a mite more sense than the rest of the gang and didn't want his face seen no more than could be helped."

"That's the way I figure him," Lance agreed.

Oscar studied the picture for a time, but Foster's face wasn't familiar to him either. The men talked a few minutes more, then Lockwood said, "I'll be busy on these reports for a mite yet. Why don't you two go get your dinner, then relieve me when you're finished?"

On the street Lance said to Oscar, "Where do we eat?"

"There's three or four good restaurants in town. There's a chili joint across the street there. The New York Chophouse serves good grub. I like the hotel dining room, too, only they take longer to serve. There's a Chink down the street a couple of blocks has right good chow."

"Let's make it the Chink's. A couple of blocks' walk will give me a chance to see your town."

They sauntered along, their high-heeled boots making hollow, clumping sounds on the raised plank sidewalk from which, in places, the broiling noon sun was drawing spots of pitch. As they crossed Laredo Street Oscar pointed out the Pozo Verde Savings Bank at the northeast corner of Main. As Lance glanced across the street Chiricahua Herrick, accompanied by a middle-aged fat man in a white shirt, was just emerging from the bank doorway. The fat man was mopping perspiration from his bald head with his handkerchief.

"That fat feller is Gillett Addison, owner of the bank," Oscar commented.

"Queer bedfellows," Lance said.

"Huh?"

"I mean it's rather surprising to see a man like Herrick consorting with the owner of a bank."

"I reckon they weren't together. Probably just came out the door at the same time. See, Addison is walking down the street alone. Probably headed for the hotel. He always eats his dinner there."

"And Herrick," Lance added, "is heading out toward the hitch rack. It sure looks like his pony had been pushed hard. Look at the poor beast. It's flecked with foam all over its forequarters. I reckon Kilby was speaking straight when he said Herrick had gone to Tipata to check up on my alibi. But why should he go direct to the bank?"

"You tell me," Oscar suggested.

"I wouldn't know. Though generally a man like Herrick don't have many dealings with a bank. I was just wondering if he had gone there to report that my alibi was airtight."

"Report to who?"

"That's something else I wouldn't know."

"Gosh, you're sure suspicious, Lance, when you start picking on one of Pozo Verde's leading citizens."

"I didn't say he'd reported to Banker Gillett. But in my game you have to be suspicious of everybody."

They walked on until they came to the Chink's restaurant. Across the windows of the building was painted the words: "Jou Low—Restaurant." They passed inside and found seats at a long counter, where presently they were served with roast beef, pie, potatoes, bread and coffee. They were half through the meal when Chiricahua Herrick entered. Spying Lance seated at the counter, Herrick stiffened suddenly, then, noting the deputy sheriff at his side, relaxed again. He nodded shortly to Oscar and spoke coldly to Lance:

"I want to see you, Tolliver."

Lance glanced over his shoulder at Herrick. "You see me, hombre. What's on your mind?" His eyes drilled into Herrick's.

Herrick opened his mouth to speak; his eyes fell momentarily before Lance's steely gaze. Finally he turned away muttering, "I'll see you later," and passed down the counter to find a seat farther on.

"I wonder what's eating him?" Lance commented to Oscar.

"He's prob'ly got liver trouble," Oscar grunted between bites of food. "He should eat more lemon drops."

They finished their dinners, drained coffee cups and left the restaurant. On the sidewalk once more, Oscar said, "I'll get back to the office and see can I help out on the sheriff's reports. What you going to do?"

"I'm going to stay here until Herrick comes out," Lance said quietly. "He opened a topic of conversation he didn't finish. I aim to learn what's on his mind."

"In that case," Oscar drawled, "I reckon the sheriff's reports can wait a spell longer. I don't think you'll start trouble, but you might have it forced on you. It's my duty to keep the peace when possible."

"Suit yourself."

They rolled and lighted cigarettes and stood leaning against the tie rail, waiting for Herrick to put in an appearance. Within a short time he emerged from the restaurant doorway, picking his teeth. His face flushed a trifle as he noted Lance and Oscar standing at the hitch rack, but he made no move to stop.

"Hi yuh, Cherry-Cow," Oscar said cheerfully. "I hear you been ridin' across the line to Tipata to check up on Tolliver's alibi—and incident'ly on Sheriff Lockwood's word. He already told you where Tolliver was the night Bowman was killed."

Chiricahua Herrick paused, spun about and crossed the sidewalk directly to face Oscar and Lance. "Who told you I'd been to Tipata?" he growled.

Lance took up the conversation. "I encountered your friend, Kilby, this morning. He spilled the beans."

Herrick's swarthy features twisted angrily. "I heard something about that encounter, Tolliver. Taken to beating up fellers when they've been drinking, eh? Is that your idea? Get 'em when they ain't steady on their pins?"

"Frankly," Lance said quietly, "I didn't want to do it. I wasn't looking for trouble. I wasn't side-stepping any that was forced upon me either. I couldn't do anything else——"

"That's your story," Herrick sneered, deceived by Lance's quiet manner

"Hell, Cherry-Cow," Oscar said disgustedly,

"Kilby's just lucky Lance didn't plug him. He was asking for it. Lance was decent to him just as long as he dared be——"

"Yaah!" Herrick said scornfully. "That's why Tolliver hit him. He wouldn't dare cross guns with George Kilby. Kilby would shoot rings——"

"Oh, cripes," Lance said wearily, "let's forget it. There was no powder burned and no one hurt to any extent. If Kilby's got any sense he'll be glad I acted as I did when he sobers up. Let's skip it, Herrick. . . . I hope you learned that I spent the night at Moreles' fonda in Tipata the night Bowman was killed."

Herrick laughed skeptically. "Yeah—that's what Moreles says, but I wouldn't believe that Mex on a stack of Bibles. You probably paid him plenty pesos for backing up your play. But we'll get the deadwood on you yet——"

"If you're trying to make trouble," Lance said firmly, "I'll do what I can to accommodate you——"

". . . and square matters for the murder of our old pal, Frank Bowman," Herrick raged on, the angry words gushing from his lips.

"Herrick," Lance asked, "you keep talking about your old pal, Bowman. Just how long has he been a pal of yours?"

Herrick paused. "Why—why," he finally said lamely, "me and the boys have only known him about a month or so, but we were right friendly. We all thought a heap of Frank——"

"I think you're a liar," Lance said quietly.

"You can't call me a liar!" Herrick flared hotly.

"I've already done it."

"That sounds like war talk, Tolliver," Herrick said menacingly.

"It's meant to be!" Lance took a step nearer Herrick. "If you don't like that kind of war talk get out your iron and go to work."

Herrick eyed Lance unbelievingly. "You're offering to cross guns with *me?*" Again he laughed scornfully. "I reckon you don't know my rep hereabouts."

"I'm not even interested in it," Lance snapped. "I don't like you or anybody that does. Furthermore, you're so damned anxious to pin Bowman's murder on me I'm commencing to wonder just who you're shielding——"

"Huh? What did you say?" A certain consternation appeared in Herrick's beady eyes. "Where did you ever get such a crazy idea as——?"

"And I'd also like to know," Lance interrupted, "just why you have to report to the bank that my alibi was airtight." This last was largely a feeler to see what it might draw forth from Herrick.

"You—you—you're crazy as a hoot owl," Herrick stammered.

"What were you doing in the bank a spell back?" Lance flashed.

"Why, I—I wasn't at the bank—I——"

"Don't lie, Herrick!"

"Oh yes, I know what you mean." Herrick's words sounded a bit crippled. "Yeah, I remember now. I dropped in to get a ten-dollar bill changed."

Oscar chuckled dryly. "All the saloons in town out of change, I suppose."

Herrick directed a look of hate at Oscar and swung back to Lance. He was regaining some of his courage now. "What in hell business is it of yours, anyway?" he demanded. "I got a right to go in the bank——"

"I'm not denying that." Lance nodded coolly. "As a matter of fact, I didn't open this conversation.

In the restaurant you said you wanted to see me. I waited here until you'd finished your dinner. So far you haven't had anything to say that amounts to a damn, aside from voicing some threats that sound pretty empty to me."

"They won't sound so empty before long," Herrick snarled, again losing his temper. "I said I was going to get you. I'm not backing down any on that statement."

"I've already invited you to pull your iron and start," Lance said quietly. "The first move is up to you!" He stood easily before Herrick, right thumb hooked into cartridge belt, waiting.

Herrick backed a step, then another. Suddenly he threw both arms wide of his sides and shook his head. "I'm not drawing now," he said thickly. "Not when you got that deputy to back your play. I'll get you sometime when the odds are even. A man can't get a square deal with the peace officers in this town."

Oscar drawled indolently, "Cherry-Cow, how would you like me to knock your ugly mug out from under your hat?"

"There you are, there you are!" Herrick spat hotly. "Like I say, the law's taking sides. I ain't fool enough to take on two men at once——"

"You're fool enough to stand here talking about it, I notice," Oscar stated disgustedly. "Go on, on your way, Herrick. First thing you know, I'll be running you out of town for good."

Herrick commenced backing away, his gaze still on Lance. "You got things your way right now, Tolliver," he grated, "but just remember, there's new cards turn up in every deal."

"I'm remembering," Lance said coldly. "Any time,

anywhere—the play's up to you. I'll meet any stakes you name!"

Herrick mouthed a muffled curse and, swinging around, strode swiftly down Main Street as though anxious to get away.

VI
Peaceful Yaquentes?

Oscar and Lance arrived back at the sheriff's office after a time to find Lockwood donning his sombrero preparatory to going to dinner. Lockwood eyed the two gravely as they entered.

"I understand," the sheriff said, "that you two exchanged a few words with Chiricahua Herrick."

"Where'd you hear that?" Lance asked.

"Herrick dropped in a few minutes back to make a complaint. He claims you tried to pick a fight with him, Lance, and you, Oscar, was ready to jump in to help. He asked that I tell you to leave him alone."

Oscar said calmly, "He's a bloody liar if he claims we picked on him. Here's what happened." He gave the sheriff the story of what had taken place.

Lockwood nodded. "I figured it was something like that. I wasn't impressed none. I told Herrick to mind his business, and you boys would mind yours. He was inclined to get a mite cocky, so I told him when he was willing to trust the law hereabouts the law would trust him. He claimed he didn't know what I meant, so I asked him what in hell was his idea riding to Tipata to check up on Lance's alibi after I'd passed my word the alibi was good. I reckon he hadn't figured on me knowing that, and he got sort of flustered. I poured it on him pretty strong, and he was glad to get out of here, I reckon."

"At that, I figure he'd be a mean man to tangle with," Lance commented.

"You're probably right." Lockwood nodded. "Well, I'm going to get some chow. My stomach is commencing to think my throat's cut. What you going to do, Lance?"

"I'm aiming to drop in on the hotel sometime this afternoon and get further acquainted with Professor Jones. I've got to see about getting a room there myself anyway."

Oscar asked, mouthing a lemon drop, as he dropped into the chair vacated by Lockwood, "You figuring to see if you can pump him about those Loafer-for-William plants?"

"Mebbe." Lance smiled. "I'd just like to get better acquainted with him."

He and the sheriff passed through the doorway and started along Main Street. Lance mentioned that he had seen Herrick leave the bank with the bank's owner, Gillett Addison. Lockwood frowned and said, "I doubt if it means anything. Gill Addison has always been on the up-and-up so far as I know. Incidentally, if you're going to see the professor you'll probably meet his niece. She's a right likely looking filly, if I ever saw one. Her father owned a ranch down in Sonora. He was murdered about a year back. Nobody ever did know who done it. Some Yaquente Indians found the body and brought it into Pozo Verde——"

"They're sure the Yaquentes didn't kill him, eh?"

"I don't know how sure they are. Being in Sonora, the whole business was up to the Mexican authorities, you know. What they ever did, if anything, I haven't heard. It was out of my jurisdiction, of course—— Say, speaking of Yaquentes—there's a couple of 'em now across the street."

Lance's gaze followed the sheriff's pointing finger and saw the two Indians. They were well set-up men, clothed in loose, flopping cotton garments, with huge straw sombreros on their heads. One was in his bare feet; his companion wore crude leather sandals. They looked much like the peons to be found throughout Mexico, though there was an air of independence about the two men that almost smacked of belligerence.

"Right peaceful-looking hombres," Lockwood muttered grimly, "but they're sure hell on wheels when it comes to fighting. You give them two a six-shooter and a carbine and a bandoleer of ca'tridges and you'd be surprised how it 'd transform 'em. I know; I fought 'em some about fifteen years back. The Mex Government has got 'em held down to some extent at present, but no man can say they were entirely conquered."

"What do you suppose those two are doing in Pozo Verde?"

"They cross the line and come to town every once in a while," Lockwood replied. "A small bunch of 'em get a few pesos and come up here for a buying spree every so often. We never have no trouble with 'em. They never do any drinking here—mostly they're satisfied to buy some beads or knives or bolts of colored cotton——"

"Here's three more of 'em," Lance interrupted, "coming along the street on this side."

The sheriff didn't seem greatly concerned. The

three Yaquentes, dresed approximately the same as the first two Lance had seen, passed them swiftly and turned in at Parker's General Store.

Lance laughed. "I hope somebody in that store can speak Yaquente."

"He can't," Lockwood said dryly. "Nobody speaks Yaquente but a Yaquente. But they get along all right. Some of those Indians can *habla* Spanish right well."

Lance parted from the sheriff at the corner of Laredo Street and crossed diagonally to the steps of the San Antonio Hotel which stood at the intersection of the two thoroughfares. As he mounted the steps to the hotel porch which stretched across the front of the building's lower floor, fronting on Main, Lance glanced along the street in either direction. From this higher point of vantage he had a clear view both ways. His eyes narrowed a trifle as he noticed on the sidewalks still more Yaquente Indians.

"Knowing what I do of Yaquentes," Lance muttered, "I sure wouldn't feel too good about 'em coming over here. Howsomever, they're peaceful now, and I reckon Ethan Lockwood knows his business." Dismissing the thought from his mind, he passed on into the hotel.

The hotel lobby reached the length of the front of the building. To the left as one entered was a doorway into the hotel bar. At the opposite end of the lobby was a staircase ascending to the rooms on the second floor. Midway between the two was a small oaken desk with behind it a series of pigeonholes for room keys and letters. Several men were seated about the lobby. Most of them, Lance decided after a brief glance, were drummers for liquor or hardware houses or cattle buyers in Pozo Verde to make contacts with the neighboring ranches.

Lance negotiated for a room and secured one on the second floor, facing Main Street. "I'll see it later," he told the clerk who wanted to show the room. "My bedroll is with my horse over at the Lone Star Livery. I'll bring over what dunnage I need later on." He signed the register, then asked, "By the way, Professor Jones is staying here, isn't he?"

The clerk nodded. "Oh yes. His room is just down the hall from the one you've taken. . . . No, I'm afraid you can't see him now. He's out, I believe, riding with his niece. You know, studying cactus——" The clerk smiled a bit superciliously. "Why anyone should bother with such plants is more than I can understand. Now, a nice geranium in a window pot—that's different——"

"Everybody to his own taste, I reckon," Lance commented. "The professor goes in pretty heavy for cactus, eh?"

"More than seems reasonable." The clerk nodded. "He's already packed three boxes with plants and has them stored in our storage room until he leaves." The clerk whirled the register around and read Lance's name. "Oh, Mr Tolliver. You're the one who found that murdered man, aren't you?—Frank Bowman?"

Lance nodded and started to turn away. "Tell the professor I dropped in, will you? I'll be back later on——"

He stopped short as a new voice broke in, "I'm a friend of Professor Jones'. Perhaps I can help you out if you'll let me know what you want. It may save you a trip back here. I'm Malcolm Fletcher. Did I understand you to say you're Tolliver?"

"I'm Tolliver." Lance shook hands with Fletcher, whom he'd noticed seated at the far end of the hotel lobby. Fletcher was a broad-shouldered, slim-hipped man with a lantern jaw, piercing eyes and brown hair, somewhere in the vicinity of thirty or thirty-five years of age. He wore high-heeled boots and corduroy trousers. A black sombrero was shoved to the back of his head. He had the appearance of a cowman, though Lance felt he hadn't worked at that trade for some time. There was an air of affluence about Fletcher.

". . . and if you care to state your business," he was saying, "I may be able to help you out."

"No particular business to state." Lance smiled. "I just met the professor on the street this morning, and he asked me to call. I'll see him later."

"It wasn't about a job as a guide you wanted to see him?"

Lance shook his head. "Why should I?"

Fletcher laughed. "No reason at all," he replied. "I just thought you were after that job Bowman had before his death. Just in case you were, I can tell you now it's not open."

"The professor decide he doesn't need a guide any more?"

"He actually doesn't, of course, around here, but he had hired Bowman to take him down into Sonora."

"I see." Lance nodded. "Has Professor Jones given up the Mexico trip?"

"Just about," Fletcher answered. "I've been against it from the first, of course. I think he'll take my advice."

"There's nothing final been decided yet, then?"

"It's practically settled."

"Why have you advised against the trip?"

"Mexico is pretty wild country," Fletcher explained. "I don't think it any place to take a girl—at least, a girl like Professor Jones' niece. There are a large number of Yaquente Indians through the section in which Jones wants to travel. The Yaquentes are peaceful enough now, but"—Fletcher shrugged his shoulders—"a man never knows what may turn up."

"You certainly said something then," Lance agreed. He turned to leave. "Well, much obliged for the information. If you'll tell the professor I called——"

"I'll tell him," Fletcher said, "though there's no chance of you getting that job even if you knew that country down there. I hope you see how it is."

"I reckon," Lance said noncommittally. He nodded to Fletcher and left the hotel. On the street he said to himself, "I'm not sure if I do see how it is. I wonder who that Fletcher hombre is, and is he making all decisions for Jones? For some reason he's none too keen for Jones to head down into Mexico. Oh well, I'll see Jones later. Maybe a mite of conversation will bring out something."

Lance next bent his steps in the direction of the railroad depot. As he entered the station old Johnny Quinn glanced up and grunted sourly. "You agin, eh?" he squeaked. "Well, I ain't remembered no more than I did this mornin', so ye're wastin' my time and yours if ye insist on hangin' round——"

"There's no law against sending a telegram, is there?"

"A telygram?" Johnny Quinn stiffened like a soldier coming to attention. "Ye want to send a telygram? Whyn't ye say so in the first place? Here's a pad o' paper. Write 'er out plain, and I'll shoot 'er off."

Lance smiled inwardly and proceeded to "write 'er out plain." When he had finished he shoved the paper across to old Quinn. Quinn snatched at the paper and started to read it. He got as far as the address, then glanced up over his spectacles at Lance, saying, "You're sendin' this to Washington, D.C., hey? Hmmm. Thet's where the President of these United States lives."

Lance nodded. "I've heard rumors to that effect before. Howsomever, it isn't being sent to him."

"Shucks all tarnation!" Old Quinn sounded exasperated. "I know thet much." He started to read on, then stopped. A frown gathered on his forehead. He squinted through his spectacles, took them off, wiped them on his bandanna, replaced them, took them off again. Finally he gave up. "Are ye drunk?"

"Haven't had a drink today."

"There's somethin' wrong with ye!" Quinn snapped. "I can read your words separate, but they don't make no sense strung out in a line. Can't make head ner tail what ye're aimin' to send."

"You can send the words just as they are, can't you?"

" 'Tain't usual!"

Lance laughed. "It is back in Washington. That's the way folks talk back there. If you're interested I can tell you what the message is about. You see, my aunt Minnie is back there suffering from a bad case of hemoglobinuria and——"

"What's thet?" Quinn's jaw sagged.

Lance laughed suddenly. "Of course, of course. I might have known you'd had that disease some time or other, so there's no need of me going into details about Aunt Minnie's case. Probably you know more about the ravages of hemoglobinuria than I do. What's that? You got it back in sixty-five? Well, well, imagine that! That's the very year Aunt Minnie was took down with it. What? You don't say so! A poultice of axle grease and horse liniment, eh? And it cured you? I'll sure write Aunt Minnie about that if she doesn't get well——What? A glass of bourbon three times a day prevents a recurrence of the disease? Sa-ay, it's lucky I ran into you. Aunt Minnie will probably owe you her life."

Johnny Quinn's eyes were glassy; his jaw hung open. He was gasping like a fish out of water. So far he hadn't said a word, but Lance's swift monologue had swept him from his feet. His brain swirled dizzily, and he was already convinced he had had the disease Lance mentioned.

". . . and I'll sure remember," Lance flowed on, "to bring you a bottle of bourbon when I come back for the answer to my telegram. I wouldn't want you to come down with hemoglobinuria again. You see, when that answer comes through I'll know if Aunt Minnie is recovering or not, so shoot my message off pronto. I'll be back later for the reply—and I won't forget your bourbon."

Five minutes after Lance had left the station old Quinn was still scratching his sparse gray hair and panting for breath. His brain whirled. "Lemme see," he gulped, "was it in sixty-five I had that hemo dis-ease?" His thin frame trembled. "By grab! I'd better get this telygram sent right to once. A case of life or death ain't to be ignored." He stumbled toward the sending apparatus muttering, "Life or death, life or death, life or death."

Lance was still laughing when he entered the sher-iff's office a short time later. Lockwood was back at his desk. Oscar Perkins had gone down to the general store for a fresh supply of lemon drops. "What you grinnin' at?" Lockwood demanded.

"I had a telegram to send," Lance chuckled. "It was in code, so I had to give old Johnny Quinn an explanation." He related what had happened.

The sheriff's laughter merged with Lance's. "Johnny's always boasting about how many different diseases he's had," Lockwood said, "so I reckon it wa'n't hard to convince him he had this here—uh—hemo—uh—what was that word? What's it mean?"

"Hemoglobinuria." Lance explained, "That's just a more scientific name for Texas tick fever." Lockwood went off into renewed gales of laughter. When he had quieted Lance asked, "Say, who's this Malcolm Fletcher staying at the hotel? I went to see Jones, but he was away digging cactus. Fletcher claims to be a friend of his."

"He might be, at that," Lockwood conceded. "I don't know. He's been right friendly with Miss Gregory—you know, Jones' niece. The two of 'em have gone riding a lot. Anyway, I told you the girl's father owned a ranch down in Sonora. Malcolm Fletcher was Jared Gregory's pardner in the ranch. I meant to tell you all this today. Then we got talking about those Yaquentes we saw, and it slipped my mind."

"You told me about Jared Gregory being murdered and brought in by the Yaquentes." Lance's eyes narrowed. "It couldn't be that Fletcher had a hand in the death of Miss Gregory's father?"

"If he did, I couldn't say. He had an alibi, at least."

"The same being?"

"Fletcher claims to be interested in both mines and ranches. At the time Jared Gregory was killed

Fletcher was this side of the border driving around and looking at properties for sale."

"You just got his word for that?"

"We got the word of Banker Addison. Addison was showing the properties which the bank had foreclosed on some time before."

"Apparently," Lance said slowly, "that clears Fletcher." Then he added, "Apparently."

Shortly before suppertime Lance entered the railroad depot, a bottle of bourbon under one arm. He placed it on the counter behind which old Johnny Quinn stood waiting with a yellow sheet of paper in his hand. "Johnny, there's your medicine. Did you get an answer for me?"

"Sartainly," Johnny replied. "I had it rushed right through."

Lance took the yellow paper and quickly perused the code message it contained. A frown gathered on his face.

"Aunt Minnie must be worse," Johnny said anxiously.

"Aunt Minnie," Lance replied solemnly, "has plumb passed away. You'd better drink your medicine regular, Johnny."

Three minutes later Lance was back in the sheriff's office. "I got an answer to my telegram," he said tersely. "I had a little checking up done on Professor Ulysses Z. Jones of the Jonesian Institute at Washington, D.C. According to my reply there never was any such organization as the Jonesian Institute, and no one down there has ever heard of Professor Jones!"

"Somebody," Lockwood said grimly, "is a blasted liar."

Lance nodded. "I figure that I'm going to get acquainted with that somebody right after supper. I'll bet he doesn't do any cactus digging at night—though he may have other activities. That's something I'm aiming to find out with no more waste of time."

VII
Guns and Mezcal Buttons

It was shortly after six o'clock that evening when a worried-looking Johnny Quinn locked the doors of his station and took his departure, with an already partly depleted bottle of bourbon under his arm. Muttering something under his breath about the sad end of poor Aunt Minnie, he hurried off in the direction of his lodginghouse to fortify his system against the dread disease that had carried off Aunt Minnie.

The rapidly descending sun touched a line of fire along the high peaks of the Saddlestring Mountains. The crimson line turned to purple, then disappeared altogether. Darkness filled the ravines and hollows, spread swiftly overhead, and night came down. A few stars twinkled into being in the eastern sky, the first vanguard of the millions to follow. Off in the hills a coyote barked suddenly and as suddenly fell silent.

In the Mexican huts and adobe houses across the railroad tracks lights shone from windows, and a smell of cooking food mingled with the fragrant odor of mesquite roots ascending from dozens of chimneys. A door opened here and there and then closed abruptly on soft snatches of conversation in Spanish. Somewhere could be heard the strumming of a guitar. For a time quiet settled on the Mexican district.

Then, gradually, as meals were concluded doors commenced to open and close again as small knots of men and girls started walking toward Main Street to end up at Tony's Saloon or the Mexican Chili Parlor, with dance hall attached, which was located across the street from the sheriff's office. There weren't so many lamps burning in the houses now.

One, two, three hours passed. It had grown darker by this time. The moon wasn't yet up. By twos and threes soft-stepping, white-clothed forms in huge straw sombreros were commencing to cross the railroad tracks, flit silently past the scattered Mexican dwellings and take their steps in the direction of a squat adobe-and-rock building situated on the southern outer fringe of Pozo Verde at the very edge of the open range. The door of the building was locked, so the white-clad figures congregated silently about the building or conversed in low, guttural tones while they waited for the white man who had promised to come.

Chiricahua Herrick, followed by several other men, suddenly took form in the darkness. He jerked out a few low words of greeting in Spanish to the waiting Yaquentes, unlocked the door of the rock-and-adobe building and stepped inside. The Indians made no move to follow. Chiricahua found a bottle with a candle stuck in one end and touched a match flame to the wick, filling the room with soft light. Chiricahua spoke to two of his followers, and burlap sacks were fastened at the two windows of the single-room building which was furnished only with a table and a couple of straight-backed wooden chairs.

Chiricahua went to the doorway. "Johnson," he said softly, "you and Ordway stay out there and keep those Injuns quiet. Tell 'em they won't have to wait long and keep your eyes peeled to tip us off if anything goes wrong—though I don't reckon it will. Anvil should be along pretty soon."

He shut the door and sat down at the table. George Kilby took a chair by his side, and Bert Ridge found a seat on the floor with his back to the wall. Cigarettes were rolled and lighted.

Chiricahua said, "George, where'd you put that box?"

"Right behind you," Kilby said, "where it will be within easy reach."

Herrick laughed a bit uneasily. "For a moment I thought you'd forgotten it."

"Not that box," Kilby stated definitely. "I might have forgotten one in the past, but that damn box of buttons caused us too much trouble to be forgotten easy."

"By Jeez!" Ridge commented. "That was once we nearly got caught. That damned Bowman would have had us dead to rights——"

"That reminds me." Chiricahua Herrick frowned. "I think that blasted Oscar Perkins has something in mind——"

"If it's anything but lemon drops"—Kilby grinned—"I'll be a heap surprised."

"Don't you grade Perkins down none." Herrick frowned. "That deputy has more sense than we give him credit for, unless"—he paused suddenly, struck by a new idea—"unless that Tolliver hombre is back of it——"

"Back of what?" Ridge asked.

"This afternoon," Herrick explained, "the barkeep of the Pozo Verde Saloon told me Perkins had been in asking questions."

Kilby asked, "What sort of questions?"

"Perkins wanted to know if there was any shooting heard out back of the saloon the night Frank Bowman was killed——"

"My Gawd!" Kilby exclaimed, and some of the color left his face. "That comes pretty nigh to hittin' the bull's-eye. The railroad station ain't much more than good spittin' distance back of the saloon."

"I've been thinkin' about that, too," Herrick growled. "I don't like it——"

"Look," Ridge broke in, "did the barkeep hear anything that night?"

"We got a break," Herrick said quietly. "Don't you remember, day before yesterday was payday for the Bar-L-Bar outfit? The whole crew was celebrating. The barkeep tells me they made plenty noise. Some of 'em was even shooting holes in the clouds. So," and he smiled craftily, "the shot that got Bowman was never noticed."

Kilby gave a long sigh of relief. "That *is* a break."

"It's too damn bad," Ridge commented, "that we couldn't have fastened that job on Tolliver."

"Tolliver will get his yet," Herrick promised darkly. "Only that I got orders from the chief not to start anything I'd slung a slug through Tolliver this morning."

"Why'd the big boss give orders like that?" Kilby asked.

Herrick shrugged his shoulders. "He gives orders, and I take 'em. I'm paid well, so I don't kick. Howsomever, he probably don't want any of us mixed into any shooting scrapes until things are all set. We don't want to attract no more attention than possible."

"I'd like a chance to put a forty-four right through Tolliver's belly," Kilby snarled. "I got to get even for the wallop he give me this mornin'——"

"I reckon you had that coming," Herrick said coldly. "Only for you getting crocked and talking more than you should nobody would ever have known I rode to Tipata to check on Tolliver's alibi. Yep, sometimes I could almost wish Tolliver had plugged you——"

"Aw, hell, Chiricahua," Kilby protested, "I told you I didn't know what I was doing. I made a mistake—I admit it."

"It'd be your neck if I told the boss," Herrick snapped. "I reckon you wouldn't last long if he knew——"

"Is that right?" Kilby said, bristling. "I wouldn't advise this boss you're always takin' orders from to get too hard with me. I know too much."

Herrick nodded coolly. "I know you do, George. There was a couple of other fellers just like you— they knew too much. That's why we had to get rid of 'em. And we didn't just tell 'em to get out of the gang. Do you see what I mean?"

Kilby gulped and shivered a little. "I see what you mean," he said shakily, and fell silent.

"Don't forget it then," Herrick said cruelly. "There's no place in our gang for hombres who run off at the head. There's more 'n one way to keep a feller from talking—but there's only one sure way."

"Sure, Chiricahua," Kilby said placatingly. "I know what you mean."

There was silence for a few moments. Kilby produced a flask and drank deeply. Herrick was restored to good humor again. "Going to keep that all to yourself?" he demanded. "Me 'n' Bert could stand a drink."

The flask was passed around until it was empty. Then Herrick said, "I don't know just what to think of Tolliver."

Ridge asked, "Why?"

Herrick shrugged. "I don't know. I got a feeling I'm due to cross guns with him. Well, the sooner the better."

There was another silence before Kilby said, "Anvil's later than usual, seems like."

"I reckon not," Herrick replied. "You're just nervous, George."

"Maybe I got a right to be," Kilby said. "If anybody ever stumbled onto us we'd have some fast explanations to make. I don't see why the big chief doesn't take the stuff over into Sonora instead of having those Yaquentes come here for it."

"The big boss isn't running any more risk than necessary," Herrick said. "The Mexican Government don't cater to those Yaquentes having guns, or buttons either. Suppose some of us got picked up in Mexico—running that stuff into the country? Anyway, don't you worry, George. I reckon this will be the last for a spell. We should have enough stuff over there now to outfit a young army."

"I still don't get the idea of the mezcal buttons," Ridge put in. "Guns, yes, that's clear, but——"

"A Yaquente will do anything for anybody that gives him a button he can dry and eat," Herrick said. "The tribe has just about cleaned out the hills in their own neighborhood and they don't like the idea of traveling farther south to get the buttons for their ceremonies——" He paused suddenly.

Outside could be heard the sounds made by an

arriving team and wagon, then loud tones as the wagon was tooled into place near the building.

"There's Anvil now." Kilby looked relieved.

"And noisier 'n hell!" Herrick said angrily. "Whoever named him Anvil sure called the turn. Loud and hard!" He jerked open the door and snapped, "Cut out the noise, Wheeler. You'll have the whole town down on us. Ridge—Kilby—get out and help Ordway and Johnson bring in them boxes."

Kilby and Ridge hurried outside. Anvil Wheeler jumped down from the wagon he had been driving and strode into the 'dobe building. He was a big, powerfully built man with a hooked nose and wide spreading mustaches. A tattered, roll-brim sombrero was yanked down on one side of his head.

Herrick said, "You're late."

"Hell's bells!" Anvil Wheeler replied. "I pushed that team right along. After all, it's quite some miles to Saddleville and back——"

"Have any trouble?" Herrick asked.

"Not none."

"All right, get them boxes open when the boys bring 'em in. Get Kilby to help you." From the doorway Herrick gave further orders. "Get them Injuns lined up, Johnson. Keep 'em quiet and keep 'em moving. We want to get away from here as soon as possible."

Pine boxes were carried into the building. Johnson and one of the other men were getting the Indians in line. There was little talking now. Anvil Wheeler and Kilby were removing covers from the boxes, Kilby with tools, Wheeler with main brute strength much of the time.

Finally all was in readiness. Herrick sat at the table again, the box of mezcal buttons within easy reach. Kilby and Wheeler stood near the boxes of rifles and six-shooters. Johnson entered from outside. He was grinning. "Them Yaquentes are ready for their 'peestols,' " he announced.

Herrick chuckled. "Damn Injuns call all shootin' irons pistols. Makes no difference if it's a rifle or six-gun. All right, let 'em come."

The Indians started entering the building. The first dark-skinned, flat-faced Yaquente came to the table at which Herrick sat. Herrick said, "What you want, hombre?"

The Yaquente's teeth flashed whitely. "Un peestol— peyote," he said gutturally.

"Here's your peyote." Herrick's hand dipped into the near-by box and came up with a mezcal button which he passed to the Indian. The Yaquente clutched it avidly. Herrick jerked one hand over his shoulder toward Kilby who stood near a box of six-shooters. "That hombre will give you your peestol," he said.

The Indian passed on to receive his six-shooter. Others came behind to receive six-shooters and peyotes. Every fifth man received a rifle in addition to his six-shooter. The Yaquentes circled the table, then departed by the open doorway.

Suddenly there was a slight commotion at the doorway. One of the Indians was arguing with Larry Johnson. Herrick growled, "What's eatin' that hombre?"

Johnson replied, "He wants the ammunition to go with his gun."

Herrick shook his head. "Tell him we'll bring the ca'tridges later. No bullets now—no slugs—no bang-bang. Savvy, hombre?"

"Savvy," the Indian grunted, and disappeared through the doorway. Once more the passing line of Indians got under way.

Finally the line came to an end. There were still a few guns and mezcal buttons remaining in the boxes. Herrick said, "Take these leftovers out and divide 'em up." When this had been done the door was once more closed. Herrick rose to his feet and stretched wearily. "A good night's work," he announced. He glanced at the empty boxes, then smiled at the words painted on them. "Canned tomatoes, eh? Must be you're going into the grocery business, Anvil."

Wheeler's loud laugh shook the rafters of the room. "That's what the freight agent in Saddleville wanted to know. What gets that hombre is that he don't know where I take all these canned goods he delivers to me."

"It's a damned good thing he don't know," Herrick said shortly. "Ordway, get outside and see if those Yaquentes are gone yet. If they ain't tell 'em to va-moose and get over the line as soon as possible. We don't want any slip-up at this stage of the game."

Ordway stepped outside. Within a few minutes he was back. "Not a Yaquente in sight," he announced. "They've plumb faded. Aces to tens they're halfway to the border already."

"I don't reckon it will be many more days before we're headed that way ourselves," Herrick said. He blew out the candle. "All right, get going. Scatter! We'll meet at the Pozo Verde Saloon and drink a long one to crime and easy money."

VIII
Another Clue

Meanwhile, after having eaten supper with Sheriff Lockwood and his deputy, Lance returned to the sheriff's office with the two peace officers to smoke a couple of cigarettes before going back to the hotel in search of "Professor Jones"—as he called himself.

"Those Yaquentes," Lance commented, "seem to have disappeared from the streets. I haven't seen one since suppertime."

Lockwood nodded. "They don't often stay in Pozo Verde after dark. I noticed a small bunch of 'em crossing the railroad tracks shortly before we went to eat. They'll probably travel all night and keep going, with but little sleep, until they strike their own country. They're tough travelers and tough fighters. They can move through a country where an animal couldn't find forage and be ready to tackle their weight in puma cats at the same time."

Oscar Perkins fumbled with his sack of lemon drops, thrust it back into his pocket and then rose and lighted two oil lamps resting in their brackets on the walls of the sheriff's office. Velvety darkness settled softly along Main Street. Occasionally the clump-clump of heavy boots could be heard passing along the raised plank sidewalks. Now and then a rider loped his pony through town, raising dust from the roadway. Across the street from the sheriff's office small knots of Mexican girls and men congregated before the chili restaurant. At the rear of the restaurant, where a dance floor was located, a string orchestra could already be heard tuning its instruments.

Lance rose and donned his sombrero. "I reckon I'll drift down to the hotel and see can I find Professor Jones. He should be through his supper by this time."

Lockwood asked, "Are you going to tell him you discovered there wasn't any Jonesian Institute in Washington?"

"And that they don't even know of a Professor Jones there?" Oscar put in.

Lance smiled and shook his head. "I won't tip my hand in that direction until I have to."

He said "S'long" to Oscar and the sheriff and sauntered along Main Street past the rows of shops and stores and saloons, many of which were brightly lighted; others were closed and dark. He crossed diagonally at the corner of Laredo Street and entered the San Antonio Hotel. There were several men lounging about the lobby when he came in. There were two women in sight. One, whom he judged to be the wife of the local minister, was carrying on a discussion with an elderly man regarding the sermon of the previous week. The other, a girl with yellow hair, in a blue dress, was seated at the far end of the lobby conversing with Malcolm Fletcher. Fletcher was talking earnestly to his companion, but the girl was smiling and shaking her head. Whatever the conversation, Lance judged Fletcher wasn't making any headway.

Looking at the girl with Fletcher, Lance paused and felt a small twinge of envy. The girl glanced up;

her eyes met his. She said something to Fletcher.
Fletcher frowned impatiently and glanced around.
His frown deepened as his gaze fell on Lance.

"You'll find the professor in the hotel bar, Tolliver," he called tersely, "if you still want to see him.
If it's a job, though, it won't do you any good."

Lance said, "Thanks," and turned toward a doorway at his left, but not before he had seen Fletcher
swing abruptly back to the girl. Passing through into
the hotel bar, Lance saw Ulysses Jones seated at a
corner table with a bottle of beer before him. At the
professor's elbow was a small cactus plant, and he
was busily engaged in transferring certain penciled
notes from a small notebook to a larger memoranda
book. Lance glanced along the bar. Some half-dozen
men were engaged in desultory conversation. The
barkeep was polishing glasses. A couple of the men
at the bar glanced at Lance when he entered, then
turned back to their drinks.

Lance approached Jones's table. "Howdy, Professor."

Jones lifted his thin face. His vague eyes settled
on Lance with a sort of irritated expression. They
cleared suddenly, sharpened; a smile crossed his
lips. "Ah, it's Mr Tolliver—right? Glad to see you. Sit
down. Drinking beer myself. Suit you? Right!" He
raised his voice. "Pat, two more of the same."

"Be right with you, Professor." The bartender
nodded.

". . . thought I'd drop in and get acquainted,"
Lance was saying. "How'd the cactus digging go today?"

"Little digging," Jones jerked out. "I only take the
rarer specimens—y'know, the unusual—that sort of

thing. Mostly study soil—growing conditions—whether in full sun or shade—surrounding brush—so on."

"The hotel clerk was telling me you already had three boxes packed in his storeroom."

Jones nodded. "Not full, y'know—not entirely. Packed in wood shavings. Nice specimens—not rare, all of them. Certain plants—necessary to complete my—our—Jonesian Institute collection. . . ."

The bartender arrived with the beer and glasses and removed Jones's empty bottle. Jones drank deeply of the foamy amber liquid, set down his glass and resumed: "You say—clerk—told you of my boxes?" Lance nodded. Jones smiled. "Fortunate I'm not trying—smuggle anything. Done, you know. Great Christopher, yes! Rare plants—smuggled one country—to another. Clerks—great source—information."

"I wasn't particularly looking for information," Lance said, "at least along those lines." He chuckled. "Fellow named Fletcher who said he was a friend of yours had an idea I was looking for Bowman's job. He told me it wasn't any use."

"Aren't, are you?"

Lance shook his head. "I saw him in the lobby when I came in tonight. He said the same thing again."

Jones frowned. "Fletcher takes a great deal on himself," he said more slowly than usual, running long fingers through his dark, gray-streaked hair. "He has no right to make decisions for me just because he doesn't favor my trip down into Mexico. Was Katherine with him?"

"Who?" Lance asked.

"Katherine Gregory—my niece—secretary."

"I saw him talking to a girl——"

"Fletcher didn't introduce you?"

Lance smiled. "Maybe he didn't think of it."

Jones laughed shortly. "More likely—wanted Katherine—to himself. Selfish brute!" His eyes twinkled. "Think Fletcher's—badly smitten. Do, for a fact."

Lance changed the subject. "So you're still planning the trip into Mexico?"

Jones nodded. "Some extent—Sonora—Chihuahua. Certain specimens—wish to study firsthand. Incident'ly"—he picked from the table the small cactus plant at his elbow and placed it before Lance— "found this today. Beautiful specimen—what?"

Lance glanced at the spines and decided not to pick it up. It was somewhat globular in shape, not more than two inches across, with eight deeply indented ribs, each rib bearing several brownish-black curved spines, its bright green surface thickly covered with tiny white dots.

Lance raised his eyes to meet Jones's. "I've seen these plants before," he said. "Not in these parts though. Let me see . . . seems like I remember seeing some over in New Mexico."

"Right, right, quite right." Jones beamed. His gaze sharpened suddenly on Lance. "Very observant, Tolliver. The *Astrophytum capricorne* is native to New Mexico. Of course—high percentage—New Mexican cacti—found in Arizona. This particular plant, however—beautiful—not found in native habitat— spines—unusual development—so young a specimen."

"Is this cactus," Lance asked innocently, "any relation to that peyote I gave you this morning?"

"The *Lophophora williamsii?*" Jones looked indignant. "Different genus entirely. As a member of the cacti family, yes. Otherwise—certainly not——" He paused. "Incident'ly—reminds me—you say you didn't find that specimen growing here? Mind—saying where—did you find it?"

Lance decided to hurl a bombshell. He said quietly, "I took it from Frank Bowman's hand when I found him dead."

Jones blinked rapidly. Then his eyes sharpened. "You mean to say you found the dead man holding that plant?"

"What's this?" a new voice broke in. Lance glanced around to see Malcolm Fletcher standing behind him. Fletcher said, "What plant was found in what dead man's hand?"

Lance wondered how long Fletcher had been standing there.

Jones was explaining, "Why, bless me, Fletcher! Tolliver says he found Bowman holding a *Lophophora williamsii*——"

"You mean that peyote thing you showed me this morning?" Fletcher asked sharply. "I thought you'd dug that up someplace." He turned suddenly to Lance. "How'd Bowman happen to be holding that thing? Where'd he get it? What was he doing with it?"

"You tell me, and I'll tell you," Lance said calmly. "I'm just telling you where I found it. Further than that I can't say. Why?—does it mean anything to you, Fletcher?"

Fletcher laughed shortly. "Not a thing. Seemed odd, that's all." He turned and started away.

Jones called after him, "Where's Katherine?"

"Gone up to her room," Fletcher answered,

scarcely waiting to reply. "If she comes down again tell her I've gone for a walk. I'll be back later." He hurried out the street entrance of the hotel bar.

Lance turned back to find Jones frowning in the direction Fletcher had taken. "Certainly seemed in a hurry to go someplace," Jones said.

Lance considered. Fletcher had heard part of their conversation. It had seemed to affect him queerly. Why not give Jones some more of the story and see if it brought any results?

"I'll tell you, Professor," Lance went on, "maybe I can give you a few more details about Bowman's death, provided you'll treat the matter confidentially." Now he really didn't care whether the man did or not as a matter of fact.

Jones looked interested. "Of course," he promised.

"Somebody," Lance commenced, "had a shipment of those mezcal buttons shipped to Pozo Verde. Now I can't tell you why Bowman was interested in that shipment, but he was shot after he'd opened the box and taken one of those plants. As he fell he knocked over a bucket of creosote on the station platform. Later, before he died, he was carried out to that dry wash where I found him. . . ." Lance went on and supplied certain other details.

When he had finished Jones's eyes were glowing admiringly. "If you're not a detective you should be," he stated emphatically. "Nice work, Tolliver. Imagine!—discovering all that from a hand painted black."

"And a pine sliver," Lance reminded. "If I could discover what the woolly threads were on Bowman's spur I might find the murderer."

Jones looked thoughtful. "The murderer sounds like a rather careless man," he put forth. "The matter of those woolly threads, for instance." He considered for several moments while Lance watched him narrowly. If Jones knew who the murderer was, Lance decided, there was nothing in Jones's face or manner to reveal it. "A very careless man," Jones repeated. "A man like that would be a menace to any gang with which he operated. A careless man might overlook other clues——"

"What, for instance?" Lance asked.

"Tolliver," Jones asked abruptly, "what's your interest in this matter?"

"Well," Lance said cautiously, "I found the body. The murderer should be found and punished. I'm interested, that's all."

"Quite so, quite, quite." Jones nodded impatiently. He appeared to consider the matter for more moments. Finally he said, "A careless man might overlook something. Undoubtedly there was an opportunity for Bowman's hand, freshly plunged in creosote, to brush against the murder's clothing when the body was lifted to the horse——"

"By cripes!" Lance exclaimed, "I've been a fool! I should have thought of that." He smiled suddenly. "If you're not a detective you should be," he said, repeating Jones's words of a few minutes before.

Jones laughed disparagingly. "Not at all, not at all. Bit of a hobby of mine—criminology—detection of crime. Only slight interest—y'understand. I merely mentioned—possibility. Something—think about. Cacti—more interesting. Incident'ly—dry talking. Drink up. . . . Pat, two more of the same."

"Coming up, Professor," the barkeep replied.

Jones had again taken up the cactus plant on the table. "This specimen—related to *Astrophytum myriostigma*—somewhat similar in form—usually only five ribs—rarely spined—sometimes called 'Bishop's Hood Cactus'—looks for all the world like a bishop's miter. . . ."

Lance only heard half of what he was saying, so concentrated were his thoughts in other directions. For the next two hours Professor Jones advocated the merits of collecting cacti. He explained various forms to Lance, told him where they were to be found, pointed out different habits of growth. Twice Lance made excuses for leaving, but each time Jones talked so fast Lance found it impossible to withdraw from the conversation—if such a one-sided monologue could be termed a conversation. Whatever Jones was, or appeared to be, Lance decided, the man certainly knew his cactus.

Lance finally made himself heard. "That's all mighty interesting, Professor. I got a good notion to pull out for Washington and take a look at your institute."

"What? What's that?" Jones appeared startled. He went on rather lamely, "Fine idea, of course. However—suggest you—postpone trip—until my return. Collection—not complete, y'understand."

At that moment the hotel clerk came into the bar with word that the professor's niece was awaiting him in the lobby. Somewhat reluctantly Jones stuffed the cactus plant into one of the roomy pockets of his tweed jacket after first wrapping it in a handkerchief, gathered up his papers and rose from the table. Lance started to leave, but Jones detained him with a "One minute. You must meet my niece. You'll like Katherine."

The girl was seated at the far end of the lobby when Lance followed the professor into the long room.

Jones performed the introduction, adding, "I believe we're going to be brother enthusiasts, Katherine. I feel Tolliver will prove a most apt pupil in the study of cacti."

All this was news to Lance. He blinked, though afterward he was never sure whether it was the professor's words or sight of Katherine Gregory that momentarily threw him off balance. He liked instantly the girl's cool, rippling laugh that greeted her uncle's words. The direct, even glance from the girl's dark, long-lashed eyes did things to Lance Tolliver. She was tall and slim and healthily tanned. Mostly it was her heavy mass of yellow hair, knotted low at her nape, that caught Lance's attention. The color was so vivid, reminding Lance of the golden pollen dust of certain desert flowers, it seemed to cast a pale shimmering light about her head.

"Uncle Uly is always trying to make converts, Mr Tolliver"—she smiled—"so don't take him too seriously."

Jones commented on the absence of Fletcher. The smile left Katherine Gregory's face. "I don't know where he is. We had a bit of an argument. To get out of it I made the excuse I was going to my room for a handkerchief. I haven't seen him since. He wasn't here when I returned."

Lance put in, "He came into the bar and said something about going for a walk."

The girl lifted one shoulder in a slight shrug. She suggested that Jones and Lance take chairs. Lance seated himself, twirling his sombrero on one finger, scarcely knowing what to say. Katherine suggested that the men smoke. That put Lance more at ease. He rolled a brown-paper cigarette while Jones stuffed tobacco into a battered and ancient-looking brier.

"By the way, Tolliver"—Jones looked slightly apologetic—"do you mind if I tell Katherine of your deductions in the Bowman killing? Very interesting. I remember you said—confidential—that sort of thing—but—but——" His voice trailed off lamely.

"Go ahead," Lance consented, feeling the professor would tell the girl whether he liked it or not if it pleased him to do so. Jones said, "Thanks," and related the story in his jerky accents. The girl's eyes widened, and something of admiration came into them as the story was unfolded. "All this—confidential—of course," Jones concluded.

The girl was still looking at Lance. "Smart—awfully smart," she said in a voice that was almost a whisper.

Lance felt a pleasurable flush mounting to his face. "It was just a matter of using my head," he said awkwardly. "Professor Jones pointed out one clue I entirely overlooked—that matter of the creosote being wiped on the killer's clothing."

"Uncle Uly always was quite good that way," Katherine Gregory said dryly. Lance didn't understand her tone at the time.

To keep the conversational ball rolling Lance asked the professor if he had ever heard of an outfit called the Southwest Cactus Company. Jones replied promptly, "Why, of course. Situated in El Paso—old company—export to Europe a great deal—all over nation, in fact. Suppose you've passed the place—traveling through—Texas——"

Once on the subject of cacti it was natural for the professor to do all the talking. It was nearly midnight by the time Lance rose to leave. Someplace during the conversation he had promised to accompany the professor the following day and study "plants in their native soil," as Jones put it. Pleading that he expected to be busy all morning had had no effect on Jones who had pointed out the afternoon would do just as well. Finally, when he had said his good nights and once more found himself on Main Street, Lance's brain was still somewhat in a whirl.

Sheriff Lockwood had gone home by the time Lance arrived back at the sheriff's office. Oscar was sitting on the cot where he spent his sleeping hours, eating from the usual paper sack. Oscar glanced up as Lance entered. "Huh, you made quite a stay. Learn anything new?"

"Maybe," Lance said noncommittally. "Oscar, do you remember how sore Kilby got when I mentioned his new overalls?"

Oscar nodded. "That was just before you hit him. Why?"

"Where would he be likely to buy those overalls?"

"One of the general stores—Parker's or Rumler's."

"Do me a favor tomorrow morning. Find out if Kilby did get his overalls at one of those places and if they know what became of his old ones. You can ask questions and get answers that might be refused me because I'm a stranger in Pozo Verde."

"Sure, I'll do that. But what's the idea——?"

"I'll tell you tomorrow. I'm working on a hunch. What time does Johnny Quinn open his station? I've got to send another telegram."

"Probably around seven o'clock. Just before the limited goes through."

"I'd better get along to bed, then, so I can rise early."

"It's an idea for both of us. By the way, did you get to meet the professor's niece?" Lance nodded carelessly. Oscar said enthusiastically, "Stunner, ain't she?"

Lance shrugged. "I didn't notice in particular."

Oscar snorted skeptically. "The hell you didn't! You can't look at that girl without noticin' in particular. Did you ever see such hair? Pretty as—as— lemon drops."

Lance laughed and said good night. He retraced his steps toward the hotel, mounted to his room on the second floor and went to bed to dream of a girl with pollen-dust hair.

IX
A Fighting Deputy

Early as Lance left his hotel room and got breakfast the following morning, Sheriff Lockwood was already at his office desk when Lance arrived. Lance asked, "Where's Oscar?"

"He's been sitting around here waiting for the general stores to open up. He just left. He tells me you wanted him to check up on overalls sales."

Lance nodded. "I'll tell you about it later. Right now I've got to dust over to the railroad station and send a telegram. See you in a little spell, Ethan."

"Right, Lance."

Lance walked rapidly along the street. As he passed Parker's General Store Oscar was just emerging from the doorway. Lance said without preliminaries, "Any luck?"

Oscar shook his head, lowered his voice and fell in step with Lance. "Kilby hasn't bought any overalls there recent. I'm going to try Rumler's next."

They parted at the corner of Laredo Street, Lance turning right in the direction of the railroad station. Old Johnny Quinn looked as though he'd had a hard night when Lance stepped into the depot. "How's your hemoglobinuria this morning, Johnny?"

Johnny Quinn raised one hand tenderly to his head.

"Poorly, Mr Tolliver. I took my bourbon last night too. Felt right pert then. But this mawnin' my head thumps fit to be tied. Tongue feels sort of dry an' parched too. Huh? Oh, my telygraph pad? Here ye are."

Lance quickly composed and wrote out his message. He passed it across the counter and put down some money. Johnny took the paper, tried to make sense of the written words, then raised his eyes accusingly to Lance.

"Same crazy words like yisterday," he complained. "Separate, I can read the words, but when I string 'em together they're jest flapdoodle. I like to know what folks is sendin'."

"I appreciate your interest," Lance said gravely. "I'm just trying to make arrangements for Aunt Minnie's funeral."

"But the address here is to El Paso," Johnny Quinn pointed out. "Aunt Minnie passed away in Washington, D.C."

"I know," Lance explained patiently. "You see, Aunt Minnie came from El Paso. They're shipping the remains home to Uncle Obadiah. This feller I'm sending the message to is a relation of ours. He's to let me know if they're going to keep Aunt Minnie in a glass coffin or call in a taxidermist and have her mounted in her old rocking chair."

Johnny Quinn's watery eyes bulged. "Whut?" he demanded in horror-stricken tones. "Ye ain't meanin' to tell me they're aimin' to stuff Aunt Minnie and keep her in the house?"

"You're being hardhearted about the whole matter," Lance said in mingled sadness and indignation. "Uncle Obadiah would miss Aunt Minnie something fierce if she wasn't around the house to keep him company. Just put yourself in Uncle Obadiah's boots. See how you'd feel!"

"I—I guess you're right," Quinn stammered weakly.

Lance made as though to brush a tear from his cheek. "I'm glad you understand," he said in broken accents. "Now, if you'll just send that telegram right away——"

"I'll do it to once, Mr Tolliver."

Lance turned and left the station. Johnny Quinn gazed after him, shaking his head. "Thet redheaded Tolliver jasper sure must have some mighty peculiar kinfolks," he muttered.

Oscar was sitting on the corner of Lockwood's desk talking to the sheriff by the time Lance returned. He glanced up disappointedly as Lance strode through the open doorway.

Lance nodded philosophically. "Don't say it, Oscar. I can tell from the length of your face you didn't have any luck."

"Not none," Oscar said gloomily. "I was sort of pinning hopes on them missing garments, too—or would you say overalls was a garment?"

"I'll tell better when we locate 'em," Lance said.

"Just what do you expect to find?" Lockwood asked.

"It's this way," Lance replied. "There was fresh creosote on Frank Bowman's hand. I was hoping that when the murderer lifted Frank to his horse some of that creosote might have rubbed on the killer's clothing. You know how such things go—a man can hardly pick up a paint brush without getting some on his clothing." He smiled. "That's always been my experience, I've noticed. . . . Anyway, George Kilby did suddenly get new overalls. When I mentioned the fact to him he sure got riled. He was drunk, of course, but——"

"You figuring Kilby killed Bowman?" the sheriff asked.

"I've got hunches that-a-way." Lance nodded. "Day before yesterday when I found the body and you rode up with Kilby, Herrick and the others I don't remember Kilby having new overalls then. Things like that stand out sometimes. At the same time, maybe he had 'em then, and I just overlooked it."

"There'd be no reason for you noticing new overalls then," Oscar put in.

"Look at it this way," Lance continued. "Bowman was killed at night. The creosote on his hand wouldn't be seen in the dark. But in the daylight, when I found the body, it was seen plain enough. All those hombres saw it. Let's suppose Kilby noticed some on his overalls and figured somebody might tie the two together. He'd want to get rid of his overalls, wouldn't he?"

"By cripes!" Oscar exclaimed, "maybe you've hit on something."

"It's no good without the missing overalls," Lance pointed out. "Besides, it wasn't me hit on it. Give Professor Jones credit for that."

"Who?" Lockwood frowned. "Did you say Jones?" Oscar's eyes widened.

"I said Jones." Lance smiled. "I took a chance last night and told him part of the story—confidentially. Maybe he'll keep it to himself, maybe he won't. I don't much care. I just wanted to watch his reactions, and damned if he didn't suggest overalls to me. Pointed out that a man who would leave part of his clothing on Bowman's spur might make other mistakes. That Jones is one shrewd customer whether we like him or not, and I've got to admit to a sneaking liking for him."

Oscar drawled, "His niece wouldn't have anything to do with that, would she?"

"Not a thing." Lance felt his face color. He went on, "I had a hunch that Kilby might have left his old overalls wherever he bought the new ones. He'd want to get rid of the old ones as soon as possible. By the same reasoning he wouldn't want to be caught carrying them down the street when he was wearing the new overalls. That might attract attention."

Lockwood cut in, "Speaking of Jones reminds me of that friend of his—Fletcher. Last night I was walking along Main, seeing that all was quiet, when Fletcher came tearing out of the street entrance of the hotel bar. He was in a hell of a hurry, looked like——"

"What time was this?" Lance asked quietly.

" 'Tween eight and eight-thuty, I should say."

Lance's gray eyes hardened. "That's just about the time he overheard me tell Jones about finding that peyote in Bowman's hand. He didn't even ask about the rest of the story. Maybe he didn't think there 'd be more. Anyway, he lit out of the bar like a bat out of hell. Where 'd he go, Ethan?"

"Down to the Pozo Verde Saloon. He was almost running by the time he got there. I dropped in a few minutes later and looked around. Fletcher was standing at the bar alone, drinking whisky. He looked worried and didn't even hear me when I spoke to him."

Oscar said, "Herrick and his gang usually hang out in the Pozo Verde Saloon—if that means anything."

"It might," Lance said, "again, it might not."

Lockwood continued, "Fletcher stayed in the Pozo Verde for some time. I know because I kept an eye on the place. Quite a while after Fletcher went in there I saw Chiricahua Herrick go in. Well, it was about second-drink time of the evening anyway, so I followed. When I came in it looked like Fletcher suddenly broke off talking to Herrick, though I couldn't swear to that. While I was in there the two men might have been total strangers as far as appearances went. Later Kilby and Ordway and some more of the gang came in, and I drifted out."

Oscar leaped to his feet suddenly and exclaimed, "Dreben's! Cripes! I forgot Dreben's! If my brains was dynamite there wouldn't be enough to blow my Stet hat off'n my head."

"What you talking about?" Lance demanded.

"Ike Dreben's Clothing Store," Oscar explained. "Mostly he carries shirts and neckties and Sunday-go-to-meetin' togs, but I just remembered he carries a line of overalls too. Don't sell much. Hereabouts folks likes the regular brands, and Dreben stocks a kind of cheap line——" He broke off and dashed through the doorway, calling back, "I'm heading for Dreben's plenty *pronto!*"

Neither Lockwood nor Lance said anything for a couple of minutes while they waited for Oscar's return. Lance finally broke the silence. "I've been thinking something, Ethan."

"Let's hear it."

Lance said slowly, "If Oscar does bring back Kilby's overalls it looks like we've got the deadwood on him. Either he killed Bowman or he was an accomplice."

"Right," the sheriff agreed.

"That first day Bowman was found a lot of folks in this town reckoned I killed him. Herrick and his crew probably did their best to spread that report.

What I'm getting at, I'd like the chance to make the arrest."

Lockwood nodded. "I get your slant: but you don't want to do it in your own official capacity. I reckon that can be arranged." He drew out a drawer of his desk and fumbled among papers, pencils, a number of forty-five cartridges and other miscellaneous articles until he had found a couple of deputy sheriff badges. He polished the face of one on a pants leg, slid it across the desk to Lance and tossed the remaining badge back into his desk. "Hold up your hand," he commenced. "Do you solemnly swear and promise to uphold and enforce the laws of Sartoris County to the best of your ability . . . ?"

The sheriff had scarcely finished deputizing Lance when Oscar came rushing in, a newspaper-wrapped parcel under one arm. "We got 'er!" he announced jubilantly. "Dreben had——Hey, what you doing, Ethan? Swearing Lance in?"

Lance explained, "I'd like to make the arrest myself, if possible."

"That's fine. But if you can get lemon drops on your expense account that's more than I've been able to do. Look here!" Oscar's indolent manner vanished as he unrolled the newspaper-wrapped bundle to display a pair of very dirty overalls. "See these marks on the right knee?"

Lance seized the right pants leg, scrutinizing the brownish-black smear on the blue cloth. He held it near his nostrils, sniffed, nodded with satisfaction as he released the garment. "You can still smell the creosote. I reckon the evidence is tightening around Kilby—providing these are his overalls."

"They are." Oscar nodded eagerly. "He bought the

new ones from Ike Dreben night before last just as Dreben was about to close up his store. I reckon Kilby must have looked himself over after he saw Bowman's right hand. It's plain why he went to Dreben's, too: he wouldn't want to go to either of the general stores where there's always people hanging around. He changed into the new overalls in Dreben's back room."

"Did Dreben know why Kilby left the old pair?" Lance asked.

Oscar shook his head. "Kilby just told Ike he didn't want 'em any more. He tossed 'em into Ike's rubbish can and told Ike to burn 'em."

"And Ike put off burning his rubbish, eh?" Lockwood said.

Oscar grinned. "He burned his rubbish yesterday—but you don't know Ike. Ike had hauled the overalls out of the rubbish can, looked 'em over and decided they was too good to burn. He was aiming to clean 'em up and get four bits from some customer. I gave him a dollar and told him to keep his mouth shut. I didn't tell him why."

Lance said, "Nice work, Oscar." He looked thoughtful, then: "What color shirt would you say Kilby wore?"

Oscar considered a moment. "Sort of brownish red—kind of a plaid with black stripes—wool——"

"Maroon, maybe." Lance nodded. "That's as I remembered it." He drew a small notebook from his pocket and took from between the leaves the woolly threads he had found on Bowman's spur. This he held before Oscar's eyes. "About this color, perhaps."

Oscar and the sheriff both nodded. "Could be," Oscar said.

"Ethan," Lance asked, "do you reckon we've enough evidence to warrant an arrest?"

"Plenty." The sheriff nodded. "Go get your man."

Lance started toward the door. Oscar said, "Want I should go with you, Lance? Kilby might prove to be a tough nut to crack."

"I'll crack him when I get him in a cell," Lance said grimly. "I figure to make him talk plenty. There's more to this than just the murder of Frank Bowman. There's a lot of things I want to know—and by the seven bald steers I'm aiming to get that information!"

He didn't say any more, just shoved his holster a trifle nearer the front and strode through the doorway.

Lockwood and Oscar exchanged glances. Oscar said, "It looks like you've taken on a fighting deputy, Ethan."

"He's got the reputation as such," the sheriff said quietly. "But he might have trouble making an arrest alone—not that I think he will, but you'd better trail along, just in case. I won't be far behind you. Get going!"

X
Hide-out Weapon

After leaving the sheriff's office Lance strode east along Main Street, unconscious of the fact that both Lockwood and Oscar were trailing him in the rear. Morning sun beat down on the dusty roadway. It was still a bit early for all the shops and stores to be open. Here and there a storekeeper could be seen sweeping out. A few pedestrians passed. There weren't many ponies or wagons at the hitch racks along the way. A man standing in the open doorway of a bootmaker's shop noticed Lance's deputy badge and said, "Good mawnin'."

Lance nodded pleasantly and passed on. He was considering now the best place to find Kilby. "Probably," he mused, "I'd better try the Pozo Verde Saloon first. That seems to be a sort of hangout for Herrick and his crowd. If he's not there I'll have to make the round of the other saloons. Next the restaurants. Maybe he's not out of bed yet. I wonder where he sleeps. Probably at one of the lodginghouses in town."

He strode on. A couple of more men spoke and wondered who the new deputy was. Lance said to himself, "Of course, there might be some trouble taking him if he's with Herrick or some more of the gang. I don't reckon so though. That crew hasn't displayed much taste for open defiance of the law. Far as I actually can *prove* right now, they haven't broken any laws. That's why I've got to make Kilby do some talking. I hope he won't put up a fight. I'd hate to have to shoot him. It isn't always easy to just wound a man—particularly if he's fast on the draw." A smile crossed his features. "Maybe I should have accepted Oscar's offer to help. I might have my hands full."

He walked steadily on, arms swinging at his sides. It was sure hot this morning. Seemed like Old Sol was doing double duty. A hard rain would feel good. Lance's eyes swept the turquoise sky. Not a fleck of cloud in sight. Just that great golden ball up there blazing down on Main Street. Golden! Yellow! Yellow hair! He wondered what Katherine Gregory was doing. Probably not out of bed yet. This afternoon. Going riding with Professor Jones. Lance smiled. Cactus hunting. That was a joke. "I'll have to make my excuses for that date, I reckon," Lance muttered. "Probably be busy with Kilby. He might break down fast though. Sometimes they do." He strode on.

He was nearing the corner of Laredo Street now. On the northeast corner stood the San Antonio Hotel. On the southeast was located the Pozo Verde Saloon. From this distance Lance could see the swinging doors of the Pozo Verde swing apart as George Kilby stepped into view and started north along Main. At that moment Kilby's eyes ranged down the street and spied Lance. Abruptly, he turned and started across the street to avoid meeting him.

"Just a minute, Kilby," Lance called. "I want to talk to you."

"Ain't got no time now, Tolliver." Kilby was increasing his gait. "I got some important business to 'tend——"

"You'd better make time pronto," Lance snapped coldly.

Kilby was half across the street by this time, but something in Lance's voice brought him to a slower pace. He stopped in front of the San Antonio Hotel and leaned against the hitch rack, with the sidewalk at his back. "Make it snappy, then," he growled in surly tones.

"We won't waste too much time," Lance said easily. He stepped to the sidewalk and came around to the other side of the hitch rack. Kilby turned to face him.

At that moment Kilby caught sight of the deputy sheriff badge pinned to Lance's open vest. "Jeez!" His face hardened. "When did you join the forces of law and order?"

"'Long about the time I decided to have a talk with you."

"Well, get on with your *habla*, Tolliver. I'm in a hurry."

Lance said, "Let me see your gun—and move easy."

"What for?" Kilby demanded belligerently.

"Let me see your gun!"

Reluctantly Kilby drew the six-shooter from its holster and passed it across the tie rail, Lance watching him narrowly as he moved. Diagonally across the street Oscar Perkins stood peering around the corner of the Lone Star Livery entrance. Two doors farther west Lockwood stood watching from a doorway. Both breathed easier as they saw the gun surrendered without trouble.

Lance was examining the six-shooter. He flipped

open the loading gate of the weapon, closed it, spun the cylinder while Kilby eyed him uneasily. "Hmmm," Lance commented. "You use a forty-four, eh?"

"Any law ag'in' it?" Kilby growled.

"Never heard of one," Lance replied quietly. "Sometimes I wonder why more people don't tote 'em. They make a nice pard for the .44-40 Winchester."

"That's my idea in carrying it. Same ca'tridges for both."

"Oh, so you're a rifle shot too?"

"I'm pretty good, if you want to know," Kilby boasted.

"I'm glad you've still got a rifle." Lance smiled thinly. "I'd sure hate to deprive you of all your weapons." He stuck Kilby's forty-four into the waistband of his overalls.

"Hey, gimme that gun," Kilby protested.

"Maybe you'll get it, and maybe you won't. I just wanted to make sure you wouldn't try anything rash. Now we can have our talk peacefully——"

"What in hell's got into you, Tolliver?" Kilby rasped. "I ain't done nothing."

"I was just thinking," Lance said smoothly, "about the weight of a forty-four slug. You know, there's only about fifty grains difference in the weights of a forty-four and a forty-five. Course, when Doc Drummond first probed that slug out of Frank Bowman everybody took it for granted it was a forty-five——"

"Hey, what you talking about?" A lot of the color had suddenly departed from Kilby's face. "You mean they've weighed that slug and found out——? Oh hell! Suppose that slug did turn out to be a forty-four? Lots of hombres use 'em. You can't pin Bowman's killing on me just because——"

"Why, Kilby"—Lance assumed a look of surprise—"I never said anything about weighing slugs. You just jumped to conclusions."

Kilby clutched at his swiftly vanishing courage. He looked uneasily about. Across the street Chiricahua Herrick and Luke Ordway had appeared on the porch of the Pozo Verde Saloon and stood looking curiously at Lance and Kilby. They couldn't hear what was being said but they saw that Kilby had surrendered his gun, so there didn't seem any possibility of immediate gun slinging.

"Speaking of Bowman," Lance was saying easily, "reminds me I wanted a look at your shirt."

"My shirt?" Kilby looked blank. "What in hell's got into you, Tolliver?"

"Turn around—slowly," Lance ordered.

Kilby obeyed. As he faced the Pozo Verde Saloon he saw Herrick and Ordway and commenced to feel better. At least his friends were near. He made a complete turn and again faced Lance. "C'mon, cut it out," he said cockily. "I ain't no time for foolishness. Gimme my six-shooter, and I'll be on my way."

"Uh-huh," Lance murmured, his eyes intent on Kilby's right shirt sleeve where a couple of torn spots showed. Lance considered. A spur could have caught in one of those spots, especially where the material was worn thin. "Just a moment, Kilby. Don't get impatient. I want to show you something." He took out his notebook and from between the pages produced a few twisted threads of dark wool. These he held against the sleeve of Kilby's shirt, then nodded with satisfaction. "Looks like the same material to me, Kilby. What do you think?"

"I think you're cuckoo in the head," Kilby snarled, losing his temper. "If you think you got something on me quit beating around the bush and come out with it. Otherwise, I'm leaving right now. I've wasted enough time."

"I'll come to the point then." Lance replaced the woolen threads in his notebook and put it away. "Those threads were found caught on Bowman's spur, Kilby. What do you know about it?"

Kilby looked startled. "Why—why, I don't know nothin' about it. You can't prove them threads come from my shirt." He backed away a step and stood nervously scuffling one booted toe in the dust of the roadway. "Cripes, Tolliver! I don't know nothin' about that killing——"

"Or about creosote either, I suppose." Lance's voice had suddenly gone hard.

"Creosote! Creosote?" Kilby's face was the color of ashes now.

"Yes, you know that stuff that was spilled at the station platform when Bowman went down. Remember? It spilled all over his hand, and when you lifted him to his horse you got some smeared on your overalls——"

"My Gawd! What are you talking about? I don't know—know—anythin'—about——" Kilby's tones sounded choked. He backed another step. "Hot—hot sun—here. Let's get across in the shade." He was still backing away, moving faster with every step.

"Stop, Kilby!" Lance snapped. "We got your old overalls from Ike Dreben. I'm arresting you for the murder of Frank Bowman. Stop, or I'll have to shoot!"

Reluctant to draw, Lance vaulted over the hitch rack and started toward Kilby who was still backing away. Abruptly a look of hate flashed across Kilby's fear-twisted features. His left hand ripped open his shirt, his right darting inside the shirt to the underarm gun hidden there. A burst of flame and smoke blossomed suddenly from Kilby's right hand.

Lance heard the bullet thud into the tie rail at his rear. His hand stabbed toward holster, came up in a swift, eye-defying arc. Lead started to pour from the six-shooter muzzle the instant it left the holster. A leaden slug threw up dust at Kilby's feet. Lance's aim lifted higher. Kilby fired again. Lance thumbed his hammer once, twice, three times.

Kilby was flung violently sidewise by the impact of the heavy slugs. For a brief moment he swayed uncertainly, then his right leg buckled, and he pitched to the roadway. For a short interval he struggled to regain the weapon that had fallen from his hand then, as Lance closed in and kicked the underarm gun out of reach, Kilby shivered and slumped in the dust.

Wild yells sounded along Main Street. Men came running from all directions. Lance was kneeling above Kilby's still form now, examining his wounds. A sudden breath of relief was expelled from his lips. Then he stiffened.

Behind him came Chiricahua Herrick's voice, violent with hate. "Damn you, Tolliver! You can't do this to a friend of mine. Now, by God! we'll see how you like the taste of hot lead!"

XI
Powder Smoke

Lance leaped to his feet but he was too late to do anything about it. He caught the complete picture in a single glance: Chiricahua Herrick's rage-contorted, snarling features as the man came plunging in, his six-shooter high in the air, already swinging down to bear on Lance!

Lance knew he'd be too late even as he started to lift his own gun. Then he saw Oscar's lanky, scarecrow figure flash in between him and Herrick. Oscar's left hand swept up to clutch Herrick's right wrist. Herrick's gun exploded harmlessly in midair. There came a swift glint of gun metal as Oscar's six-shooter barrel crashed down on Herrick's head. Herrick's legs slumped, and he pitched on his face.

Sheriff Lockwood's stern words cut in, "Back, everybody! Ordway! Keep your hand away from that gun!"

"Ain't figured to draw it a-tall," Ordway replied sullenly.

Others of the Herrick crew were near now, but none of them made movements toward weapons. A crowd was gathering swiftly.

Oscar had shoved his gun back in holster and stood looking down at Herrick, one fist doubled menacingly. "Get up, you low-lifed varmint," Oscar was promising, "and I'll give you some more!" Herrick didn't stir. Oscar looked disappointed. "Hell! You ain't as tough as I reckoned you were."

A man in the crowd commented laughingly, "That deputy can sure coldcock 'em. I'll betcha Herrick's lamp is put out for an hour."

Oscar came ambling toward Lance. Lance said, "Much obliged, Oscar. You sure moved fast. That was nice work. Herrick would have got me."

"You did some pretty nice work yourself—dropping Kilby," Oscar replied calmly. "You were sure shellin' out lead faster 'n I ever see before. Is he dead?"

Lance shook his head. "Just fainted from the shock of the slugs. I reckoned to get him in the leg and shoulder." He added meaningly, "I didn't want him dead, you know."

He again dropped at Kilby's side. Kilby had a wound in his right thigh, and his right shoulder had been smashed. His eyes were closed. "Oscar, get me some whisky, will you?" Lance requested.

Oscar left the circle of men around Kilby. Lance asked the crowd to get back and give the man air. The crowd backed reluctantly. Lockwood took a hand in the proceedings. "Go on, get back!" Lockwood snapped. " 'Way back! Show some speed before I throw half a dozen of you hombres in the cooler on a charge of defying an officer. Go on, scatter!" The crowd commenced to move back. Lockwood added, "And take Herrick's carcass with you. Lay him over there near the sidewalk."

The crowd moved well back out of earshot, a couple of men taking Herrick with them. Now only Lance and the sheriff stood near the unconscious Kilby.

Lance said, "Much obliged, Ethan. When Kilby comes to maybe we can make him talk. I'd just as soon too many folks don't hear what he has to say."

Oscar came hurrying back with a flask of whisky. Lance knelt again at Kilby's side and forced a few drops of the fiery liquor between the man's lips. Kilby swallowed convulsively. Then he choked, gagged. His eyes opened. For a moment he gazed vacantly at Lance, then a look of mingled fear and pain swept his features. "You—you——" he mumbled, and shrank back. A mask of sheer terror replaced his look of fear.

Lance said quietly, "I reckon I didn't get to make that arrest, after all, Kilby, but it was your own fault. I was willing to give you a chance and a fair trial. You see, your pals didn't come to your rescue. They left you to go it alone. You don't owe them anything. How about 'fessing up? We've got the evidence we need to prove you killed Bowman but we want the whole story. Who helped you?—Herrick, Ordway, some of that crew?"

Kilby shook his head. "Didn't have nothin' to do with it——"

"Don't lie, Kilby. We want the truth."

Kilby said weakly, "You're right. I killed Bowman. We took his body out—to that wash. It was—too dark for us—to notice that peyote he had——Gimme another drink, eh?"

Lance held the flask to the man's lips. Kilby swallowed deeply. When he had done his voice came strong. "Hey, how about getting me to a doctor?"

"We'll take you to a doctor when you've finished talking."

"But—but I might bleed to death."

"You're not hit that bad," Lance said grimly, "but it's up to you. The sooner you decide to talk the sooner you'll get medical aid. And we want the truth. No stalling. Why did you kill Bowman?"

"We had him figured for a dick," Kilby answered, apparently anxious now to give Lance the desired information. "He was always asking questions about the freight shipments that came to—that came in——"

"Came in to who?" Lance asked quickly. "What were the freight shipments?"

"Peyotes—mezcal buttons—for the Yaquentes. That night I killed Bowman he kept hangin' around the box at the depot. Later we caught him opening it. I had to stop him. Then we——"

"Who's we?"

Kilby's eyes shifted uneasily. "I don't dare tell——"

"Yes, you do. We'll see you get protection. Talk up, Kilby. It's for your own good. What sort of game have you been playing here? I want the name of every man that's behind you."

"All right, I'll give you the whole damn story," Kilby said suddenly. "They haven't helped me none, so——" He stopped abruptly.

Lance saw the sudden hole appear in Kilby's breast even before he heard the report of the gun. A cry of anguish was torn from Kilby's lips. Blood seeped swiftly into his shirt front. His eyes closed, then opened again, already growing glassy.

"Like hell you'll protect me," he muttered. His eyes closed again, and his head fell to one side.

Lance was already on his feet, looking right and left. A startled row of onlookers were ranged along the sidewalk on either side. A confused clamor filled the air.

"Where 'd that shot come from?" Sheriff Lockwood bellowed.

"That's what I want to know," Lance snapped.

"Sounded like it come from over that-a-way," Oscar stated, jerking one hand toward the hotel.

Lance glanced at the hotel building. A line of men were ranged along the porch, looking above the heads of the men crowded on the sidewalk. High up above the top of the building Lance glimpsed a vagrant wisp of smoke. Powder smoke? He couldn't be sure. Even while he looked it disappeared in thin air. The smoke may have come from farther down the street. Lance studied the second-story windows in the front of the hotel. There were five of them. All windows were lowered to keep out the heat of the day.

"Ethan"—Lance spoke swiftly—"I'm going over to that hotel. You see can you bring Kilby back to consciousness, though I'm afraid it's too late. Oscar, you question that crowd standing in front of the hotel."

Turning swiftly, Lance ran across the street. On the porch of the hotel he found the hotel clerk. "C'mon, you," Lance snapped, "get your house keys. I want to examine those front rooms upstairs."

"You certainly won't," the clerk stated indignantly. "Some of those rooms are occupied. I can't——"

"I figure one of 'em must have been," Lance cut in. "I'm going to have a look at all of 'em."

"I can't have strangers entering guests' rooms——"

"Damn it, march!" Lance growled, impatient at the time being wasted in meaningless bickering with the stubborn clerk. He tapped the deputy sheriff badge on his chest. "Maybe you'd like to face a charge of obstructing justice, mister. Either you do as I say or I'm putting you under arrest——Oh hell!" He seized the angry clerk by the coat collar and forced him into the hotel lobby. "Now you get your keys. You and me are going upstairs, and I don't want to lose any more time."

The clerk was quite pale by this time. He secured the necessary keys from behind his desk and led the way to the second-floor hall. "Who's occupying these front rooms?" Lance asked.

"Miss Gregory has the corner room—number 201," the clerk replied. "Professor Jones is in 202, Mr Fletcher has 203——"

"I have 204," Lance cut in.

"And 205 is vacant," the clerk finished. "There are only five rooms facing on Main Street——"

"I guessed that from the number of windows. Get a move on, will you? Is the professor or Miss Gregory or Fletcher in this morning?"

"Miss Gregory and the professor are out in the hills. They left word, in case you called, they'd be back by dinnertime. Mr Fletcher is in, I believe. At least, I didn't see him go out, though he may have by this time——"

"Open up Fletcher's room."

The clerk halted before number 203, thrust a key into the door and turned the knob. "Mr Fletcher," he called. There was no answer. He flung the door wider, and Lance stepped inside. The room was empty, furnished about as his own room was with a bed, dresser, two chairs and a small washstand. There were curtains at the window which was shut tightly.

Lance stepped back to the corridor. "Try 205 next."

The vacant room also was empty and didn't appear to have been occupied for some time. Dust was heavy on the dresser and washstand. Lance led the way back to the hall. "Now, my room."

The clerk thrust the key into the lock, then paused. "Why, this door is unlocked."

"It could be," Lance agreed. "I might have left it unlocked."

Nothing in that room to furnish a clue to the mysterious shot either. Lance and the clerk next entered Professor Jones's room. Here the table was littered with books and papers. A trunk stood in one corner, but there was no sign of a human having been in the room within the last ten minutes at least.

Once more in the hall, the clerk said, "That leaves only Miss Gregory's room. Surely you don't intend to enter——"

"Open it up," Lance said grimly. He could feel his face growing warm. A trunk stood in one corner of the girl's room, as in the room occupied by Jones. Articles of apparel hung on a clothes rack. There were some ribbons on the dresser. The room seemed faintly scented. But no clue here. Lance backed out as swiftly as he could, the clerk right after him. The door was re-locked.

"Well, I hope you're satisfied," the clerk said righteously. "The idea! Entering a young lady's room——"

"You make another crack like that," Lance threatened, red faced, "and I'll mop up the floor with you." He left Katherine's door and swung at right angles into another corridor. At the end of the corridor he saw a stair well. "Where does that lead to?" he demanded.

"That's a back entrance from the alley at the rear of the building."

"Door unlocked?"

"It's left unlocked during the day."

Lance hurried down the steps and opened the

door on the alley. He scrutinized the earth in the vicinity of the door, but too many people had passed there to leave any definite sign. Slowly he retraced his steps up the stairway, his keen eyes looking for some evidence of the killer's having come this way, but again the search was without result.

"Is that all?" the clerk asked when Lance had rejoined him.

"I reckon that's all," Lance said disappointedly. He followed the clerk along the corridor and descended the stairs to the lobby once more. As they stepped into the lobby Lance saw Malcolm Fletcher just entering. Malcolm nodded and started to pass.

Lance caught his arm. "Where you been?" he asked.

"Out on the street," Malcolm said in surprised tones. He smiled. "I guess the rest of the town is out there too. Nice bit of shooting you did awhile back, Tolliver."

"Somebody else did some shooting, too," Lance said grimly. "That's the hombre I'm looking for."

"Mr Fletcher," the clerk put in, "this fellow insisted on entering your room. I told him——"

"What's the idea?" Fletcher demanded of Lance.

"Looking for the man who fired that shot," Lance said coldly. "I figure it came from the direction of this hotel. I looked in all the front rooms. I wasn't overlooking any bets."

Malcolm laughed shortly. "I guess there was no harm done. I see you're wearing a deputy's badge. You won't have to go after Bowman's job, after all."

"Fletcher, I never intended going after Bowman's job. I got this badge for the purpose of arresting Bowman's murderer. That part is accomplished. Somebody killed Kilby——"

"Who is Kilby?"

Lance stopped. "Kilby is the man who finished Bowman—just in case you don't know."

"Surely you're not suspecting me of having a hand in the affair?"

"I'm suspecting damn near everybody until I get to the bottom of things. Just where were you before that shot was fired?"

"Which shot—yours or the one that got Kilby?"

"Mine got him first," Lance growled, "but you know damn well I'm talking about the shot afterwards—the one that came from the direction of this hotel." Lance felt himself growing angry.

"Oh, I see." Fletcher looked amused. "In other words, you want to know what I was doing at the time and so on."

"Exactly."

"Here goes. I had finished my breakfast and was sitting in my room when I heard some shooting. I looked out of the window and saw one man down and you running toward him with your gun in your hand. I jumped up, ran downstairs and went out to the street——"

"Wait a minute." Lance turned to the hotel clerk. "Did you see Fletcher leave?"

The clerk shook his head. "But that doesn't mean anything. I ran outside, myself, when I heard the shot. Naturally I'd——"

"All right," Lance cut in, turning again to Fletcher, "all right, you're out on the street now. What happened?"

"I saw another man try to shoot you," Malcolm said coolly. "Herrick, I understand, is his name. But that other deputy prevented that. Later you'd started to talk to Kilby when that shot came from down the street——"

"From down the street?" Lance frowned. "From this direction, you mean."

Smiling, Fletcher shook his head. "No, I don't. That sound seemed to come from west of here, say, in the direction of the bank building. Of course, I couldn't say for sure."

"You probably couldn't," Lance said ironically. "Then what?"

"I saw you come running over here. I hung around down on the street for a while, then decided to come back to my room. I'd just entered the lobby when you grabbed me and started to ask questions. Now you've got it, what are you going to do with it?"

"I'll tell you later," Lance replied quietly. He brushed past Fletcher and the hotel clerk and stepped out to the street once more. A few minutes later he found Oscar.

Oscar said, "Learn anything?"

Lance shook his head. "All I know is somebody could have fired that shot from one of those hotel rooms, closed the window—it wouldn't have to be open very far—and made a getaway down the back stairs of the hotel. Did you pick up anything?"

"Nothing but confusion," Oscar said wearily. "No two men in the crowd have the same idea regardin' the direction that shot came from—east, west, north or south. There's them that claim somebody in the crowd did the shooting. I can't see that. It sounded like a rifle to me, and a rifle would be noticed pronto. Hell! It all happened so quick! We were all watching you and Kilby."

"It sounded like a rifle to me too. I talked to Fletcher in the hotel, and he thinks—or claims to think—that the shot came from near the bank building or even farther west."

"There y'are. Nobody can agree on it." Oscar scratched his blond head and glanced toward the bank building. "Maybe so," he commented dubiously, "but I'd bet against it."

"We've got to admit it was damn accurate shooting, anyway," Lance said ruefully. "I've a hunch it was done to keep Kilby from spilling what he knew."

"Maybe you've hit it. By the way, Kilby died almost instanter. Never recovered consciousness. It's a tough break."

Lance nodded agreement. He and Oscar joined the sheriff standing near Kilby's lifeless form. Lockwood glanced at Lance's face, saying, "I figure you didn't have much luck."

"Not any," Lance replied. "Jeepers! One minute I thought we had this case all sewed up. The next, it blew wide open."

"It's not a total loss, anyway," Oscar reminded. "Kilby confessed to Bowman's murder. That's one scut out of the way."

Lockwood nodded, then said, "I reckon we'd better get this body off'n the street so the crowd can go about its business. Lance, it looks like Herrick has come to life again. What charge you want placed against him? He might have killed you."

Lance glanced across the street. Herrick was seated at the edge of the sidewalk in front of the Pozo Verde Saloon holding his head and taking but little interest in his surroundings. Lance smiled. "Oscar, you sure take the fight out of 'em when your gun barrel lands."

"It takes more than one jolt to take the fight out of Herrick's breed," Lockwood growled. "Oscar just softened him up temporary. Wait until we get him in a cell——"

"Ethan," Lance proposed, "let's not arrest Herrick. I've got a hunch we may learn more by letting him run loose. You know, give a man enough rope and he'll hang himself."

Lockwood looked surprised. "We-ell, sure, if you want it that way. But s'help me I'm going to give him a talking to and warn him that next time . . ." Muttering angrily, the sheriff started toward Herrick.

Oscar groped in a pocket for his sack of lemon drops. "Me, I never believe in givin' a sidewinder a second chance—but maybe you know best, Lance."

"I'm hoping I do. After all, Herrick didn't do me any damage—thanks to your quick work. Maybe, if we let him run loose, I'll meet him again with drawn guns. I have a hunch I will—and the sooner, the better!"

XII
"You're Covered!"

The remainder of the morning was consumed by Lance, Lockwood and Oscar in an attempt to discover some clue regarding the person who had fired the rifle, ending George Kilby's life. Men on the street were interviewed, shop- and storekeepers talked to, but without result. Lance made another more thorough examination of the earth back of the rear entrance to the hotel, but without success. It was nearing noon when Lance made a trip to the railroad station to learn whether or not an answer to his telegram had arrived, but Johnny Quinn had nothing to give him as yet. Quinn would have liked to detain Lance to discuss Aunt Minnie, but Lance managed to break away and directed his steps toward the Pozo Verde Savings Bank.

At the bank, after waiting a few minutes, he was admitted to the private office of Gillett Addison, owner of the bank. Addison was of medium height, fat and bald, with small, squinty eyes. He appeared to be very busy, and Lance gained the impression that Addison felt valuable time was being wasted on the inquiry.

"No, no—sorry, I can't help you," Addison said brusquely. "I wouldn't have any idea of the direction from which that shot was fired. Matter of fact, I wasn't paying too much attention when the shot came. Oh yes, I was out on the steps of the bank, watching the excitement. To be frank with you, Tolliver, if I had to place a bet on the matter—though I want you to understand I'm not a betting man—I should say the shot came from over near the railroad tracks somewhere."

"And," Lance said dryly, "the bullet passed right through the Pozo Verde Saloon building, I suppose, and struck Kilby in the chest. Kilby, of course, was stretched on the ground when the shot came."

"I'm not arguing the matter," Addison said stiffly. "I'm simply giving you my impressions. Perhaps the shot came from the saloon."

Lance said ironically, "Thanks a lot," and, after a few more words had been exchanged, left the banker's private office, closing the door behind him.

On the way through the bank proper he stopped at the cashier's window. Behind the grill was a tall, thin young fellow with a pale complexion. Lance approached the cage. "You're Elmer Manley, I take it. Sheriff Lockwood was telling me about you——"

"I'm Manley, Deputy Tolliver." The young fellow smiled. "I hope you or the sheriff aren't after me for anything?"

"Not at all." Lance laughed. "I'm talking to as many folks as possible, trying to get an idea from which direction the shot was fired that killed George Kilby. Did you happen to be on the street when that happened?"

Manley nodded. "It sounded to me as though it came from the direction of the hotel. Of course, I couldn't be certain. I'm not supposed to leave my cage here at all but I did dash out to take a look for just a second. Just as I reached the doorway I heard the shot. I really haven't much idea of what happened, except what I've gathered from others. . . . You don't remember me, do you, Mr Tolliver?"

"Should I?" Lance scrutinized the man more closely. There was something vaguely familiar about Manley's features.

"Think back about five years," Manley suggested. "The Dankerker counterfeiting case in St Louis——"

"Sure enough," Lance exclaimed, his brow clearing. "You were a witness for the prosecution. You helped us convict——" He paused suddenly. If this man knew him . . .

"Trust me, Mr Tolliver," Manley said. "I've an idea what brought you here and what brought Frank Bowman here. I haven't said a word to anyone—and I don't intend to."

"That's a relief," Lance said ruefully. "You could upset a lot of plans."

"I don't intend to," Manley repeated, and somehow Lance felt he could put faith in the man. Manley went on, "You wouldn't want two five-dollar bills in exchange for a ten, would you?"

"I might at that," Lance said slowly. What was the fellow up to? Lance drew a ten-dollar bill from his wallet and passed it through the grill.

Manley reached below his counter and secured two fives which he exchanged for the ten. Lance glanced at the numbers on the bills. Then he looked up, his eyes meeting Manley's. Manley nodded slowly. Lance tensed. "Where 'd you get these?" he demanded.

"I can't talk now," Manley said, low voiced. "If I could meet you someplace after work——?"

"Anywhere you say. How about the sheriff's office?"

Manley shook his head. "Somebody might see us. I wouldn't be able to meet you until tonight. It's getting along toward the end of the month, and I'll have to work fairly late. Do you know where Tony Pico's saloon is? How about meeting me there? That's the last place anybody would expect to see me——"

"Who do you mean by anybody?"

"Can't tell you now. I'll see you there tonight around nine o'clock——" He stopped abruptly.

The door of Gillett Addison's office had opened suddenly, and the banker emerged with his hat on. He frowned upon seeing Lance at Manley's window.

"I doubt Manley can tell you anything, Tolliver," he stated coldly, crossing over. "He scarcely stuck his head out the door."

"I just learned that much, Mr Addison," Lance said quietly. He still held in his hand the bills Manley had given him.

Addison spied the bills. His features tightened a bit, then he forced a cold smile. "Transacting a little business?"

Lance laughed. "Two-dollar bills are bad luck. I was just exchanging one for a couple of aces." By this time Lance had thrust the two fives out of sight. He said much obliged to Manley and started toward the door with Addison by his side.

Addison said, "I'm just going out to my dinner. Have you tried the hotel yet? I'd be glad to have your company. I'd like to get better acquainted with the town's new deputy."

"Thanks, no," Lance refused. "Some other time. I'm going to be right busy for a spell." He wondered what had made the banker suddenly grow so genial. Probably the man wanted to question him, pump him. Or maybe it was just his imagination, Lance considered. On the street he said good-by to the banker and headed toward the sheriff's office.

Lockwood and Oscar were waiting there when he arrived.

"Looks like you didn't learn anything new?" Lockwood said.

"Regarding that shot, I didn't," Lance replied. "Did you two?"

"Nary a thing," Lockwood stated gloomily.

Oscar shook his head. "From the various yarns I've listened to, I'm commencin' to think that shot come down from the clouds."

Lance asked, "Ethan, who is Elmer Manley? I know he's cashier at the bank, but what do you know about him?"

"We-ell," Lockwood said slowly, "I always figured Elmer was a right nice hombre. I can't say I know much about him. He came to Pozo Verde about four years back—came out here for his health, he claimed. I reckon he was by way of becoming a lunger back in St Looie. That was his home. He told me one time he used to work for the First National Bank there. I'd be willing to take his word for that. 'Bout the time he arrived out here Gill Addison needed a cashier. Elmer landed the job. I don't figure Gill pays him much, but I do think Elmer does most of the work around that bank. That bookkeeper they got in the bank—well, Elmer just about taught him to run the books from what I've heard. Yep, I figure Addison would miss Elmer was the boy to leave sudden. What about him?"

"He knows who I am."

Lockwood whistled softly and in some consternation. He said finally, "What's he going to do about it?"

"Manley says he doesn't intend to reveal the information. I hope I can trust him. He wants to see me. I'm to meet him tonight in Tony Pico's saloon."

Oscar chuckled. "That 'll be a surprise all around. I don't reckon Elmer knows what the inside of a bar looks like—let alone Tony Pico's place, which is patronized almost solely by Mexes."

"I'm betting," Lockwood stated seriously, "that Elmer has something important to tell you. Me, I'd trust that fellow."

"You sound encouraging, anyway"—Lance smiled—"so my stomach will probably enjoy that dinner it's been craving. Either of you ready for chow?"

"Both of us already et," Oscar said, "before we come back to the office. Figured you might do the same."

"Shucks"—Lance laughed—"if I'd known I wasn't going to have company I'd have taken Banker Addison up on his offer. He asked me to eat with him at the hotel."

Oscar choked on a lemon drop. "By cripes," he gulped, "I never knew that tightwad to buy anything for anybody before. There must have been a catch in it someplace."

"If Gill Addison offered to buy your dinner"—Lock-wood frowned—"you can depend on it he had something in mind. He always gets double value for whatever he gives."

"Maybe I made a profit by refusing then." Lance laughed. "As a matter of fact, he didn't urge me very hard. . . . By the way, Ethan, you're going to have to get along without one of your deputies this afternoon. I'm going with Professor Jones, you know—though I don't know how much good it will do me."

"You'll probably get stuck on one of two things," Oscar prophesied: "cactus spines—or a girl with yellow hair. One nice thing about cactus spines—you can recover from their wounds."

Lance flushed. "I doubt very much that Miss Gregory will go with us."

"T'hell she won't," Oscar denied. "She's a secretary, ain't she? She usually does go riding with him."

"In that case"—Lance grinned—"maybe the afternoon won't be a total loss. Well, I'm going to hunt me a flock of food. See you later."

He left the sheriff's office and walked down Main Street to the Chinaman's restaurant. Twenty minutes later he emerged and started toward the Lone Star Livery where his horse was stabled. He was still a couple of doors east of Laredo Street when he saw Chiricahua Herrick standing before the Pozo Verde Saloon talking to a Yaquente Indian. The two were having an argument of some sort. Lance paused and stood before a store window watching. The Yaquente appeared to be stubbornly insisting on something to which Herrick violently shook his head in the negative. Once Herrick raised his clenched fist with the quirt dangling from his wrist, but the Indian refused to give ground.

Lance mused, "Now I wonder what palaver Herrick could be having with a Yaquente. . . ."

At that moment Herrick broke into a fit of cursing. Toward the end of a savage tirade Lance caught a few words: ". . . and I told you last night you couldn't have any bullets. Understand, you low-down, flat-faced, greasy son of a bustard! I meant what I said! Now you get outa town and stay out. . . ."

Herrick's fist suddenly shot out and caught the unsuspecting Yaquente alongside the head. The Indian's huge straw sombrero tumbled off. He staggered back, tripped and fell flat on the sidewalk. Instantly Herrick was on him with tigerish ferocity. Twice the quirt at the man's wrist cruelly rose and fell, and each time it left a livid streak across the Yaquente's face. Lance could hear the whistling hiss of the split leather, metal-pointed end of the quirt as it swished through the air. The Indian covered his face with his arms. Herrick shifted his sadistic attack to the man's body. Crimson streaks appeared on the Yaquente's thin cotton shirt.

"I'll teach you, you——" Herrick was snarling as Lance closed in. The quirt was just raising in the air when Lance seized Herrick's wrist and forced it down.

"Better take it easy, Herrick," Lance snapped.

Herrick stiffened, twisted his head to see who had stopped him. Then as he recognized Lance a look of extreme malevolence appeared in his bloodshot gaze. He jerked savagely free from Lance's grasp, fell back three paces. Swiftly his right hand dropped toward his holster.

"Hold it, Herrick!" Lance's tones were like chilled steel. His six-shooter was already out. "You're covered!"

Herrick paused with his gun half clear of holster. He tried to keep his eyes steady on Lance's, but something in Lance's piercing gaze sent chills coursing down Herrick's spine. He could see tiny, flickering, angry blue flames in the relentless eyes, warning him that this tall, redheaded deputy had the law on his side—more: that Lance Tolliver, if pushed to the limit, might prove as much of a killer as Herrick himself. Herrick's eyes widened at this discovery.

Involuntarily he commenced to back away. The fingers of his right hand spread, relinquishing their hold on the gun butt, and dropped to his side.

"Reach!" Lance jerked out. "Reach high, you scut!"

Herrick's hands came into the air above his Stetson. A shiver flashed along his backbone. He felt something jab, hard and sudden, into his middle. Looking down, he realized that Tolliver's gun muzzle was boring in between his ribs.

Lance's left hand moved forward, jerked the six-shooter from Herrick's holster. Then he stepped back. "This seems to be your day for getting jammed up, Herrick," Lance commented coldly as he thrust the captured gun into the waistband of his overalls. "First thing you know, you're going to get into trouble—and I mean trouble! Beating up a helpless Indian seems to be just about your speed. I'm warning you not to go too far."

"By God, Tolliver!" Herrick flamed. "I'll get you for this if it's the last thing I do——!"

"You had your chance," Lance snapped, "but you lacked the nerve. I figure you're yellow clear through!"

A small knot of men had collected. Ordway, Anvil Wheeler, Ridge and two or three others of Herrick's gang had appeared on the porch of the Pozo Verde Saloon. Lance watched them warily while still keeping an eye on the fuming man before him. None of the gang attempted to take a hand in the affair.

The Yaquente had by this time climbed to his feet and stood stolidly by, blood running down from the angry lashes across his face. More blood was seeping into his clothing.

Lance glanced at the man and felt a sharp anger

run through his body. For a brief moment his gun barrel raised a trifle toward Herrick. Herrick quailed back. "My God! You wouldn't shoot a defenseless man!" he exclaimed in terror.

Lance laughed shortly. "Yellow clear through," he repeated. "No, Herrick, I'm not aiming to shoot you, though you deserve just that."

Herrick glanced at his gang on the porch at his rear and could see the beginning of a certain contempt in their eyes. He gathered his fleeing remnants of courage and forced himself to meet Lance's angry gaze. "Sometime," he grated, "I'll show you if I'm yellow or not. Don't think you got me bluffed, Tolliver. Right now my hands are tied." This for the benefit of his friends on the porch. "But my time will come. The time just ain't ripe yet. But you'll see. I'll blast you so wide open that——"

"Cut it," Lance said sharply. "Cut out your boasting and tell me what all this is about. What's the idea of beating this Yaquente?"

"None of your damn business," Herrick snarled.

"Maybe"—Lance's gun tilted threateningly— "you'd like me to make it my business."

Fear appeared in Herrick's face. "All right, if you got to know," he said sullenly. "This flat-faced Yaquente was begging ammunition from me. I told him I wouldn't give him none. He made a blasted nuisance of himself, hanging around."

"Is that straight?" Lance asked.

"Hell!" Herrick jerked one angry thumb over his shoulder. "You don't need to take my word. Ask any of them fellers. They heard the whole thing— how this Yaquente has been hanging around all day——"

"That's right," Herrick's pals chorused. "Chiric-ahua's throwing a straight loop, Tolliver."

Lance glanced scornfully at the knot of men on the porch, then turned to the Yaquente standing near. "You understand this, hombre?"

The Yaquente burst into a guttural flow in his own tongue.

"Whoa, whoa!" Lance exclaimed. "Hold it, Injun. Now, listen careful." Lance tried the man with a few Spanish words and saw his face light up. "You understand that, eh?" Lance asked. The Indian nodded. It appeared after a moment that he also had a few words of English. "All right, we're getting straightened around now," Lance said. He repeated certain words.

Again a volley of Yaquente verbiage mingled with Spanish and a spattering of English assailed Lance's ears. He turned to Herrick. "The Injun says you promised him some ammunition for a gun."

"He's a goddam liar," Herrick growled.

"How about it, Yaquente?" Lance asked.

The Indian glanced at Herrick's friends on the saloon porch, next at Herrick. Something in their eyes made him change his mind, apparently. He finally grunted, "Forget eet, señor. Ees not'ing."

Lance shrugged his shoulders. Time was passing. "What's your name?"

The Indian replied promptly. Lance smiled. "Maybe you're right, but it sounds like Horatio to me."

"Ees good name." The Yaquente showed white teeth from his bloody countenance.

Lance took a half-dollar from his pocket and gave it to the Yaquente. "Here, go get your face washed and a bellyful of chili. Then you'd better light out for home, savvy?"

"I'm—savvy. Gracias, señor." Obediently the Yaquente turned the corner and stalked off in the direction of the railroad tracks.

Lance turned to Herrick. "You'd better keep off my path for a spell, Herrick. I won't be pushed much farther."

"I want my gun——" Herrick commenced.

"Want and be damned," Lance said wrathfully. "You can have it when you learn how to act civilized. Just remember what I've told you. Don't cross my trail any more than you can help."

He left Herrick standing on the corner cursing under his breath and started once more for the livery stable. Here he saddled up and headed toward the sheriff's office. When he arrived there he didn't dismount, but drew to a halt before the tie rail and called to Oscar. Oscar came out of the office.

"Hell's bells!" Oscar said, "ain't you left yet? I figured by this time you'd have dug up half the cactus in Sartoris County."

Lance took Herrick's gun from his waistband. "Here's your friend Cherry-Cow's gun," he said. "I told him he could have it when he learned to behave himself."

"Cripes A'mighty! You had another run-in with Herrick?"

Lance smiled. "I had to prove to him I didn't always need you for protection." He related what had taken place.

When Lance had finished Oscar said indignantly, "The dirty sidewinder. I'm sorry you didn't plug him. Taking his gun won't do any good."

"It 'll make him buy another, leastwise," Lance said, "if he needs one right away. And now"—

touching spurs to his pony's ribs—"I'm off to the cactus party." He moved down the street.

Oscar called after him, "Better take along some lemon drops. They're right beneficial for sunstroke."

"It's not the sun I'm afraid of." Lance laughed back.

XIII
Hot Lead!

Katherine Gregory and Professor Jones were mounted, waiting for Lance, by the time he arrived at the hotel. He apologized for being late but asked to be excused on the grounds that he'd had some business to attend to.

"Yes"—Jones nodded—"we were watching you from the hotel-lobby window. You seemed quite busy for a few minutes with that fellow—Herrick—or some such name——"

"In fact," Miss Gregory put in, "the hotel clerk tells us there's been quite a bit of excitement around town while we were out in the hills this morning——"

"I hope you had a good time," Lance mumbled sheepishly, sensing what was coming.

". . . and I was quite surprised to find I had a visitor," Katherine continued, apparently not noticing the interruption. "If I'd only known you were coming——"

"Look here, Miss Gregory," Lance protested, growing red in the face, "I'm plumb sorry I had to go in your room this morning, but it was all in the line of duty. I inspected every room in the front of the hotel. I just had to—somebody fired a shot and—and"—he commenced to stammer and paused to get a grip on himself—"and, anyway, I didn't look at anything. I just looked for the hombre who might have fired a shot. I—I——" Again he paused, feeling perspiration forming on his forehead.

Something very near to a giggle reached Lance's ears. He glanced at the girl and saw she was having difficulty smothering her laughter. "Look, Mr Tolliver," she said frankly, "it really didn't make a speck of difference. I know you had to do what you did. It was the hotel clerk who was indignant, not I. Honestly, I didn't believe our famous deputy sheriff could be so easily upset after all I've heard about him."

"Aw, shucks," Lance said awkwardly, "let's forget it. I'm just mighty glad you weren't really sore——"

"Think we—should make a start," Professor Jones broke in. "Plan—cover—eight—ten miles today. Let's go."

The three horses moved west along Main Street, Katherine riding between the two men. The girl wore a corduroy divided skirt, mannish flannel shirt and high-heeled riding boots. A black Stetson adequately covered her heavy yellow hair. Jones wore his usual riding breeches, knee-laced leather boots and tweed jacket. His saddle was equipped with roomy saddlebags for holding his notebooks and any small specimens he might collect. At the cantle was a rolled burlap sack. From one of Jones's jacket pockets projected the wooden handle of a trowel. Lance was surprised to note that both Jones and Katherine carried thirty-eight six-shooters in holsters at their sides. He wondered if they knew how to use them. Whatever his thoughts, both guns and holsters appeared well worn.

At the edge of town Jones turned in a northwesterly direction. The horses were moving at an easy lope. Lance had to admit that both Jones and Katherine were good riders. For a time there was silence between the three as they moved across the semi-desert country toward a row of low foothills. Yucca and prickly pear and cholla dotted the landscape, with occasional bunches of dry, wispy sagebrush. Overhead the sky was a great blue, inverted bowl. Far on the western horizon fleecy white clouds floated above the highest peaks of the Saddlestring Mountains.

When five miles had passed to the rear the horses were pulled to a walk. Jones reopened the talk of the morning's happenings. Apparently he and the girl were interested in learning firsthand the details of Kilby's death and of the events leading up to the disarming of Herrick a short time before Lance joined them at the hotel. Lance gave brief details, but he could tell when he had finished that Jones wasn't satisfied.

"It's very—queer—very"—Jones frowned—"this Kilby fellow—found time to say nothing. You're sure—didn't let drop anything—to incriminate his gang?"

"Nothing a man could tie to," Lance evaded. "Anyway, you don't want to be bothered with such stuff. Remember, you were going to teach me something about cactus this afternoon."

"Quite so, quite." Jones nodded. "At any rate—I imagine this—Kilby fellow—put out of the way—by one of his gang. Logical, what?"

"Logical," Lance agreed.

"Feel sure—someone in hotel—responsible for that shooting—from all I hear." Jones looked sharply at Lance to see if he agreed.

"It's logical," Lance said dryly.

Jones said, "Humph! Like drawing cactus spines from one's fingers—get information from you." He smiled suddenly. "All right, cacti it shall be. Over that way"—he swept one arm to the left—"small stretch—haven't investigated yet."

He touched spurs to his pony, and the three horses lengthened their gaits. For twenty minutes they rode through a series of low-lying foothills. Once Jones drew to a halt, and the other two followed suit. Jones directed Lance's attention to a slender, many-branched plant covered thickly with pale yellow spines. "What, for instance," Jones asked, "do you call that?"

"Cactus, I suppose," Lance guessed, though he usually thought of cactus as the prickly-pear variety.

"Right. Which genus—what kind of cactus?"

"I've always known it as cholla," Lance answered.

Jones frowned. "Yes—and no. Not the true cholla. That particular specimen—*Opuntia bigelovii*—more spiny than the true cholla. Remember that next time."

Lance said meekly, "Yes sir," feeling like a small boy in school.

The horses moved on. They were crossing gravelly soil now. Outcroppings of granite rose at places and barred the way, necessitating wide swings to the right or left, as the case might be. Here and there Lance noticed barrel cacti growing along the way. Here at least he would show his knowledge. He spoke to the professor.

"You tell me if I'm right about those cactuses——"

"Cacti," Jones corrected, frowning.

". . . those cacti over there. In the Southwest we call 'em 'barrel' cactuses—cacti. They are also known as 'viznaga'——"

"And 'biznaga.'" Jones was quick to take him up.

Katherine put in, "And 'mule' cactus."

"*Ferocactus wislizenii,*" Jones snapped.

Lance laughed weakly. "Anyway, they're all *Fero*——Whatever that word was, Professor."

"Wrong," Jones jerked out. "Only tyro—think them all—same. Many of them—*Ferocactus lecontei.*"

"Well"—Lance laughed—"they look the same to me."

"Not if—examined closely. The *lecontei*—narrower plant—spines not so hooked."

"Have it your way," Lance said helplessly.

"Uncle Uly"—Katherine laughed—"quit pestering Lance."

Jones grinned suddenly. "He's not too young—to learn."

He moved his pony to a faster gait. Lance hadn't overlooked the use of his first name by Katherine. He wondered why the girl appeared so friendly. What was back of all this? Lance felt sure Jones hadn't brought him 'way out here simply to teach him the botanical names of certain species of cacti. He glanced back over his shoulder once and unconsciously moved his holster a trifle nearer the front.

Katherine didn't miss the movement. She said dryly, "We really didn't bring you out here to assassinate you, you know."

Lance flushed. What he might have answered he didn't know. At that moment the professor drew his pony to a halt at the entrance to a low rocky canyon descending sharply to an old river bottom. He motioned for Katherine and Lance to dismount. He pointed to a plant a few feet away. "There's your true cholla, Lance. *Opuntia fulgida.* Beyond that— see—with the red and yellow flowers—clump—

Opuntia versicolor—remarkable color range—of bloom——"

"Look," Katherine exclaimed, "a dove just flew out of the *versicolor.*"

"Nest probably there—spines protection—certain enemies. Katherine—suggest you and Lance—rest here—wait for me—get acquainted, y'understand." Jones paused awkwardly.

"Where are you going?" the girl asked.

Jones jerked one thumb over his shoulder. "Down into that canyon—gravelly limestone soil—evidence presence—perhaps—*Echinocactus horizonthalonius*—valuable field observation—that sort of thing, y'understand——" Jones was moving off, burdened with notebooks and trowel, even before he finished talking. Within a few minutes he had passed from sight around a high shoulder of rock.

Katherine sighed and dropped to a sitting position on the earth. "Well, there doesn't seem anything else to do, does there?"

"Suits me." Lance dropped down a few feet away.

"Poor Uncle Uly." Katherine laughed ruefully. "Sometimes I think he's plain batty on the subject of cacti——"

"At the same time," Lance said directly, "he didn't bring me out here to just educate me along those lines."

Katherine's blue eyes met his a moment, then dropped before his steady gaze. Suddenly she lifted her head. "Lance, we haven't fooled you a moment, have we?"

"How do you mean?"

"You know how I mean. You've been suspicious right from the start. I've felt it. Uncle Uly felt perhaps

I could persuade you better than he—you know"—
the girl's face crimsoned—"turn on my winning
feminine charm or something of the kind. I can see,
now, it was all so silly."

"I think," Lance said directly, "that if anybody
could persuade me to anything it would be you,
Miss Gregory."

Katherine smiled. "Very nicely put, Lance, and
you can dispense with the 'Miss.' I'm plain Katherine to my friends. And that's not part of the charm.
At least I'm sincere in that."

"Just what," Lance asked, "are you supposed to
persuade me to do?"

"Uncle wants," the girl replied, "a guide to take
us down into Mexico."

Lance considered. Just what was back of this? Why
should anybody try to persuade him to leave Pozo
Verde? He said, "So your uncle is going through with
the Mexican trip. I had understood from Fletcher that
he wasn't going——"

"Mr Fletcher is against the trip. He says it is no
place for me to go."

"For once I think I agree with Fletcher."

The girl made an impatient little gesture. "I've
been able to take care of myself for a long time," she
said slowly. "I don't believe I have anything to fear
from Mexico."

"Even so, why should your uncle want me for a
guide? I've been all through Sonora and Chihuahua,
of course, but I don't count myself as thoroughly familiar with that country down there. You could probably find dozens of men around Pozo Verde who'd
make far better guides than I."

"That may be," Katherine agreed, "but it isn't so
much a guide as it is a man to manage the trip. There

'll be wagons to buy, men to hire; someone to handle them is necessary. Uncle says you're smart. He likes you. He said he considered the trailing down of Frank Bowman's murderer one of the finest pieces of detection he ever heard of."

Lance smiled. "I reckon your uncle isn't too familiar with the business of detection."

"He might fool you."

"He might, at that." Lance added after a minute, "And you're going to the expense of such a trip just to collect and study cacti? Do you expect me to believe that, Katherine?"

The girl was silent for several minutes. Lance rolled and lighted a cigarette. Finally Katherine spoke. "Maybe I'd better give you the whole story. You've probably heard that my father owned the Three-Cross Ranch down in Mexico—and that he was killed down there?"

"I've heard that." Lance nodded. "I believe the Yaquentes brought him to Pozo Verde, and nobody ever discovered who did it."

"That's correct. Father was given that ranch years ago in return for certain services he rendered the Mexican Government's Bureau of Mines. Father was really a mining man, you see. He didn't know very much about cattle raising but he wanted to try. Things didn't go as well as he hoped, though he made a good living for us. Then, when I was fifteen, Mother died. There was a revolution brewing in Mexico at the time. Father thought it best if I return to the States. He sent me up to San Francisco, where I lived at a school for girls, to complete my education."

"And you haven't been back to the ranch since?" Lance asked.

Katherine shook her head. "I never saw Father

again. That's nearly seven years ago. He was always promising to get away from the Three-Cross and come to San Francisco to visit me, but the ranch always needed him. He was still working hard to put it on a big-paying business, and I guess it wasn't easy. I wanted to be with him, but he always refused to let me come to the ranch until, as he said, he could furnish it fit for a lady. That was foolish, of course, but, after all, he was the boss."

Lance ground out his cigarette butt in the sandy soil at his feet and waited for the girl to continue. In a few moments she went on, "A little over a year ago I had a letter from Father. He seemed more cheerful than usual and enclosed a draft on the Pozo Verde bank for five thousand dollars, which he wrote was to make up for the years of doing without things—though that was another foolish idea. I may not have had as many clothes as other girls at the school but I wasn't doing any protesting. He said that before long he would be sending for me."

"That was the last letter you had from him?"

"The last." Katherine nodded. "He explained that for twenty-five thousand dollars he had sold a half-interest in the ranch to a man named Malcolm Fletcher and that they intended to buy some blooded bulls and raise the quality of their stock. Father appeared very cheerful about his new pardner and mentioned that he'd made a discovery that might make us all wealthy. He didn't mention what it was but said he was sending a present that might give me a clue."

"What was the present?"

Katherine unbuttoned the sleeve of her shirt and rolled it up to display a heavy silver arm clasp about two inches wide. She slipped it off and handed it to

Lance who examined it curiously, conscious of its warmth from the girl's arm. It was of extremely fine workmanship and looked like pure silver. Its surface was almost entirely covered with an orderly series of strange symbols, arranged in straight lines, down and across the armlet, raised slightly above the level of the silver.

Lance scrutinized the markings. "Looks like Indian work," he said dubiously, "though I don't know."

"Uncle Uly thought they were Aztec symbols, if not of an earlier race."

"I'd take the professor's word for it if he knows about those early races the way he does cactus—cacti. I suppose your dad had this made up someplace. What was his discovery?—a silver mine?"

"That's what I'm inclined to think, but I don't know. Mr Fletcher claims he never heard anything of the discovery."

"Where does Fletcher fit into this story? Does he deny your ownership of half the ranch—or anything of the sort?"

Katherine shook her head. "Not at all. He's really been very kind about the whole business. In a way I feel obligated to him. You see, it was he who wrote me of Father's death. Mr Fletcher wasn't at the Three-Cross when it happened. Some Yaquente Indians found Father's body and brought it to Pozo Verde. It was Fletcher who arranged to have it shipped to San Francisco for burial. He intended coming with it but at the last moment telegraphed me he was unavoidably detained but would come later to see me and tell me what he knew——"

"Did he know anything?"

"Nothing, except that the Yaquentes had found Father's body a short way from the ranch house. He had been shot. But I didn't verify that until we arrived in Pozo Verde and I met Fletcher personally. You see, he'd kept writing from time to time that he was coming to San Francisco, and I kept postponing my visit here while awaiting his arrival. A whole year passed in such fashion. Finally I made up my mind to come here. Uncle Uly was about to start his cactus expedition, so we decided to make it a joint affair. He'll look for cactus, and I'll see what, if anything, I can learn regarding Father's death."

"The professor came on here from Washington, of course?" Lance said.

"Why—oh yes, of course." Katherine appeared flustered. She went on, "And Uncle decided you'd be the man to accompany us on the trip into Mexico. Will you?"

Lance slowly shook his head. "I'd like to, but I can't just see my way clear." He tapped his deputy sheriff's badge. "You see, I couldn't very well resign after just taking on this job. It may prove to be a big job before I get through with it. If you're bound to go down there it seems to me Fletcher is the man you want. He knows the conditions and the country down there. Probably he'll be all right when he understands you insist on going."

"I'm afraid not," Katherine said, flushing a little. "You see, he's against my going there in the first place, and in the second—well, we quarreled over it—and something else. You may as well know. He asked me to marry him, and I refused."

"What! I don't blame you," Lance blurted.

Katherine smiled. "You don't like him, do you?"

What Lance might have answered the girl never knew. At that instant there came a sudden silvery flattening of lead against a large chunk of granite situated near the girl's left shoulder. Almost instantly the report of a high-powered rifle reached their ears. A second shot whined viciously close to Lance's face, then a third!

XIV
Manley Disappears

Lance threw himself swiftly across the stretch of sandy soil intervening between himself and Katherine, threw one arm around her waist and forced her to the earth. Then he half dragged, half carried the girl behind the shelter of an upthrust of granite rock. Even as he moved another leaden missile scattered dust and gravel close to his body.

"You stay there—down, out of sight!" Lance snapped.

Turning, he sprang to his pony, gathered the reins and leaped into the saddle without touching stirrup. The roan gelding needed no more than a touch of the spur to get into motion.

"Lance," Katherine wailed. "Come back! You'll be hit!"

"You stay out of sight," Lance yelled back over his shoulder.

He was riding low in the saddle, crouched behind his horse's head. Those shots had come from an easterly direction, and Lance was heading toward a brush-covered ridge from which he calculated the shots had been fired. It wasn't easy going. There was too much brush and cacti barring the way.

"Damn cactus!" Lance growled, and touched the gelding again with his spurs.

He was nearing the side of the ridge now, momentarily expecting to ride straight into a hail of rifle fire. Lance's six-shooter was out, but he could see nothing at which to shoot. His eyes were intent on the ridge ahead. No further shots were forthcoming. Lance wondered if the hidden assailant was holding his fire for close-up work. The tough little gelding dug in its hoofs and scrambled, panting, up the side of the steep slope.

It was slow going, but finally horse and man reached the crest. From this position Lance had a wide view of the surrounding country, but there was nothing to be seen except a vast sea of mesquite, paloverde trees, creosote bush and cacti, with the hot sun making shimmery waves of the distant landscape.

Suddenly a dark, racing figure caught Lance's eye. It disappeared behind tall brush, again came into view farther on and once more disappeared, moving fast. It was a rider, all right, but too far away to be recognized. Lance swore softly under his breath. "That coyote is heading for Pozo Verde but he's got too much of a head start for me to overtake him before he gets there. Cripes! Once in town, he'd quickly lose himself. I reckon I'd better go back. This might be a trick to draw me off. After all, that first shot came a heap closer to Katherine than it did to me. I wonder which one of us that sidewinder was aiming to get. Maybe both. It was dang good shooting, at that. Blast the luck! There are too many good riflemen not getting caught."

He turned his pony back down the ridge and

started toward the spot where he had left Katherine.
The sun was swinging wide to the west by the time
he returned. The girl was waiting anxiously, and a
look of relief swept across her face as his pony moved
out from the tall brush.

"Lance!" she exclaimed. "Thank heaven you didn't
get hurt. Who was it?"

Lance shrugged his shoulders. "I couldn't find
anybody. Probably just some fool hunter trying to
get a brace of quail for supper——"

"Lance! You know that's not so. People don't hunt
quail with rifles—not generally. I've hunted enough
to know that much. Somebody was trying to shoot
you."

"Anyway, he didn't succeed, so there's nothing to
worry about. The professor not back yet?"

Katherine shook her head. "He's probably neck-
deep in cacti someplace. Even if he'd heard those
shots he'd be so interested in his notes they wouldn't
register on him. He should be along soon though.
The afternoon's going."

Jones put in an appearance in a few minutes
though. He looked somewhat relieved at seeing Lance
and Katherine. "I thought I heard some shots a time
back," he said. "Probably mistaken—what?"

"You're not mistaken." Lance shook his head.
"Some hunter was potshooting around. Anyway, it's
about time to start back, I reckon."

"Confound that hunter!" Jones exclaimed crustily.
"I thought—something wrong. Very awkward. I'd
just discovered—beautiful *Echinocereus fendleri*—very
unusual—late for bloom, y'understand—but just
covered—magnificent magenta flowers. But, Katherine, you'll never believe it"—Jones's tones took on
enthusiasm—"I found an almost perfect specimen of

Homocephala texensis—most unusual—these parts. That spot down there—veritable botanical garden. I've brought with me an *Echinocereus rigidissimus* and a *Neomammillaria macdougalii*—just seedlings— y'understand. Must return—tomorrow. Be no end interesting—stay beyond nightfall—any number *Penicereus greggii*—due for blooming. Night bloomer, Lance—y'understand——"

"Uncle," Katherine said impatiently. "Lance is not telling the truth. Somebody was shooting at us."

"What, what! Bless me—can't believe it. No. I——"

"I wouldn't say for sure they were shooting at us, whoever it was," Lance said quietly. "Howsomever, I figure we'd better be getting back."

Jones was considerably upset at the news. Saddle cinches were tightened. Jones gathered his papers and specimens into saddlebags, and they mounted and turned the horses' heads toward Pozo Verde.

A mile or so was covered in silence before Katherine spoke. "It wasn't any go, Uncle Uly," she said. "Lance refuses to take the job as our guide down into Mexico."

"Ridiculous," Jones snapped. "Nothing else to do—far as I can see. Is there, Lance? Any number men—for deputy jobs. You'll reconsider?"

Lance, smiling, shook his head. "No can do. I'm no guide——"

"Great Christopher! No need of a guide. I can get into a saddle and ride. Need a man to—hire crew— wagons—buy supplies—that sort of thing. We need you——"

"Sorry, Professor." Lance shook his head. "I'm not so sure Katherine should go down there either."

Katherine said "Fiddlesticks!" Jones continued to insist. Finally, to get his mind off the subject, Lance pointed to a tall, polelike cactus some short distance off. "I suppose you'll be telling me that's not an organ-pipe cactus. The Mexes call it *pitahaya dulce*, meaning 'sweet fruit' or something of the kind."

Jones glanced briefly at the plant in question. "Only one of the organ pipes," he jerked. "That one— *Lemaireocereus thurberi*. Now when we get down into Mexico I hope to show you a *Pachycereus marginatus*— some term it—true organ pipe——"

"But I'm not going to Mexico," Lance insisted.

Jones fell into a moody silence, for once, apparently, not content to discuss cacti. Four or five more miles drifted to the rear. Abruptly Jones broke the silence. "I still don't understand"—he appeared to be choosing his words with care—"that man Kilby not having time to tell you a few things about his gang before he died. You're quite sure, Lance, he didn't reveal anything of import?"

"Darn little." Lance's irritation showed in his words. He hated to be questioned. He considered. Something might turn up if he told the professor what Kilby had said. "Kilby refused to talk about the gang at first," Lance continued. "He confessed to killing Bowman and taking the body out to that wash. I remember Kilby mentioned something about it being too dark to notice the peyote in Bowman's hand— —" Lance paused, struck by a sudden thought.

"What's that you said?" Jones pounced on Lance's words. "Too dark to notice—peyote in—Bowman's hand?"

Lance nodded. "And that's queer, too," he said slowly. "There's been so much action today, I reckon my mind isn't working straight. I never thought of that until now——"

"Great Christopher, yes!" Jones exclaimed. "How

many men knew that you found that peyote in Bowman's dead hand?"

"Sheriff Lockwood, Oscar Perkins," Lance said, "Katherine and yourself."

Jones interrupted, "Fletcher overheard you telling me last night. Remember how he hurried from the hotel bar?"

"I'm thinking of it now," Lance said ruefully.

Jones said quickly, "Only five people knew—one of them—told Kilby. Which one?"

Katherine put in, "It looks like Fletcher to me."

"Couldn't be—anybody—else," Jones said.

Lance nodded. "Let's push along. I'm aiming to talk to Fletcher when we get back——" Again he paused, wondering if he was telling Jones too much. After all, Kilby had confessed that somebody was supplying peyotes to the Yaquentes. Peyotes came from a cactus company. The professor could order those peyotes with immunity, so far as being suspected was concerned.

Jones said shrewdly, "Guilty conscience, what? Wondering if you've—revealed secrets—to me?" He laughed shortly. "Can't say—much interested in peyote cactus—that standpoint."

"Whatever I'm thinking"—Lance smiled—"I've got to admit this much. Maybe you haven't improved my brain so far as cactus is concerned this afternoon but you sure started it working in another direction. That's twice I'm indebted to you."

"Perhaps"—Jones returned to the old subject—"make further improvement—if you decide—come to Mexico with us. Mutual improvement, what?"

"Sorry." Lance's lips compressed tightly. "I'm not going to Mexico. That's out, Professor."

Jones sighed. He didn't press the matter further.

The remainder of the ride to town was made in quick time. Arriving in Pozo Verde, Jones and Katherine offered to take Lance's pony to the livery while Lance went directly to the hotel in search of Fletcher.

"Sorry," the clerk informed Lance, "Mr Fletcher isn't in. No, I can't say where he went. I saw him riding a horse earlier today. If he's returned, I couldn't say. I haven't seen him. He may be eating his dinner."

Lance left the desk and went to the hotel dining room. There was no sign of Fletcher there. He returned to the street and visited all the restaurants in town, then the saloons. He kept a sharp eye for those passing along the street, but of Fletcher there didn't seem to be any sign. Lance finally gave up the search and ate his own dinner. It was dark now. He finished his food and went to the sheriff's office. Oscar and Lockwood were there.

"Ah, the return of the cactus hunter." Oscar grinned. "Did you get your itsy-bitsy hands full of nasty old spines?"

"No, but I dang nigh got my carcass full of lead," Lance said.

"You don't say!" Lockwood sat straighter at his desk.

"Somebody tried to dry-gulch me—or Miss Gregory," Lance said grimly. "I'm not sure which. I just know the slugs were too close to both of us to be comfortable." He told the rest of the story, ending with, "And now I want to talk to Fletcher."

Lockwood frowned. "If Jones has got a tie-in with Fletcher why in the devil does he suggest things that make you suspicious of Fletcher?"

"For that matter," Oscar put in, "it was Jones suggested you look for creosote on the overalls of Bowman's killer. What's his game—if any?"

"You got me." Lance shook his head. "Maybe he's just what he says he is. Somehow I've got a hunch to the contrary but I'm damned if I can put a finger on anything definite. Of course, there was that remark he made last night about a gang getting rid of careless members, or something of the sort. Incidentally, have you hombres seen anything of Fletcher this afternoon?"

Oscar said, "I saw him mounted, riding west along Main, a short time after you pulled out with the professor. I don't know where he went though."

"I might make a guess," Lance said darkly, "but I've no proof to back it up. At any rate he's not back yet, according to the hotel clerk."

"Cripes!" Lockwood growled, "that wooden-faced hotel clerk don't know what's going on anyway." He paused, then: "By the way, Lance, I checked up with Johnny Quinn as you asked me to. There's no answer to your telegram yet. Johnny's quite put out about the whole business. Says he had a notion not to close the depot until he learned just what was to happen to your aunt Minnie."

Lance smiled. "Thank your stars there's something left in this world to laugh at. Things are so muddled in my brain that I can't seem to figure anything out. F'rinstance, why in the devil is Jones so anxious to have me guide him down into Mexico?"

"Maybe he figures there isn't so much law down there." Oscar chuckled. "Up here, in the States, we sort of enforce the law concernin' assault and battery. What I want to know, where does Jones' niece fit into the picture?"

"I'm betting that girl's straight," Lance said earnestly.

"You would." Oscar grinned. "I know—pure as

the lily in the dell. But a lily might get the wool pulled over her eyes."

"By the way," Lockwood put in. "I was passing Smith's Gun Shop this afternoon. I glanced through the window. Chiricahua Herrick was looking at six-shooters. I reckon he figured I wouldn't give him back that weapon you took off him, Lance."

"That reminds me of something else," Lance said gloomily. "I've been thinking I should have held that Yaquente that Herrick was beating up today. I let him go, at the time thinking it wouldn't be much use questioning him, but I should have tried."

"It wouldn't have done you any good." Lockwood shook his head. "I know those hombres. They don't talk unless they feel like it, and wild horses couldn't drag any information out of 'em."

Lance nodded. "Just about what I was afraid of. This whole damn business is a puzzle. I'm just hoping when I meet Elmer Manley tonight he'll have something to say that will give me a lead. By the way, where is Tony Pico's saloon?"

Oscar jerked one thumb toward the doorway. "That Mex joint across the street. You won't have far to go. You weren't to meet Manley until nine o'clock, were you?"

"Nine," Lance said. "What sort of joint does Pico run?"

"Tony's all right," Lockwood said. "He obeys the closing law on time. There's never any fights in his place. By Hanner! If all of the people in this town was as law-abidin' as our Mex population we wouldn't have any trouble."

Shortly before nine o'clock Lance crossed the street to Pico's saloon. Oscar went with him. Pico proved to be a round-faced, grinning Mexican who immediately insisted on buying drinks for Oscar and Lance. Oscar didn't drink. This didn't at all stop Tony. Grinning widely, he reached to his back bar and handed Oscar a paper sack of lemon drops. "I'm know someday you come een my bar, Os-cair, so I'm prepare' for any emergen-cee."

"By cripes, Tony"—Oscar laughed—"you're a man after my own heart. Take care of my friend, will you? He's aiming to meet somebody here."

Oscar departed. Lance waited. A few Mexicans strolled in from time to time and drank beer or tequila. Lance carried on a desultory conversation with Pico. Pico happened to mention that a great many Yaquentes were being seen in Pozo Verde the last few months. Lance pricked up his ears and asked Pico if he knew the reason. Pico shrugged. Apparently he knew nothing much about it. "Good fightairs, those Injun," he commented.

"So I hear." Lance nodded. He ordered another bottle of beer. By this time it was nine forty-five, with no sign of Elmer Manley. Ten o'clock came and passed, then ten-thirty. There were more Mexicans in the saloon now; the place was filled with smoke. Lance stepped out to the sidewalk in front to get a breath of air. He wondered why Manley failed to put in an appearance, and there was growing concern in the thought.

A few lights, here and there, still shone along Main Street. Across the roadway oil lamps burned in the sheriff's office. Now and then Lance could hear Oscar's laugh. Lance breathed deeply of the cool night air. Footsteps sounded along the sidewalk. A familiar figure took form.

"Why, hello, Lance." It was Professor Jones. "Waiting for somebody?"

"Just enjoying the cool of the evening," Lance evaded.

"Looking for you—you know," Jones went on. "Intended visiting—sheriff's office——"

"Now, look, Jones," Lance said wearily. "I'm not going down into Mexico with you."

"Quite so, quite. Great disappointment. Not what I wanted to see you about—at all. Fletcher not back—yet. Thought perhaps—you'd be—interested."

"Fletcher hasn't come in yet?"

"Not yet. Strange, what?" Jones puffed smoke from his brier, and the glow from the bowl lighted his face. "Thought you would care to know."

"Well, yes, much obliged."

The professor appeared to want to talk further but when Lance showed no inclination to continue the discussion he said good night and turned back toward the hotel. "Now what"—Lance frowned, looking after the professor's disappearing figure—"did you want? Or are you just being friendly? I don't know whether to be ashamed of myself or not."

It was after eleven o'clock by this time. Oscar came across from the sheriff's office and stood talking to Lance awhile. Lance told him about the professor. Oscar said, "Damn! I wish I could figure that coot out. Looks like Manley isn't going to show up either. I'll tell you what I'll do, Lance. I know where Manley lives. I'll go see if he's home. You wait here in case he shows up." Oscar hurried off down the street.

Within fifteen minutes he was back. "Manley has plumb disappeared," he announced. "About six o'clock he hired a horse and buggy at the Lone Star Livery."

"Did he happen to say where he was going?" Lance asked quickly.

"Not definitely. Just told the livery man he wanted a horse and rig that could make a quick trip to Saddleville."

"How far is Saddleville?"

"About eighteen miles. I went to his boarding-house first. They hadn't seen him since breakfast."

"How'd you happen to go to the livery?"

"Dropped in there on my way back to see if Fletcher had put in an appearance. He hadn't. Fletcher got his horse this afternoon and hasn't been back since."

"I wonder if there's any connection between the two?" Lance frowned. "Oh hell, nothing works out right. I'm going to bed. Maybe we'll have better luck tomorrow——"

"Wait," Oscar interrupted. "Here's the rub. The horse and buggy Manley hired is back. The horse came wandering in about an hour ago. But Manley wasn't with it. There's a suitcase in the rig. That's all."

"Nope, I'm not going to bed," Lance said wearily. "I reckon we'd better saddle up and see if we can find Manley along the Saddleville Road. There's no rest for the wicked, Oscar."

"You mean," Oscar pointed out, "the wicked don't seem to give us any rest. All right, let's go."

XV
Traced Shipments

They hurried across the street to inform the sheriff what had happened. Lockwood looked concerned. "I don't like it. All right, you boys get going. I'll see what I can do at this end."

Lance and Oscar hurried to saddle up. Within five minutes they were riding out of town on the Saddleville Road. Lance felt from the beginning such efforts were futile, but it was part of the routine that had to be gone through.

Lance proved to be right. Gray dawn was lighting the silent streets of Pozo Verde when they returned and put their ponies up at the livery stable. Then they hastened to the sheriff's office. Lockwood had spent the night there sleeping on Oscar's cot. He sat up, rubbing his eyes. "Any news?" he asked.

Lance shook his head, his eyes dark with fatigue. "We went all the way to Saddleville. It was too dark to see any tracks, of course. When it did commence to get light this morning on the way back the road was too chopped up to figure out anything anyway, even if we knew exactly at what spot to look. Course, we were half hoping we might find Manley's body along the way someplace—but no dice. We had the ride for nothing."

"Did you learn anything, Ethan?" Oscar asked.

"Not much. I got Gill Addison out of his bed last night after you left and queried him some. He didn't know where Manley was. He said Manley left the bank about five-thirty or a quarter to six to get his supper. As Addison tells it, Manley was due back at the bank to put in another hour or so on the accounts. Addison was plumb riled he didn't come back."

"Manley told me," Lance said, "that he had to work some last night."

"Here's something," Lockwood went on. "I opened up that suitcase that was in the buggy. It was filled with old newspapers."

"Newspapers?" Lance exclaimed.

"Newspapers." Lockwood nodded. "What do you make of it?"

Lance shook his head. "It's got me down. There's just this much to it. If Manley had suddenly decided to leave town he certainly wouldn't pack his suitcase with newspapers——"

"Unless," Lockwood put in, "somebody exchanged suitcases with him and he didn't notice the exchange. What would the employee of a bank have in a suitcase maybe?"

"Money," Oscar said promptly.

"That's what Gill Addison thought too." Lockwood nodded. "He got dressed to once and hurried down to his bank. He was here just a few minutes before you boys arrived. He couldn't find any money missing, so he felt better. But he's still peeved at Manley. I could tell it in his manner when he left to go back to bed."

"Did Manley have that suitcase with him when he hired the horse and rig?" Lance asked.

"I asked the livery man about that," Lockwood replied. "He doesn't remember for sure, but he thinks not. Doesn't remember seeing it leastwise. What do we do now?"

"I'm going to the hotel and grab a couple hours of shut-eye," Lance replied.

Lockwood nodded. "It's a good idea. Oscar, you tumble into your cot. I've managed to get in several hours, so I won't bother going to bed."

The lobby of the hotel was deserted when Lance opened the door and quickly ascended the stairway to the upper floor. He paused a moment, listening, outside of Fletcher's door. He could hear nothing from the room beyond. Then he knocked. There was no answer. Lance frowned. "I wonder if that hombre didn't come back all night either?"

Turning, he let himself into his own room, undressed and went to bed. He didn't sleep long but he felt refreshed by the time he again descended to the street. It wasn't eight o'clock yet. He found Oscar already having breakfast in the Chinaman's restaurant when he stepped in.

Oscar grinned and said, "Hope you had pleasant dreams."

"I slept like a log while it lasted." Lance gave his breakfast order to the slant-eyed Oriental behind the counter, then turned back to Oscar. "Anything new show up?"

"Not much. I talked to Ethan just before I came in here. He's been over to Manley's boardinghouse and asked questions but he didn't uncover much. He examined Manley's room. All Manley's clothes and things were there. Either he didn't expect to stay away long or——"

"He didn't expect to leave," Lance finished the thought. "I don't like it, Oscar."

Ham, eggs, coffee and bread were placed on the counter before Lance. The two men ate in silence. Oscar finished first. He said to Lance, "Well, where do we go next?"

"There's much to be done, but damned if I know where to start," Lance answered. "We can't do anything about Manley's disappearance until we dig up a clue or something to go on. Suppose you go to the bank and talk to that bookkeeper. Manley might have let something drop that will help. If you know anybody else that was close to him see what you can dig up. I can't help feeling his disappearance is mixed up in this whole business—peyotes, stolen money, Bowman murdered. Jeepers! What a mess. And I don't know where to start to dig myself out. If Kilby hadn't been shot——"

"I know," Oscar put in, "and if Manley had met you as he promised and if you only knew something definite about Jones—— Shucks! What are you going to do?"

"I sent a telegraph to our operative in El Paso. Maybe by this morning Johnny Quinn will have an answer. If he does maybe we'll know who sent for that shipment of peyotes."

"I'll give you odds Jones is the man."

Lance smiled wryly. "I don't like to take any man's money on a sure-thing bet, Oscar. I'd bet in a minute if I thought there was a chance of your losing——"

"I know what's eating you," Oscar said. "You don't like the idea of Katherine Gregory being mixed up in the business."

Lance reddened and drained his coffee cup. "Hell!

I don't even like to think the professor is mixed into it. In spite of myself I like him."

They slid down off the stools and went out to the street after paying for their breakfasts. Lance rolled and lighted a cigarette. Blue smoke floated in the bright morning sunlight. Lance said, "It's going to be hot today."

"By cripes!" Oscar said, "it's been hot every day since you hit this neck of the range. And I'm not talking about sunshine."

They walked west on Main Street, nodding absentmindedly to the few people they passed. The minds of both men were full of thoughts of the things that had happened. They weren't much inclined to talk at the moment. Reaching the corner where the Pozo Verde Saloon was situated, Lance left Oscar and cut off in the direction of the T.N. & A.S. station.

As he entered the small depot old Johnny Quinn was standing behind the counter impatiently awaiting Lance's arrival.

"Crackee!" Johnny grumbled. "Where ye been? I thought ye was never goin' to get here."

"Got a reply to my telegram?" Lance asked.

"Sartain. It arruve not five minutes ago." He passed the sheet of paper across to Lance. "Quick! Whut about Aunt Minnie?"

Lance accepted the telegram. It was rather lengthy and required some time to decipher. Johnny Quinn fidgeted impatiently. Finally Lance glanced up, his forehead creased with frowning concentration.

"Well, well, speak up," Johnny snapped anxiously. "Whut they aimin' to do with Aunt Minnie? Ye looked sorter shocked."

"Maybe I am," Lance said slowly.

"Whut's it to be?" Johnny demanded querulously. "Glass coffin or stuffed in th' rocking chair?"

Lance managed to bring his thoughts back to the conversation. "Neither," he said solemnly. "It's too late."

"Whut! Whut? Speak up! Ain't there goin' to be no funeral for Aunt Minnie?"

"There ain't no Aunt Minnie," Lance explained gravely. "You see, that hemoglobinuria disease just wasted her body away until there wa'n't nothing but a couple fingernails an' a tiny patch of skin left. Them 'll be cremated."

Johnny Quinn gasped. His face went pale. He tried to talk, but his teeth were chattering violently. "Whut—whut a turrible end," he quavered. "You got my sympathies in your bereavement."

"I appreciate that, Johnny," Lance said sadly. "And I'm much obliged for handling all these telegraphing details like you did. It's mitigated my sorrow more than you'll ever understand. I'll mention your help in my next letter to Uncle Obadiah."

"Thankee, Mr Tolliver. An' I hopes as how he'll be mitigated too."

"He's sure to be." Lance turned and left the office. Two minutes later he ran into Sheriff Lockwood sauntering along Main Street.

"You look like you'd learned something," Lockwood commented.

"I did," Lance replied tersely. "I just got an answer to that telegram I sent our El Paso operative. It's taken them quite a spell to run down what I wanted, but here's the facts. That box of mezcal buttons was ordered from the Southwest Cactus Company by Malcolm Fletcher——"

"T'hell you say!" Lockwood exclaimed. "But why? What's the idea? What's he do with 'em?"

"I don't know for certain, but it's my guess he's furnishing 'em to the Yaquentes. That's why you've seen so many of those Indians in Pozo Verde of late——"

"Cripes!" Lockwood protested. "Those Indians have been coming here for two, three months now——"

"And that," Lance stated grimly, "is just about the length of time Fletcher has been ordering peyotes from the cactus company. There's been more than one shipment. I've got the list when the peyotes were ordered and when they were sent. Now you tell me just why Fletcher is supplying peyotes to the Yaquentes. What's back of it all?"

"You got me." Lockwood frowned. "The best thing to do is ask Fletcher."

"Fletcher hasn't been back to the hotel since yesterday."

"He's back," Lockwood stated. "I met Doc Drummond on the street just a few minutes ago. Doc was returning late from a case early this morning. As he passed the hotel he saw Fletcher just going in."

"Good!" Lance exclaimed. Then he scowled. "It's damn funny! If Fletcher got back, why didn't he answer my knock when I stopped at his door this morning just before I turned in?"

"Maybe he didn't hear you. He might be a sound sleeper."

Lance shrugged his shoulders. "Could be," he admitted. "Well, maybe we're getting someplace at last. I can tell better after I've had a talk with Mister Malcolm Fletcher—and I figure to find out just where he was yesterday afternoon when somebody threw lead at Miss Gregory and me. Oh yes, I'm going to tie Fletcher down, hard and tight, this time. No more of his uppity airs for me. He's going to talk or else!"

"Or else what?" Lockwood asked.

"Ethan, I've a hunch you're going to have a guest in one of your furnished, steel-barred apartments by tonight. Will you please see that there's lots of hot water and clean sheets?—particularly hot water!"

"Go to it, Lance." Lockwood nodded, tight lipped. "I'll back up any play you make."

"Thanks." Lance turned, swung diagonally across the street toward the San Antonio Hotel. He was about to enter the building when a voice hailed him from near the hitch rack. Professor Jones was just climbing into his saddle. Lance halted.

"Oh, I say," Jones asked, "feel inclined—continue—study of cacti—this morning?"

Lance crossed to the hitch rack. "I do not," he said emphatically. "I've got other business."

"Quite so." Jones smiled. "However—no necessity to—snap my head off. Just suggestion, what? No harm done."

"Not at all." Lance softened a trifle. "I didn't intend to snap your head off. I was thinking about something else."

"Quite so, quite. I intend returning—spot we studied—yesterday. Unusually rich territory. Wide variety—genera."

"Going alone?" Lance asked.

Jones gave a quick, short nod. "Katherine remaining here. Advised her—not accompany me. Suggested she—start packing—Mexican trip. Plain subterfuge, of course. I consider it—safer in Pozo Verde. No blasted hunter's bullets—flying about. Bad situation, that. Very!"

Lance pointed out, "It doesn't seem to worry you any."

"Don't like it at all." Jones frowned. "But—can't risk—losing desired specimens. Only yesterday I—noticed exquisite clump—*Opuntia macrocentra*. Must make notes. Very queer—yellow flowers—turn red when dry. Such observation extremely important."

"Oh, extremely," Lance said ironically. "See you later, Professor." He entered the hotel thinking that Jones either felt certain no one would shoot at him or that the man's enthusiasm for cacti was worth the risk. "Maybe he's just a nut—I hope," Lance mused.

At the desk in the hotel lobby Lance told the clerk he wanted to see Fletcher. "And," Lance added, "don't stall me off. I know Fletcher got back last night. If you know what's good for you you'll send word up to him pronto—or run up to his room and——"

"But, Deputy Tolliver——"

"Never mind your 'buts,'" Lance snapped. "Do as I tell you—— What!!! He's not here?"

"If you'd listen to reason," the clerk said in chilly accents, "instead of rushing in like a mad bull, you'd understand what I'm trying to tell you. At my last hotel in Boston such an attitude would never be tolerated——"

"Never mind Boston," Lance fumed. "Where's Fletcher?"

"I haven't the least idea. He checked out last night—I should say, early this morning, around three o'clock. Roused me out of my bed to settle his account. He left a note for Professor Jones. Perhaps the professor may know of his whereabouts. I'm sure I don't. And furthermore . . ."

What more the clerk said Lance didn't hear. He

was already hurrying out of the lobby and down to the sidewalk. A look of relief crossed his features when he saw Jones still mounted at the hitch rack.

"Why didn't you tell me Fletcher left?" Lance demanded.

"You didn't ask." Jones appeared slightly amused at something in Lance's attitude. "Had an idea you—looking for Fletcher. Waited to see——"

"You know where he went?" Lance commenced to cool down.

"Faint idea at least. Left note for me. Note explained—Fletcher reconciled to idea—our trip to Mexico. He's left to prepare Three-Cross ranch house—for visitors. Note stated—considerable cleaning up necessary—that sort of thing."

"Well, I'll be damned!"

"Oh, quite likely." Jones smiled cheerfully. "Enjoy yourself first, though—what? When I see Fletcher—tell him you were sorry—miss him—all that sort of thing."

"Dang right I am," Lance said coldly. "I wanted to ask him why he's been having mezcal buttons shipped in."

The smile left Jones's face. "What's that?" he cracked out.

Lance repeated the words, closely watching Jones's face meanwhile. "Certain shipments have been traced direct to Fletcher," he added. "Does that mean anything to you?"

Jones's eyes had a narrowed, faraway look. A frown creased his forehead. His horse shifted weight suddenly, jogging Jones's mind back to the present. He smiled thinly down at Lance. "It means one thing, Lance," he said slowly. "Your information places me in the clear."

Lance looked startled. "What do you mean—places you in the clear?" he demanded.

"Surprised," Jones murmured absent-mindedly, "Fletcher didn't—cover tracks better."

Lance repeated his demands.

"It's this way," Jones replied. "Now you'll no longer suspect me—— No, wait! Don't deny it. Natural thing. Peyote cacti shipped here. Only normal for you—assume—I'm guilty party. Admitted?"

"Admitted," Lance said sheepishly.

"Thought so." Jones smiled. "Better friends now, what? By the way, Fletcher has gone to Mexico. If you must see him—make the trip, eh? Still need that guide, y'understand."

Lance laughed softly. "Professor, you've hired a hand—providing I can pick my own crew."

"What!" Jones's face beamed. "Excellent! Must tell Katherine. Good news." He got down from his horse and gripped Lance's hand, then started toward the hotel entrance. At the doorway he paused, looked back. "Pick your own crew—naturally. Suit yourself."

Lance said, "If you're going after cacti I suppose you'll want men who 're handy with shovels."

"Talk it over with me—tonight. Already—wasted part of the day. And—er—er—you mentioned shovels. Not so important. Prefer men—thoroughly familiar—six-shooters."

And with such surprising statement Jones disappeared through the hotel doorway.

"Now what in the devil"—Lance frowned—"did he mean by that?"

He turned and hastened back to the sheriff's office. Oscar and Lockwood were seated in straight-backed wooden chairs, tipped back against the wall of the building. Lockwood said, "Did you see Fletcher?"

Lance shook his head and told them about Fletcher leaving during the night.

Oscar said, "I'd just like to know if he took Herrick and his gang with him. I haven't seen one of that crowd this morning."

"Maybe I'll find out soon," Lance replied.

"What do you mean?" Oscar asked.

"I'll tell you in a few minutes. Oscar, did you learn anything about Manley?"

Oscar shook his head. "I talked to a lot of folks. Nobody saw him leave town. The bookkeeper at the bank didn't know anything about it. He'd stepped out for his supper a short time before Manley left. After supper the bookkeeper worked an hour or so on his books. Then he ran into some sort of a snag that Manley wasn't there to explain. So the bookkeeper went home."

"I reckon we'll have to leave further work to Ethan—so far as the Manley case is concerned. Ethan, I'm resigning from my deputy job."

"Didn't expect you to continue on with it. You leaving Pozo Verde?"

Lance nodded. "I'm going to guide Jones on that trip into Mexico. Bowman must have expected skulduggery from that direction. I'm going to see if I can pick up where he left off."

"Maybe you've got the right hunch." Lockwood nodded.

"We'll sure miss you, feller," Oscar said sincerely.

"Maybe *you* won't," Lance replied. "Ethan, you said once that the taxpayers thought you could get along without a deputy in Pozo Verde. I'd like to take Oscar along with me—if he'll take the job."

Oscar's chair bumped down suddenly on all four legs. A wide grin spread over his features. "If I'll take the job?" he exclaimed. "Man alive! All you got to do is let me have lemon drops on my expense account, and I'll follow you to hell and back."

"It 'll be a relief to get rid of him"—Lockwood laughed—"I get so damn tired of that crunch-crunch-crunch of lemon drops all the time."

"When do we start?" Oscar asked.

"Two, three days, I figure," Lance said. "We've got to buy equipment, hire men and so on. Oscar, you should know a few cow hands hereabouts who'd like a trip down into mañana land."

"Yeah, I do—several," Oscar said warily, "but they'd be fighting men. They wouldn't take kindly to breaking their backs with a shovel in a cactus pasture."

Lance laughed. "What the professor wants is men who can handle six-shooters."

Oscar's jaw dropped. He slumped down on his chair. "Well, may I be hung for a tobacco-eatin' sheepherder," he said weakly.

Lockwood frowned. "Men who can handle six-shooters? Hmmm! Must be Jones is expecting trouble down in Mexico."

"Well"—Lance smiled thinly—"I never yet heard of anybody shooting cactus out by the roots!"

XVI
Captured!

Mexico. Land of sun and dust and soaring-buzzard shadows across alkali wastes, of purple mountain peaks and broiling deserts and coppery skies. A country of romantic laughter and music and wood smoke under starry nights. A gargantuan arena running crimson with the blood of revolution. A vast region of the oppressed; an indolent realm of soft laughter. A paradoxical land of dreamers and noble warriors, of poets and seraped centaurs. Mañana land. Land of tomorrow. Mexico: a saddle for *el diablo*, a sombero for the *buen Dios*. Where—it is said—nothing ever happens, and where life—and even death—is in a state of unceasing flux. A nation whose battle-drenched soil is all things to all men. Mexico: land of perpetual contradiction.

Thus the thoughts coursed through Lance Tolliver's mind, entirely excluding that other Mexico to the far south, the Mexico of high plateaus and humid jungle lands. Here the country through which the little caravan passed was one of sand and spiny vegetation that marched solemnly through the undulating hills. Huge black rocks or massed phalanxes of Spanish bayonet broke the monotony from time to time, with always, overhead, that burning metallic sun. In the veins of man and beast and plant ran an unceasing desire for rain.

It was the fourth day out from Pozo Verde. It had required three days to outfit the expedition, during which no sign of Herrick or his gang had been seen. Nor had any news been received regarding the sudden disappearance of Elmer Manley who, by now Oscar had decided, had just lost his nerve and "run out" on his promise to talk to Lance, an opinion in which Lance Tolliver concurred not at all.

Meanwhile Lance and Oscar had been busy—the professor was too occupied in the hills near Pozo Verde to take any real part in the outfitting—though Lance had found it necessary on frequent occasions to consult Katherine Gregory, much to Oscar's amusement. To Oscar had been delegated the job of hiring men and the two wagons that accompanied the expedition. Oscar's idea it was that resulted in the employment of two ordinary cow-country chuck wagons. One was rebuilt to furnish sleeping quarters for Katherine Gregory, its tarpaulin-covered bows providing adequate shelter from early-morning suns or chill night winds. The remaining wagon was left "as was" and carried supplies, bedrolls for the men (who slept in the open), the professor's notebooks and a pine box filled with wood shavings from the Pozo Verde Builders' Supply Company—this last to be used to pack such rare specimens as the professor might find.

The men Oscar had picked were six, all of them lean, hard, weathered individuals who talked little unless they had something to say. To Cal Braun fell the job of driving the chuck wagon and preparing food, a task at which he was a master. Tom Piper drove Katherine's wagon and looked after the horses.

In addition to these two were Trunk-Strap Kelly, Hub Owen, Luke Homer and Lanky Peters. Lanky Peters was built like a fence rail and as tough as rawhide; he knew that section of Mexico to which the party was going and, most important and surprising, possessed a smattering of the Yaquente language, being himself of one eighth Yaquente blood—just about enough, as Lanky drawlingly expressed it, "to fill a whisky glass." A dozen saddle horses accompanied the expedition, those not in use being tethered to the wagons.

Forage and water were none too plentiful along the dim trail they were following, but they managed to make out. A few squalid towns had been passed. Now on this, the fourth day of the journey, they were headed toward the town of Muletero, a few miles beyond which was situated the Gregory Three-Cross Ranch. It was expected to reach the ranch by night. Horses and men—and Katherine—were covered with dust, but everyone was in high spirits. Particularly the professor. Each day of the trip he had ranged ahead of the wagons and, accompanied by Katherine and one or two of the men, had made excursions along the hillsides in search of precious specimens or material for his notebooks. There hadn't been any attempt to make speed on the journey.

It was still early, only half an hour after the morning start. Katherine, Jones, Oscar and Lance rode ahead. The others and the wagons were strung out behind. On either side—and often directly in front—huge sahuaro cacti raised gigantic heads above their surrounding vegetation. There seemed to be thousands of them growing in the coarse outwash soil swept down from the sheltering hills.

Oscar had been watching them for some time as

his body moved easily to the motion of the horse. "The feller that named them sahuaros 'Sentinels of the Desert' sure said a mouthful, Professor. Watch 'em for a spell and you'd almost believe they were ready to come alive. They got personality, I claim."

"Over in western Arizona," Lance put in, "there's a lot of those sahuaros. The Papago Indians up that way dry out the fruit and then grind the seeds into a sort of meal——"

"For a fact?" Jones demanded quickly. "Lance, why haven't you told me this before? I must make a note——"

"You never asked me." Lance grinned. "There's quite a few things like that we Southwesterners know, but, Professor, you got us where we're almost afraid to open our mouths about cacti. You know too much for us. For instance"—pointing to a cane-branched opuntia a short distance from the side of the trail—"if I told you that was called a 'tesajo' you'd give me some other long, unpronounceable name."

Jones glanced briefly at the plant in question. "I think you're right—for once." He smiled. "Cholla family, of course. Probably—*opuntia emoryi*. Not certain, of course, without closer observation."

Katherine's laughter joined Oscar's. Lance said ruefully, "You see, I'm always being corrected."

"Someday," Katherine said, "when I build a house of my own, I'm going to plant a sahuaro in my garden." She paused at exclamations from the others. "Lordy, no!" She smiled. "Not one of those huge things. I want one just large enough to give me those luscious creamy blossoms and have woodpeckers nest in it like they do in the desert."

"Incident'ly"—Oscar frowned—"I don't ever remember seeing a small sahuaro. They're all full size by the time they come on view. I ain't never seen a baby giant cactus."

"Not likely to," Jones said. "Hard to find—possess ability—hide among rocks and brush. Often—ten, twenty years old—before they push up above their surroundings. Grow rapidly—from then on." He paused, then added, "Grew one from seed—five years ago. At two years it—looked like—small green ball—three-quarter-inch diameter. Long yellow spines . . ."

Horses and wagons moved on under the hot morning sky. Behind the riders listening to Jones's dissertation on cacti there sounded the occasional squeak of a wagon wheel or the creaking of saddle leather. The way was leading into higher terrain now. The slopes on either side were spotted with ironwood and paloverde trees. There was more rock than seen on the previous day and the vegetation had a greener look. An occasional organ-pipe cactus appeared.

Jones pointed one out. "There, Lance—true organ pipe—*Pachycereus marginatus.*"

The procession moved around the shoulder of a rock-cluttered hill. Ahead and to the left a long, gradual slope lifted to dizzy peaked heights scarred with dark ravines and hollows. Jones eyed the scene with fresh interest. "Some timber up there," he announced. "Think I'll have a look. Come on, Katherine. We'll pick up the wagons later. Want to come, Lance?"

Lance hesitated. Ever since he'd crawled from his bed at sunrise he'd had an uneasy sensation of being watched by unseen eyes. Just what it was he didn't know, but some premonition of approaching danger warned him to go slow.

"We-ell, I don't know." He hesitated. "Why not pass up the cactus hunt for the day, Professor? I feel we should push along to the Three-Cross. We should get there tonight. Once you've established your head-quarters you can roam around this country to your heart's content."

"Maybe Lance has the right idea," Katherine commented.

"Nonsense!" Jones said impatiently. "No time like the present. Such observations as I make along the way will save later repetition."

"Suits me." Katherine nodded. "Lance, it's not really necessary you should go if you feel you should stay with the wagons. Oscar or one of the other men can go."

"I'd better stay with the wagons," Oscar said. He slid a paper bag from his pocket and put a lemon drop into his mouth. "You ought to take one of these. They're sure good for cuttin' the dust in your throat."

They talked a few minutes more. Jones was intent on his cacti search and wouldn't be swayed from his determination. Reluctantly Lance decided to go with them. He turned, frowning, to Oscar. "We'll try to pick you up by dinnertime. Don't go on until we show up."

"You'll pick us up by dinnertime," Oscar scoffed, "providing the professor doesn't forget the time like he did day before yesterday."

"I apologize again"—Jones smiled—"for that tardiness. But—opportunity of lifetime—*Astrophytum myriostigma*—such variety—three-ribbed specimen—worth being two hours—late for dinner. You don't understand."

"I'm afraid I don't," Oscar said dryly.

"Well, see you later." Lance nodded. He put spurs to his roan gelding and pushed up alongside Katherine, who rode between him and the professor. They jogged along the ancient wagon trail for an hour where it wound between hills and around huge blocks of black basalt rock. The ponies climbed steadily. Once, looking back and down, Lance saw the wagons and riders of the expedition, tiny in the sun-drenched distance.

Finally the professor led the way from the old trail up a gradually ascending slope. He wound in and out among clumps of paloverde. There were no more of the big cacti to be seen now, though an occasional growth of prickly pear or cholla pushed up through the brush. In time they commenced to see stunted pine trees and scrub oak and piñon. Quail whirred out of the brush, and startled jack rabbits scurried frantically for shelter. Rocks the size of an ordinary house bulked huge in every direction. Here and there scarred watercourses, made by the rainy seasons' runoff, cut deep ravines and gulleys. The trees grew taller too.

The riders pulled to a halt to rest their ponies. Lance said, "I've got to admit a mite of shade goes right good after the heat down on the level. But if it's cacti you're looking for, Professor, I'd figure there's too much shade up here to furnish much success——"

Jones broke in impatiently, "Don't know where people—get ridiculous idea—cacti need full sun. Only about fifteen per cent—various species—do without some shade." He dismounted from his horse. "Wait here. I'll cast about a bit and see—anything to be learned. If I want you—give a hail, what?"

Lance dismounted and helped Katherine down from the saddle. They found a smooth slab of rock to sit on. The professor moved slowly away, closely scrutinizing the earth in all directions. A trowel hung in a scabbard at his belt. Under one arm he carried a notebook, under the other a small roll of burlap sacking.

Katherine smiled. "Two bits to a dollar we don't get back to dinner in time."

Lance laughed. "The old bloodhound's on the scent. He won't quit until he finds something. Then we'll have to listen to more big words."

"He's a dear, though," Katherine said.

"He's regular. But sure batty on the subject of cacti." Lance rolled a cigarette. Blue smoke spiraled up to be lost among the branches of trees overhead. His eyes were still on the professor wending his way slowly through the brush. Finally Jones disappeared around a shelf of protruding rock.

Lance's eyes darted continually here and there. He still had that feeling that someone was watching him from cover. Twice he arose and moved around. There was nothing unusual to be seen. He came back to the rock where Katherine waited. She commented on his uneasiness. He laughed that off and sat down again. His cigarette burned down. Finally he ground it under his toe. He was finding it difficult to make conversation, though more and more these days he found enjoyment in the girl's company.

"Lance," Katherine said suddenly. "You are uneasy about something. I can tell from your manner. To tell the truth, I've felt sort of queer today. . . . Oh, I don't know. As if—as if someone were watching me all the time. Every time I glance around I half expect to see a pair of eyes peering from the brush—

but there never are. I've had that feeling of someone following along at the side of our trail watching every move we make."

"Maybe we're not living right or something." Lance laughed. "I wonder if lemon drops would help us. My gosh! You should have seen the stock Oscar laid in. He won't run short. By the way, do you remember what sort of town Muletero is?"

Katherine shrugged her trim shoulders. "Not much of a town," she admitted. "Just a typical Mexican settlement—a handful of shops and houses built of adobe. It's less than five miles from the Three-Cross. We'll be able to buy a few supplies there. But I think you'll like the Three-Cross. Part of it is in the state of Chihuahua, you know. It's good grazing country, Father claimed——"

Lance said suddenly, "What's that?"

They both listened. Again came a startled, high-pitched cry. It seemed to come from some distance off.

"It's Uncle Uly!" Katherine cried. "Something's wrong!"

They leaped to their feet and dashed off in the direction from which the call had come. Prickly bushes caught at Katherine's shirt. Luckily the denim overalls she had insisted on wearing didn't impede her progress. Lance ran ahead to break trail. Once they raised their voices to call again. This time there was no answer. They plunged on.

Suddenly Lance and Katherine emerged into a small clearing. Lance saw the professor first. The man was crawling about on hands and knees closely studying the earth in all directions.

"What's wrong?" Lance yelled. "Rattler?"

Jones didn't even raise his head.

"Uncle Uly," Katherine exclaimed sharply, "why don't you answer us? Are you hurt? Quick! What's the matter?"

Jones reluctantly gained his feet. "Hurt?" he queried vaguely, seemingly unable to comprehend. His thin features were ashen; his hands trembled with excitement. His knees quaked as he approached. "Katherine—Lance," he stated solemnly, "this is the greatest day of my life. Look!" He led them to a spot a few yards away.

Lance looked. Katherine looked. The professor looked—with something of mingled awe and adoration in his gaze. There, at their feet, grew a globular-shaped cactus with many slightly waved ribs, each rib lined with black spines. It was about the size of a small orange, deep green, and from either side rose two deep blue, funnel-shaped flowers with yellow centers. Yellow, Lance thought, like Katherine's hair.

Katherine gasped suddenly and went off into paroxysms of laughter. "D-do you mean to s-say this is what you g-g-got us so excited about? We thought you were hurt." She dropped weakly to the earth, still laughing. Lance grinned with sudden relief.

"I'm admitting those flowers are plumb pretty," he said, "but do you think it's something to get worked up about?"

"Worked up?" Jones sounded indignant. "Can't you realize I've found a new, unknown genus? An *Echinopsis* north of the Andes! I predict—entire cactus world—worked up! Y'understand it's a marvelous discovery. Think of it—an *Echinopsis*—here in Mexico! And with *blue* flowers. Why—why, it's unheard of!"

"All right," Lance said genially. "It's unheard of. But why?"

Jones looked his exasperation. "In the first place"—trying to conceal his impatience— "the *Echinopsis* family does not grow in this continent. None has ever been discovered north of South America. And—what is more important"—Jones's voice dropped to an awestruck whisper—"did you ever in all your life see, or even hear of, a cactus with a *blue* bloom?"

"I reckon I didn't," Lance admitted.

"Now you know." Jones breathed a long, happy sigh. He dropped onto his knees to inspect the plant at closer range. Almost Lance expected him to bow down and give worship. After a few minutes he commenced making notes in a shaking hand, regarding the type soil in which the cactus had been discovered, amount of sun, shade and so on. He produced a small steel scale and made measurements. Lance could hear him muttering to himself as he made notes: "Ribs—fourteen. Areoles—seat of buds. Spines—black. Flowers—blue. Pistil—cream. Stamens—yellow——" He looked up suddenly. "Katherine, my dear. These flowers—like your eyes. I think I shall name this cactus—in honor—you and your father. *Echinopsis gregoriana*. How's that?"

"It sounds very grand, Uncle Uly," Katherine said soberly.

Jones colored self-consciously. "The name—Ulysses Zarathustra Jones—will take its place—among great—world cacti authorities." He paused, then: "I fear this specimen—only one of its kind—hereabouts. Already searched for more. No luck. Katherine—Lance—look about like good folks—see if you can find—further specimens—er—*Echinopsis gregoriana*."

Lance and Katherine moved away, scanning the earth in all directions, but without success in finding more specimens of the desired plant. The professor continued muttering to himself and making notes and measurements. Katherine whispered to Lance: "Finding that plant means the realization of an old ambition to Uncle Uly. He's always wanted to discover a hitherto unknown genus."

At length they returned to the professor. He had finished his notes and was engaged in digging a small trench about the plant. He had already packed loose grass about the blooms. A solid clump of earth remained about the base of the plant. "Mustn't disturb roots." He smiled at Lance. "Employ every care—this specimen. Must take earth." He tore into narrow strips the burlap he had brought and covered the balled earth about the plant's roots. Producing a few lengths of hemp twine from his pocket, he proceeded to tie the burlap firmly in place. Now the plant was ready to be lifted from its resting place. Jones smiled happily.

"Extreme care—necessary in handling," he said. "If I should stumble and drop this—break earth from roots——" An expression of pain at the very thought of such calamity crossed the professor's face. "Lance—a favor, please. Can't risk handling this—like ordinary cacti. Like a good fellow—bring up my horse. I think this may—fit snugly into one of my saddlebags. More secure, what? No risk at all."

"Sure, I'll get your bronc." Lance nodded and left Katherine listening to further happy utterances on the part of the overjoyed professor. He started back to the spot at which the horses had been left.

Five minutes later he arrived and found the ponies peacefully cropping near-by vegetation, with the reins dangling from their heads. The professor's gray pony stood near a great shelf of overhanging rock, beside which grew a narrow clump of trees. Lance gathered the reins in his hand. Then he stopped, thinking he had heard a movement from overhead. He stepped back, but the move came too late. He had only a brief glance of a hurtling brown form, in flapping cotton garments, as it projected itself from the shelf above his head. He caught a quick glimpse of wild black hair, angry eyes, a red, open mouth. Then something crashed heavily on his head and a curtain of black, black velvet folded sickeningly about his fading senses!

XVII
Temple of the Plumed Serpent

Lance awoke slowly. At the first move he made a dull ache permeated his head. His tongue felt thick and furry; his mouth was parched. He moved one hand exploringly and discovered he was stretched full length on a flat stone surface. He tried to make out where he was, but only the faintest light was to be seen, and that far above him.

"Jeepers!" Lance muttered. "What a head. If I didn't know myself I'd sure think I'd been on one wild brannigan. What in the devil happened to me? Where am I? What time is it?" Memory's fingers feebly commenced to trace certain patterns on his mind. "Lemme see. I remember going after the professor's horse and then——Oh yeah, I looked up just in time to see that hombre leaping down on me from above. He looked like a Yaquente. There was two Yaquentes anyway. I remember seeing a second man looking down over the shoulder of the first just before he jumped. He must have had a rock in his fist. . . . I know something came down awful hard on my head."

He raised one hand and felt tenderly of the lump high above his right ear. "Whew! What a wallop! Dammit! I had a hunch there was something wrong—a feeling like somebody was watching us. I'll bet those Yaquentes have been following us ever since we left the border. Maybe not though. Maybe just since yesterday. Or was it yesterday? When did this happen?"

Lance came slowly to a sitting position. A flash of pain shot through his head. "Ooo!" He winced. "What I would give for a drink of water. Where am I anyway?"

His right hand, still exploring, suddenly encountered a small can of water. That brought further memories. This wasn't the first time Lance had regained consciousness. He recollected now finding that water before. It had been pitch dark then. The water had had a queer, bitter taste, and Lance had swallowed only a little, fearing it might be drugged.

"By cripes!" Lance grunted, "it was drugged too. I remember starting to slip off right after the first sip. Somebody must be figuring to keep me unconscious. Why?" Fearing that thirst might induce him to drink even the remainder of the drugged water, Lance quickly emptied the can onto the floor upon which he lay. "That's settled, anyway," he said grimly. "I may go out thirsty, but I'll know what's going on anyway. . . . Who in the devil brought me here anyway? Those Yaquentes, I suppose. But what is the idea?"

He gained his feet, took a single staggering step, then another. A wave of dizziness swept through him. After a moment his head cleared, and he commenced to feel better. He took a few more steps and suddenly encountered a rock wall. It was too dark to see, but his fingers told him the wall was built of flat blocks of stone smoothly set together. He took more steps. There were three more walls. He paced

off the distance. Overhead, far overhead, he could
see a faint, grayish square of light.

"Looks to me like I'm at the bottom of a pit," Lance
muttered. "Offhand, I'd guess it's about ten feet
square and thirty or forty deep. This is certainly one
hell of a fix. I wonder what happened to Katherine—
and the others."

For a moment he felt horribly afraid. Something
of panic took possession of his senses. Frantically
he strove to scramble up the side of the nearest wall.
It wouldn't work. He couldn't find a projection on
which his fingers could seize, let alone a foothold.
The walls were too smooth for that. Perspiration
rolled from his forehead; his entire body was soaked
with sweat. His fingernails were broken; the skin at
the end of his fingers felt raw and scraped. Finally,
exhausted, he sank back to the floor of the pit.

Only then did he come to his senses. "Lance Tolliver," he told himself disgustedly, "only a damn fool
would lose his head that-a-way. Get a hold on yourself. You're still alive. If those Yaquentes had wanted
you dead they'd killed you long ago. That means
they want you alive. They put you down here for safe-
keeping. That means somebody will come back for
me sometime. If they want me they'll have to pull me
out. Once I'm out of this hole, then we'll face the
next problem."

He smiled in the darkness and pulled himself to
a sitting position. His gun had been taken, but an
examination of his pockets showed nothing else
had been touched. They'd even left his cartridge
belt about his waist. He found his sack of Durham
and papers and matches. Once he'd commenced to
inhale tobacco smoke he felt immeasurably better.
He held the lighted match to examine the walls.

Then he struck more matches. He laughed at himself. "You jug-headed idiot, Tolliver, trying to climb a wall of glass wouldn't be much worse than those. Let this be a lesson to you. Hereafter, when you get in a tight, stop and think things over before you let yourself be stampeded into such damn fool actions." He felt around and found his sombrero.

When the first cigarette was finished he rolled and lighted another. He was halfway through a third smoke when he heard a slight sound overhead. Peering up through the gloom, he thought he could make out a head peering down into the pit. Then he heard a voice. There was a queer hollow, ringing sound to the tones as though they'd been spoken in a stone-vaulted chamber.

"Yeah, I'm still here," Lance called back. "Who is it?"

There was no answer. Lance called out again. Something struck the side of his head and fell away. Lance put out one hand and grasped the end of a rawhide lariat. Now he caught the idea. "Just a minute, I'll be with you."

Knotting the lariat tightly about his shoulders, beneath his arms, he commenced to climb. At the same instant the unseen benefactor above started to haul on the rope. Halfway up, the rawhide changed to hemp. Lance judged it had been necessary to knot two ropes together. He was making fast time now, moving hand over hand.

A few moments later Lance's hands encountered the edge of the pit. He hauled himself out and scrambled to his feet, quickly unknotting the rope about his shoulders and prepared to fight if need be. It was lighter up here. Lance looked at his rescuer. The Yaquente looked familiar. He was in loose cotton garments. Beneath the big straw sombrero was a stolid brown face with two cruel, healing scars across the nose and high cheekbones. Suddenly there came the flash of white teeth in the brown features. Only then did Lance remember the Yaquente he had saved from the quirting at Chiricahua Herrick's hands.

"Horatio!" Lance exclaimed. He shoved out one hand, and the Indian grasped it. Next he handed Lance his six-shooter. Gratefully Lance shoved the gun into his holster.

"It is bes'"—the Yaquente struggled with the words—"you go 'way queeck—pronto! Savvy?"

"Savvy." Lance nodded. "Gosh, Horatio, I sure owe you a lot. What happened to my friends? Where are they?"

"Nozzing is 'appen. No kill. You find friends Three-Cross Rancho. You go 'way queeck now."

"Right. I'll get moving."

Still he didn't start. While the Yaquente waited uneasily beside him Lance glanced around. His eyes widened in amazement. He was standing in a huge vaulted chamber built of oblong-shaped blocks of granite. Here and there massive stone pillars supported the ceiling. The walls were covered with elaborate frescoes in faded pigments. Certain patterns in mosaic work carried a frieze around the chamber. A design depicting a snake seemed to dominate the decorations.

"Say," Lance exclaimed, "what is this place?"

The Yaquente frowned. "You go 'way queeck. Many men soon come. I be kill', you find here. You help me. Me help you. Go 'way queeck!"

"A lot of men coming, eh? All right, we'll get moving in a minute."

Lance took a last look around. The only light in the big chamber entered through a wide doorway at the opposite end of the huge room. Lance and the Yaquente stood at the inner end. Lance glanced down at the pit from which he'd been rescued. A few yards away from the pit stood a large block of stone, the surface of which was intricately carved with various symbols. Seeing them, Lance was reminded of the symbols on the armlet Katherine's father had sent her. He gazed again on the huge stone block. It looked to be some sort of altar.

Then he looked closer. Here and there a brownish stain had seeped into the stone. Comprehension came to Lance. He spoke to the Yaquente. "Blood, Horatio?"

"Blood. Men have die there. You nex'. Go 'way queeck!"

"I'm next!" For an instant a chill of fear ran along Lance's spine. Then he grinned. "Maybe I'm next. I'll be with you in a minute."

He had noticed a small door leading to another chamber back of the altar stone. With the Indian following reluctantly at his heels, Lance decided to investigate. He stepped into a smaller room. It was too gloomy to see much, but Lance had time to see some stacked pine boxes. At the opposite side of the room was another smaller box.

"You come 'way—queeck." The Yaquente was growing more insistent. He tugged at Lance's arm. "You be kill'. I be kill'." He forced a wan smile and managed to get out, "Hell to be paid!"

"There sure would be hell to pay." Lance chuckled. "All right, Horatio. I'll make my getaway."

They left the small room and emerged into the big chamber. The Yaquente led the way past the bloodstained altar and down the length of the long room toward the open doorway. Dust lay thickly on the floor but it was printed with the marks of hundreds of feet, both bare and booted. This much Lance gathered as he followed the Indian toward the doorway.

Once he paused and examined one of the many paintings of snakes along the walls. The paint had faded and was chipped off at several spots, but Lance had no trouble making out the outlines of a rattlesnake, rattles and all. What he didn't understand was that the reptile seemed to have a ridge of feathers growing from its body.

"What's the idea of this?" Lance asked, pointing to the snake painting.

The Indian looked uneasy. "Quetzalcoatl—him—great god—— Him——" He broke off. "Come 'way queeck!"

Lance frowned. "Say, when are the men coming back here?" He had to frame the question in two or three different ways before the Indian understood.

"Come here—tonight," the Yaquente finally answered.

"Tonight, eh? I reckon I'll be on hand for the show."

Whether he understood the words or not, the Indian certainly gathered Lance's meaning. An expression of horror crossed his face. "No—no—no!" he said emphatically. "Come 'way——"

"I know," Lance cut in, grinning, "queeck! All right, Horatio, lead the way. I won't hold you back any more."

The Yaquente hurried now. Their footsteps, despite the heavy dust on the floor, echoed queerly in the great chamber. Scattered along the floor near the walls Lance saw ancient fragments of pots and bowls. Some were too gray with the dust of centuries to tell anything of the color; on others faint traces of red or blue or black showed.

The big chamber was probably seventy-five or eighty feet long and nearly as wide. They were nearing the entrance now. Ahead Lance could see bright sunlight on gravelly soil. The sun had never looked so good to him. They reached the wide doorway which was shaped something like a triangle with the apex removed. The next instant they were in the open air. Lance drew great draughts into his lungs. Air had never before seemed so sweet.

The Yaquente kept urging Lance to hurry. Lance glanced at the sky. He judged it to be about three-thirty or four in the afternoon. He glanced back at the building from which he had just emerged. With surprise he saw it was built much like a pyramid. On the entrance side a flight of broken steps ran completely across the face of the pyramid. Where the steps led to it was difficult to say. The top of the structure was earth covered, furnishing a foothold for the trees and brush that grew there. On either side the earth was stacked to the top of the building. Lance couldn't quite decide whether the pyramid had been cut into the side of a ridge or if earth had settled or been stacked against it at a later date.

Large blocks of rock lay scattered over the earth, some still in the natural state; others had been sculptured by ancient tools into the form of huge building bricks.

Now, Lance saw, there appeared to be a sort of wide roadway leading to the pyramid. Along both sides of this road, spaced at intervals, were great slabs of graven stone covered with serried squares of symbols similar to the ones Lance had seen on Katherine's armlet. Some of these great rocks lay flat; others still stood erect, embedded in the earth; still others were tilted crazily to one side or the other like tombstones in an ancient graveyard. Lance felt like a pygmy wandering through the burying ground of some age-old, gigantic race. The symbols on the stones were worn almost smooth by centuries of erosion and sandstorms. Lance quickened his step to overtake the hastening Yaquente. "Hey, what is this place?" Lance asked.

"You come 'way queeck. I tell," the Indian promised.

Gradually, using both English and Spanish, and with the aid of signs, Lance managed to get the information. It appeared that the pyramid was a place of Yaquente religious services known as, so far as Lance could make out, the Temple of the Plumed Serpent. Lance frowned.

"You savvy, huh? Him great god."

Getting further information proved even more difficult. Lance followed the Indian through a thick tangle of high brush, asking questions as they proceeded. He realized suddenly a path had been worn through here at some previous, more ancient time. They topped a low ridge covered with brush and prickly pear. Lance glanced back. He couldn't see the temple now, so thickly was it screened by the brush and trees through which they'd passed. They dipped down across a hollow, Lance still asking questions and eking out, little by little, certain information he desired.

By this time he had learned that the Yaquentes had followed the expedition since the day it left the border, looking for an opportunity to capture Lance. It was on the previous day Lance had been knocked on the head and carried to the pit where the Indian had found him.

"But why capture me?" Lance asked.

The Yaquente shrugged his shoulders. "Big chief, him point out you. Call you man with hair like fire. I'm see you when you brought in. I'm remember how you save me from whipeeng. I'm save you from *sacrificio*. I'm no *obligación*——"

"Whoa! Sure, your debt's discharged, if that's what you mean. But I don't get this." Lance asked more questions. Gradually it dawned on him; his eyes widened. "Me?" he exclaimed. "A human sacrifice to your god—that snake with feathers?"

The Indian nodded stolidly, then went through the motions of cutting open his breast and tearing out his heart. Lance shivered. The Yaquente's appearance of uneasiness increased. Now he hurried faster. He refused to reply to more than a few of Lance's questions. Abruptly they arrived at a steep incline covered with loose rock. Together they clambered up the face of the incline. Great boulders were at the crest. There seemed to be some sort of twisted passage among the boulders. Eventually they arrived at a point where a great plain opened up before them. Lance saw grazing country and a few cows scattered here and there. Then his heart gave a great leap. Not ten miles away he saw a group of adobe buildings, tiny in the bright, sunlit distance.

"Your friends there," the Yaquente grunted. He started to follow a steep path down to a clump of trees at the bottom. Lance followed closely on his heels. Finally they stopped at the foot of the descent, and there, under a mesquite tree, Lance saw his roan gelding tethered. "Jeepers!" Lance exclaimed. "Horatio, you don't forget anything. The *caballo!* Horse!"

The Yaquente grinned. "I'm steal heem from corral," he stated proudly. "You ride. Leave countree. Not safe. Go 'way queeck!"

Lance shook hands again. He invited the Indian to get up behind him on the horse, but the Yaquente refused. "Adiós!" he said, and stepped into a clump of high brush. The next instant he had disappeared. Lance called to him twice, but there was no answer. The Indian had taken his departure with all the stealth of the snake he worshiped. Lance waited a minute longer, then mounted and turned the horse's head in the direction of the ranch buildings he had seen.

XVIII
Risky Business!

Lance strode steadily for some time. The Three-Cross buildings were nearer now. He could make out a clump of cottonwood trees and a windmill whirring in the breeze. From time to time he had passed a few cattle bearing on the left ribs the Three-Cross brand. Other cattle were unbranded. None of the animals appeared to be of high-grade stock. As he drew nearer the ranch buildings Lance saw a long adobe ranch house fronted by a gallery that stretched across the entire front of the structure. There were a bunkhouse, corrals and other miscellaneous buildings. There were a few horses in one of the corrals, but of human life about the place there was no sign.

Lance dismounted before the house, mounted two low stone steps and strode across the flag-paved gallery. A door stood slightly open before him. He pushed it the rest of the way and found himself gazing into a long room with many Indian rugs scattered about on its beaten earth floor. There was a big fireplace at one end. On the white-washed walls were a couple of mounted deer heads and one or two framed pictures. Here and there a *chimayo* blanket made a vivid splash of yellow or scarlet to add to the decorative effect. Comfortable chairs, well worn, and a long, low table holding a clutter of miscellaneous objects helped fill up the room. There seemed to be a great deal of dust over everything, and it didn't look as though the ranch house had had a good sweeping in some time.

"Huh," Lance grunted, "if Malcolm Fletcher pulled out of Pozo Verde in such a hurry to come down here and get the place ready for Katherine it sure looks like he forgot his good intentions before he arrived." He walked on into the room, closing the door behind him, and raised his voice: "Anybody home? Hey! Katherine! Oscar! Professor!"

His call received instant results. He caught a startled cry, and a door at one end of the room burst open. Katherine stood there, her long yellow hair loose and hanging below her waist. She was still in overalls, dusty, torn overalls. Her face was smudged with dirt. The girl paused in the doorway, her deep blue eyes growing wider and wider. "Lance? Lance! Is it really you?" she half whispered. Suddenly a glad cry was torn from her lips, and she came forward.

Things happened pretty quick after that. Before he realized what he was doing Lance moved toward the girl, and his arms whipped hungrily about her. Her face lifted to his. Thereafter there was silence for some time. Finally Katherine broke away, her face crimson under the smudges of dirt.

"Yeah, it's me—I'm back." Lance grinned.

Katherine said, "You certainly came back with a rush. Lance! Things happened to us all of a sudden, didn't they? I didn't know I was going to do that and then—then——"

"I know." Lance grinned happily. "I hadn't intended to say a thing until—until after things get straightened out but I kind of got swept off my feet."

"You did a good job of sweeping yourself, mister." Katherine smiled. "And look at me! I'm a sight."

Lance started toward the girl again, arms outstretched, but Katherine warded him off. "Sight or no sight"—Lance chuckled—"isn't there a saying to the effect that a new broom sweeps clean?"

At that minute a door at the opposite end of the room opened, and Professor Jones appeared. "Bless me!" he exclaimed. "Thought I heard your voice, Lance. Couldn't believe it." He paused, noticing their blushing faces and taking in the situation at a glance. "Look groggy—both of you." He smiled. "Sudden triumph for the emotions, eh? What? Don't blame you. Young myself once, y'understand. Katherine— I—both worried. Lance! Where in hell you been?" He had Lance's hand in his by this time, shaking it soundly.

"It's sure a relief to find you two," Lance said, "but where's all the rest? I'll tell my story in a minute."

"Everybody else is looking for you," Katherine said. "We've all been out all night. Uncle Uly and I just got back. Oscar was with us. I simply had to clean up. Then I heard your voice. Oscar's gone to Muletero to see if he could learn anything. It's only about four miles from here, you know. Lordy, I'll bet I've tramped and rode a hundred square miles of brush country."

It appeared that when Lance hadn't returned with the professor's horse the previous day Katherine and Jones had finally come to look for him. All three horses were as they had left them. Katherine had mounted and raced down the mountainside to catch up with Oscar and the rest of the wagon train. While two men stayed with the wagons the rest had ascended the mountain to look for traces of Lance. That continued until darkness when the search was temporarily halted, and the party came on to the Three-Cross. Then the men had once more started out on a search for Lance that had lasted the rest of the night and was still continuing. Oscar, Jones and Katherine had finally returned to the Three-Cross to see if the rest had put in an appearance with news.

"I can't understand why"—Lance frowned—"some of them didn't find sign where I was standing when it happened."

"Oscar did," Katherine said. "So did Lanky Peters. They found 'sign' where two men had waited on a shelf of rock above the horses. One of them had apparently leaped on you. We figured you were knocked unconscious and carried away. Footprints showed where they had taken you down through a narrow gully. Then, due to the scattered rock footing, the prints entirely disappeared. And so much time had already been lost——But, Lance, what did happen to you?"

Lance told his story while he smoked a cigarette. Katherine's eyes grew wider and wider while she listened. Jones grew more and more interested. When Lance had finished:

"No end remarkable," Jones commented. "Amazing, what? This Temple of the Plumed Serpent—I know very little about archaeology, but jewels and gold often found in such places. Aztec, no doubt. I knew the ancient Aztec people worshiped a god named Quetzalcoatl—called Plumed Serpent——"

"That's what Horatio called him—"Quetzalcoatl," Lance put in.

"Quite so, quite. Those overgrown tombstones—you mention—quite probably stelae—records, calendar, history of the race and so on. I should like to see them."

"You won't have to go far," Lance stated. "It's on Three-Cross property, the whole setup, temple and all, but so well hidden behind trees and brushy ridges that you'd never know it was there unless you stumbled on it by accident or found it as I did."

Katherine put in, "Lance, that armlet Father sent me—it must have come from the feathered snake temple."

"That's my idea." Lance nodded.

Katherine smiled suddenly. "Lance, Uncle Uly was so upset over your disappearance yesterday that he clean forgot his precious cactus discovery."

The professor flushed to the roots of his hair. "Ridiculous, eh?" Jones smiled wryly. "Another example—triumph of emotions over ratiocination. Must have—completely lost—head. However, we returned—today. *Echinopsis gregoriana*—safely in my possession—now."

"We returned to the place where you disappeared," Katherine explained. "Oscar wanted another look at the earth to see if he had overlooked anything. He hadn't—but I had to remind Uncle Uly to bring his precious plant this time."

"By the time we returned here"—Jones changed the subject—"Oscar discovered—your horse—missing from corral. Thought perhaps you had come or someone in Muletero had stolen it. Went to Muletero to see——"

"It was Horatio who took the horse," Lance said, "and he didn't take it to Muletero—thank heaven!"

Oscar arrived and was overjoyed to find Lance.

"By cripes!" Oscar said earnestly, "we were sure upset. I betcha I ate two pounds of lemon drops. You know, nothing like lemon drops to keep a man's courage up."

Lance had started to tell his story when, one by one, the others of the expedition put in an appearance. They were gray with dust and fatigue, but sight of Lance quickly restored them to normal. Lance went over and over his story. Darkness fell, lamps were lighted, while the men sat talking in the big room of the ranch house. Lance suddenly remembered Fletcher and asked if they'd seen him.

"He's out looking for you," Katherine said.

"Fletcher is?" Lance said unbelievingly.

Katherine nodded. "That's where he said he was going anyway. He was here last night when we arrived. We told him what had happened. He left almost immediately—alone. Said he knew this country and he might learn something. Before he left he advised us all not to leave the ranch. Fletcher said the Yaquentes are very dangerous hereabouts and to leave everything to him. He hasn't returned since."

Lanky Peters growled, "I can't say I liked the way he advised us not to leave the ranch. It sounded to me like a command. Course, we didn't pay no attention. Just before I returned here I paid a visit to the Yaquente camp. Them Injuns is living in a canyon about a quarter of a mile east of Muletero. I rode through the camp. Nobody paid me any real attention, but I did get some dirty looks. A lot of them Yaquentes looked sort of hopped up, like they'd been eating mezcal buttons or something. You've heard of 'em doing that, haven't you?"

Lance said, "Yes, I've heard of it being done." Oscar and Jones exchanged glances. So far as Lanky and the rest of the employees knew this was a cactus-hunting expedition, nothing else.

Oscar frowned. "Something else I don't like: when I was coming through Muletero I saw Chiricahua Herrick just coming out of the local cantina. Probably his whole gang is here too."

Lance asked quickly, "Did Herrick see you?"

Oscar nodded. "He said hello, in fact, genial as you please. He didn't seem none surprised at seeing me here either. I don't like the setup. Between Herrick and his crowd and the Yaquentes, it looks like we might be kept virtual prisoners here at the ranch."

The men quickly exchanged looks. Lanky Peters and the other hands appeared puzzled. Lance said, "Lanky, you and the others might as well know it now. The main object of this expedition was to hunt cacti, I suppose, but there's two or three other things in the wind to be settled. There may be some fighting before we get through. If anybody feels the job might get too tough he's free to get his horse and leave now—and there'll be no hard feelings." Lance waited. None of the crew showed any signs of leaving. As a matter of fact they appeared to take a fresh interest in the proceedings. Lance went on, "I can't go into details now, but you'll get the whole story eventually. Isn't that right, Professor?"

Jones looked startled. "Bless me, I suppose it is. I'm interested, however, in nothing but cacti——"

Katherine interrupted by rising from her chair and saying, "I've simply got to go and clean up. When do we eat?"

Cal Braun nodded. "I've been thinking it's time I started to get supper. Give me a half-hour, Miss Gregory."

"One minute," Lance said. "If Fletcher does return here, and I have a feeling he may not, I'd just as soon no one told him what happened to me. You know, regarding that snake temple and so on. If he wants to know what happened tell him to see me. I'll tell him as much as I think he should know."

"It's all right with me," Lanky drawled. "I didn't like that Fletcher's looks from the first minute I saw him——"

Lance cut in, "There's some sort of queer setup around here. Maybe Fletcher hasn't a thing to do with it, but I'm not taking chances."

Katherine left to go to her own room. Cal Braun departed for the kitchen. The rest sat around and smoked. No one said a great deal. Fletcher didn't put in an appearance. Lance wondered where he was, what he was doing. He felt quite sure Fletcher wasn't carrying on any intensive search of any sort.

Cal Braun finally announced that supper was ready. The meal was eaten, more or less, in silence. When it was concluded Lance went to the doorway and glanced outside. It was clear and starry. A wonderful night on which to point out to a certain girl the beauty of starlight on the mountains. Lance steeled himself against the thought and smiled at Katherine who may have had something of the sort in her own mind. Lance stood in the open doorway. Eventually he caught Oscar's eye and pointed to Lanky Peters. Oscar caught the idea and nodded. Lance passed through the doorway and outside.

He made his way down to the far end of the gallery and rolled and lighted a smoke, shielding the flame of the match between his cupped hands. Within a few moments Oscar put in an appearance. "What's on your mind, Lance?"

Lance asked if Lanky was coming. Oscar said he was.

Lance said, "Let's wait for him. There's no use me repeating what I have in mind."

Lanky came strolling along the gallery, his lean frame bulking big against the light shining from windows of the ranch house. The three men squatted down against the adobe wall of the building at the far end of the gallery where the shadows were thickest.

"I didn't give out all the details," Lance commenced, "when I was telling my story. That Yaquente—I call him Horatio—feels sort of grateful to me because I saved him from a beating at Herrick's hands a spell back. Well, Horatio has squared his account. If he hadn't I'd been the victim in a ceremony that's due to be held tonight——"

"Victim?" Oscar asked.

"There's a human sacrifice to be staged. I was to be it. Horatio was double-crossing his own people by aiding me to escape from that pit. Boys, he was plenty scared too."

Lanky drawled, "You'll never realize, Lance, until you know the Yaquentes like I do, how much nerve it required for Horatio to do that. But that's a Yaquente for you. They're willing to die to repay a debt."

Lance nodded. "That's the way I figured Horatio. Like I say, it was right hard carrying on a conversation with him, but I gathered he wasn't entirely sold on the setup. That beating Herrick started to give him that day has sort of destroyed Horatio's faith in things maybe. What it's about I don't know, but there's some white man working the Yaquentes up to do some deviltry. I don't know what the game is but I'm betting there's more than religious ceremonies involved——"

"You think Herrick is the white man in question?" Oscar asked grimly.

"I don't know. I keep remembering that Kilby confessed someone was furnishing peyotes to the Yaquentes——"

"T'hell you say!" Lanky ejaculated. "That means religious ceremonies sure as hell." In the faint starlight that fell on the gallery his face looked uneasy. "I had an idea those Yaquentes were getting mezcal buttons someplace from their looks when I went through their village today. 'Nother thing I didn't like—they all wore six-shooters, and the guns looked new."

Lance considered Lanky's words. "Somebody must be furnishing 'em firearms too. It's my understanding that the Yaquentes aren't supposed to wear guns to any extent. The Mexican Government tries to hold 'em down——"

"You give a Yaquente a gun and keep him supplied with mezcal buttons," Lanky said, "and he won't give no damn about any government. Sure as hell those Injuns are getting ready to blow off steam. I don't like it."

"Here's something else I haven't told you," Lance went on. "There's a smaller room off that big chamber in that snake temple. I looked in there and saw some boxes. They hadn't been opened, but I didn't have any trouble guessing what they held—ammunition and gunpowder. There was another smaller box there with a few small holes bored in it. It might have held snakes."

"Snakes?" Oscar asked blankly.

Lance nodded. "One thing that's got the Yaquentes impressed as hell is the way this white man handles snakes. They don't bite him. Furthermore, Horatio swears they're snakes with feathers. The Yaquentes are commencing to believe sure as hell that their god, Quetzalcoatl, has come back to lead them."

Lanky nodded. "I've heard of that Quetzalcoatl god and how the Yaquentes feel about snakes. They think they're sacred. Funny thing, for all his nerve, no Yaquente likes to get near a snake—especially a rattler. Well, Lance, what you aiming to do about it?"

Lance smiled thinly. "Lanky, you know some of the Yaquente language, I understand."

"I can make out with it," Lanky said warily, "though I don't claim to be expert. My great-grandmother was a full-blood Yaquente, y'know."

"Lanky—Oscar," Lance said. "There's a powwow being held in that snake temple tonight. I've got to know what it's all about. Lanky, you know the language. Are you game to go with us? How about you, Oscar? Take a chance with me?"

Oscar nodded. Lanky rose slowly to his feet. His face was white. "I reckon you don't know what it means if we get caught, Lance. It's risky business. White men have snuk into Yaquente ceremonials before—but they never lived to tell what happened. Their bodies were found later—and they weren't nice to look at."

Lance said, "I figure we need your knowledge of Yaquente to see us through."

"I'm with you, of course," Lanky said courageously. "My seven eighths white blood says stay here, but the one eighth Yaquente says take a chance. But, hell, Lance, we couldn't just walk in on their church meetin'. We'll have to fix up like Yaquentes. And how in hell do you figure to disguise that red hair of yours? And that straw-colored mop of Oscar's? I can get by, of course."

"Axle grease and black powder and dirt,"—Lance smiled—"can disguise a man's features pretty effectually."

Lanky forced a wan smile. "Sounds like you'd had experience."

Oscar put in, "Down in the bunkhouse I saw some of them baggy cotton garments like Mex peons and Yaquentes wear. And there's some of them big straw sombreros. I reckon they were left here by the hired hands back in the days when this ranch was a going concern. It's sure gone to hell lately. Hardly any cows left that I can see."

"Probably the hired hands you mention," Lance commented, "ran off the cows and bought new clothes with the proceeds. Katherine thought she had a ranch here. From all I understand it was deserted except for Malcolm Fletcher when you folks arrived last night. C'mon, let's go get those togs in the bunkhouse. Then we'll saddle up and ride. No use telling those in the house where we're headed. We'd just waste time with explanations."

"I'm ready when you and Oscar are," Lanky said. "What the hell! I can't lose more than one life and I always did have a hankerin' to know just what my ancestors did with their religion. Let's go. We'll never die any younger!"

XIX
War Drums

There wasn't much moon. What there was was partially obscured by drifting clouds. It was past midnight. Only a pale light filtered down on the great stone slabs that flanked the roadway leading to the Temple of the Plumed Serpent. The doorway of the temple stood black and forbidding. In the brush along the roadway only insects of the night made the faintest sounds. The place seemed deserted.

And then from the brushy ridge north of the temple two forms in white cotton garments appeared. Three more appeared. Then another and another. More followed, all walking silently in the direction of the temple. Occasionally one would break into a high-pitched chant. Two or three more would join in the weird sounds, then the song would die away and there'd be silence again. The road was filling rapidly with white-clothed forms now. All wore six-shooters at their waists; some carried Winchester repeaters.

More and more appeared until the whole roadway leading to the temple was filled from side to side with a vast undulating sea of straw sombreros. Now lights appeared in the temple as the first to arrive filed inside. The roadway was a packed mass of jostling

Yaquentes, many of them swaying unsteadily as they progressed toward the Temple of the Plumed Serpent from which now came the muffled, steady beating of drums. The Yaquentes quickened step to crowd through the temple doorway.

From the thick brush at one side of the roadway emerged three forms clad like the Yaquentes. They mingled quickly with the moving throng without being noticed. In that faint light there was little to distinguish the three from genuine Yaquentes. One of them even took up a few notes of the high-pitched, weird chant. Indians near the singer joined in the haunted, uncanny song which suddenly died away as abruptly as it had been started. The white-clothed procession moved nearer the temple doorway.

Lance was wondering now as, accompanied by Lanky and Oscar, he pushed along with the Yaquentes if any sort of password would be necessary to gain entrance to the ceremonies. If so they'd have to do some fast thinking—and perhaps shooting. He felt a trifle more assured at thought of the six-shooter at his waist. He pulled the big straw sombrero lower on his face and noticed Oscar was acting likewise.

There was a momentary pause at the entrance, the crush increased, then Lance and his companions were inside the temple. The place was filling fast. Lanky took Lance's arm and led him and Oscar to a position at one side within easy reach of the doorway. "Just in case we have to try for a quick getaway," Lanky whispered. His voice sounded shaky.

At the opposite far end of the big chamber pine torches burned in the stifling air, casting a flickering, unreal light over the bloodstained altar and throwing into hazy relief the faded frescoes on the walls. The temple was filling rapidly with humanity. A strong sweaty odor filled the big room. Lance and his pardners stood in the shadow of one of the great stone pillars. All around was a milling mass of Yaquentes, every eye intent on the altar beneath the flaring torches. Lance glanced at the Yaquente who stood nearest him. The man was muttering rather crazily to himself. His eyes had a strange gleam in them. He looked to be either drunk or under the influence of some powerful narcotic. Now Lance noticed other Indians with the same expression on their faces. Lanky whispered to Lance, "Most of this gang are hopped up on mezcal buttons. That's lucky for us; they ain't so li'ble to notice anything out of the way."

The drums near the altar throbbed continually. They weren't loud at first, but their steady insistent beat seemed to permeate Lance's blood and pulse through his whole body. The tempo lifted gradually, growing faster and faster. A harsh, dry, rattling sound augmented the accelerated rhythm now. Lance understood when he saw two Yaquentes manipulating gourd rattles.

The drums came louder now and still louder, the sounds beating with monotonous intensity against Lance's ears. Suddenly a pair of Yaquentes leaped to the center of the stone floor before the altar and, side by side, commenced a queer shuffling dance. Round and round they went, incorporating at regular intervals a jerky hippety-hop step. Other Indians joined in until a large circle of shuffling, hopping Yaquentes was revolving before the altar, keeping time to the beaten drums: shuffle, shuffle, shuffle, hippety-hop, shuffle, shuffle, hop, shuffle. . . . Their arms flopped loosely at their sides as though strung on wire. They threw their heads high, emitting a few notes of the weird chant they'd sung along the roadway, then dropped them again.

Round and round they went. The drums beat faster and faster. Here and there a Yaquente dropped out of the dance. Others leaped quickly in to take their places. The flaring torches cast gigantic moving shadows on the walls. By this time the whole chamber seemed to reverberate with the insidious throbbing of the Yaquente drums. Even Lance felt his blood moving faster and faster. He glanced at Lanky. The man's forehead was dotted with tiny beads of perspiration. His swarthy features had a strained look. For a moment Lance half expected him to leap in and take a part with the revolving, shuffling dancers. The strong odor of human bodies increased in the heavy atmosphere. Occasionally now a wild yell left the throat of one of the Indians. They were fast working themselves up to fever pitch.

Oscar said suddenly in a lowered tone, "Cripes! Look at that."

A tall figure in a long robe of feathers had passed just a few feet away. On his head was a sort of helmet-shaped crown decorated with more feathers, both black and white. He had entered from the back and was making his way toward the altar. Accompanying him was a smaller man in the customary cotton clothing and straw sombrero.

"There's your big white chief," Lanky whispered to Lance.

As the man in the feathered robe neared the altar the dance stopped. The drums faded away to a dim monotonous beat that could be barely heard. Gradually the Yaquentes fell silent before the spell of the newcomer. They eyed him with something of awe in their gazes and watched closely while he leaped lightly to the altar stone and stretched forth both arms.

Lance looked narrowly at the man. Something familiar about him all right, though it was impossible to make out his features. His face was entirely framed, saving the eyes and nose, with a circle of buzzard feathers. His crown was trimmed with more feathers, one of which, standing erect in front, was dyed a brilliant crimson. He threw back the robe to display a magnificently muscled torso bare to the waist. A sort of half-skirt of white eagle feathers hung to his knees. On each sinewy arm was a wide silver armlet. Again Lance was reminded of the armlet Katherine's father had sent her.

A great cry arose from the assembled Yaquentes: "Quetzalcoatl-l-l!"

The man with the helmet spoke three brief words. Instantly the Yaquentes fell silent. Lance hadn't understood the words but he recognized the intonations.

"By God," he whispered to Oscar; "that's Fletcher."

Oscar nodded, eyes glued to the scene under the flaring torches. He spoke softly from one corner of his mouth. "Even with that befeathered derby hat on and that bunch around his face I figured the same way."

Lance moved a step nearer and spoke to Lanky. "Remember that hombre's face, Lanky?"

Lanky's reply just reached Lance's ear. "It's that Fletcher feller, ain't it?"

There was some commotion around the altar now. A pine box had been brought out to Fletcher. Fletcher threw back the cover and thrust one arm inside the box. When his hand emerged it was clutching the writhing coils of a diamondback rattlesnake.

Lance's eyes widened. A ridge of feathers seemed to be growing from the reptile's backbone.

The Yaquentes near the front fell back. A deathly silence fell over the big chamber. Now the dry rattling of the snake's rapidly buzzing tail could be heard in the sudden quiet. Its heavy, sinuous body flowed up Fletcher's right arm and around over his shoulders. Fletcher seized it to prevent escape. The rattler made no attempt to strike. The drums commenced a soft throbbing.

Even while the snake was still moving Fletcher commenced to speak in what Lance judged was the Yaquente tongue. The words came in slow, halting fashion, and there seemed to be a great deal of repetition in the delivery. Sudden wild yells shook the chamber. The drums increased their tempo and again died away.

Lanky whispered to Lance, "He don't know much Yaquente. He's repeating the same thing over and over again. It's a war talk. If the Yaquentes follow him, Fletcher is saying, they'll win a big victory. That's about all there is to his speech."

Now the smaller Indian who had accompanied Fletcher into the temple commenced to interpret. Fletcher would say something to him; the interpreter would turn and harangue the assembled Yaquentes at great length, stopping every so often to receive fresh instructions from Fletcher. Suddenly there came a change in the interpreter's manner. He appeared to be explaining something.

A sudden muttering arose among the Yaquentes. Apparently they didn't like what was being said. The interpreter consulted Fletcher. Fletcher talked steadily for nearly a minute. The interpreter repeated the words. Lance glanced around. He could see scowling faces on every side. Lanky nudged Lance. "I know that interpreter by sight," he whispered. "He used to hang around Pozo Verde. He's only half Yaquente—other half is 'Pache."

The interpreter was talking again. Two of the Yaquentes in the audience stepped forward and spat a flow of deep gutturals. Lance suddenly recognized one of the Yaquentes as Horatio. Apparently some sort of argument was taking place, and Horatio was voicing a vehement protest. The chamber seethed with resentful mutterings now. The interpreter and Fletcher held a quick discussion, then the interpreter turned and harangued the Indians some more. Some of the resentment died away, though the Yaquentes were surrendering reluctantly to whatever offer Fletcher was making.

Lance felt Lanky's hand on his arm. Lanky was drawing him toward the doorway. Lance said, "Let's wait a minute more."

"We better go now while we got a chance," Lanky whispered in Lance's ear. "Pass the word to Oscar. Those Injuns all got their eyes to the front. Now's the time to light a shuck outa here."

Lance nodded. The three commenced to edge back toward the doorway. Yaquentes were all around them, but so intent were the Indians on the scene at the altar that they didn't notice Lance and his companions gradually moving away. The distance to the outside wasn't more than ten or twelve feet, but to Lance it seemed they'd never make it. Inch by inch they moved back. At the altar the interpreter was finding new floods of oratory for which Lance and his companions were duly thankful.

Finally, one by one, they slipped around the edge of the entranceway and instantly melted into the thick brush at the side of the road without their exit being noticed. Lanky dropped limply down onto the earth, screened by a thick shelter of mesquite brush. "Mister, I'm plumb thankful that's over! Them damn drums were getting me down. Just about one bite on a mezcal button and I'd have sloughed off seven eighths white man. I'm glad we're shet of that snake temple. I don't want no more!"

Now that they were outside, breathing the clean night air, Lance and Oscar were commencing to feel the same way.

XX
Revolution

They sat deep in the brush talking in hushed tones and smoking cigarettes, the glowing ends of which they kept well shielded within their cupped hands. From the temple came the steady beating of drums, but they sounded faint and far away now. The cool night wind filtered through the brush, sweeping away the cigarette smoke.

Oscar spoke, low toned. "I wonder how much longer that ceremony in there is going to last.

Lanky said scornfully, "That wa'n't no real ceremony like I've heard they have. That was just the start. You know—that dance and the drums and all—that wasn't really getting down to business. That was just the start, like a young cow hand feelin' his oats on a Saturday night. Come Saturday he likes to go out and get liquored up and do some dancing. Human nature is pretty much the same, red or white. Them Yaquentes just use mezcal buttons instead of liquor."

"If you hadn't insisted on us leaving," Lance said disappointedly, "I would have stayed. I was plumb eager to see how Fletcher would act when it was discovered I wasn't down in that pit back of the altar."

"Hell's bells," Lanky said. "He knew you'd

escaped—leastwise I figure he did. I took note, none of those Yaquentes got very near the altar. There may have been a few in the know, but——"

"Just a minute." Lance frowned. "You say Fletcher knew I'd escaped from the pit—before he got here?"

"I figure he must have," Lanky replied. "Leastwise—why did he have that interpreter announce there wouldn't be any human sacrifice tonight?— 'sacrifice of the bleeding heart,' they called it. That's what all the row was about. The Yaquentes didn't like him breaking a promise he'd made 'em. Lance, they were all set to do a job of carving on you until Fletcher told 'em the time wasn't right. He handed 'em a lot of superstitious bosh about waiting until the moon was ten days nearer the full. He was just stalling for time, of course——"

"Hold on a second," Lance interrupted. "I want to get this straight. How many people knew I'd escaped from the pit? Us three, the folks at the ranch and Horatio. How did Fletcher know I'd escaped?"

"Horatio wouldn't tell him," Lanky said quickly. "He wouldn't dare for fear the rest of the tribe would learn about it—and that would mean the end of Horatio."

Oscar said, "That leaves Miss Gregory, the professor, Trunk-Strap Kelly, Tom Piper, Hub Owen, Cal Braun and Luke Homer. Take your choice, Lance, but remember, I'm betting those hands I hired are on the level."

"I'll swear to that part myself," Lanky agreed.

Lance stared in silence at the darkness surrounding them. Finally he changed the subject. "Start at the beginning," he said wearily, "and give us the whole story, Lanky. Just what was said in that temple?"

"To cut a long story short," Lanky said, "Fletcher is working the Yaquentes up to start a revolution in Mexico and overthrow the present government. He's getting at them on the standpoint of their religion—the ancient Aztec religion that called for worshiping a snake with feathers on and had mezcal buttons as part of their ceremonial feasts. Fletcher has been furnishing the peyotes——"

Oscar cut in, "That rattler Fletcher had was feathered."

"I've been thinking about that"—Lance nodded—"and wondering where Fletcher got the nerve to handle that diamondback. Me, I wouldn't crave to do it. But the snake acted like it was afraid of *him*. No wonder the Indians are impressed. Go on, Lanky."

Lanky continued, "Like I say, Fletcher is working on their religion, telling them all Mexico must be made to return to the old beliefs. The poor ignorant suckers drink it in. The plan is to make war on the small towns first and gain supplies and converts. It'll be a case of being converted or killed. Gradually the movement will gather strength, Fletcher claims, and eventually they'll be strong enough to capture Chihuahua City. Once the state of Chihuahua is in their hands, Fletcher told 'em, the rest of Mexico will come easy. And the Yaquentes take it all as gospel truth, thinking he's a sort of direct voice from Quetzalcoatl, the snake god."

"So that's Fletcher's game," Lance mused. "I'll admit that such things have worked before."

Lanky went on, "There was to be a big ceremony tonight, until your body couldn't be produced for sacrifice, Lance. That gummed matters up plenty. The Yaquentes didn't like it. They thought you were still down in the pit, unconscious, and Fletcher took good care not to let them get close enough to the pit to learn you weren't there. For a few minutes Fletcher was in a tight spot. The Yaquentes got sulky and refused to go ahead with the ceremony. Two of those Indians were right stubborn and insisted that Fletcher keep his promise regarding the sacrifice."

"So that's what it was, eh?" Lance said. "One of the two was Horatio. He knew damn well that Fletcher couldn't produce me. It looks to me like he was trying to put Fletcher on the spot. I wonder why?"

"Maybe he's losing faith in Fletcher," Lanky suggested. "That other Indian was yelling for ammunition if he couldn't have the human sacrifice. It seems Fletcher has been giving them guns but no cartridges to shoot. Anyway, he compromised by promising to let them have ammunition and thereby wiggled himself out of a bad spot. I bet he'll think twice and some more on top of that before he gets 'em into the temple for another promised sacrifice."

"Listen," Oscar said suddenly, "the drums are stopped."

They listened intently for a few minutes. Lanky drawled, "Prayer meetin' must be over. They'll be coming out right quick. We'd better douse our cigarettes and lay low."

They put out their cigarettes and crouched low in the brush. After a few minutes several white-clad forms emerged from the temple carrying pine boxes. Lance whispered to Oscar, "There goes that ammunition and powder they had stored in that small room off the big one."

Fletcher, still wearing his long white-feathered robe, followed closely on the boxes. They could hear him urging the men to hurry. He strode along at a stiff pace beside them.

Oscar's lips were close to Lance's ear: "I reckon he's got to get ahead with that bunch and change his clothes. I'd like to learn where he keeps his horse and steal it so he'd have to return to Muletero in that outfit."

More Yaquentes were emerging from the temple now. The torches had been put out. Once more the roadway was packjammed with white-clothed figures. There was a good deal of muttering among the Yaquentes. To Lance it sounded like grumbling. The bobbing straw sombreros flowed steadily past. Finally the procession commenced to thin out. A few stragglers still came on behind. Now they hurried to catch up with the rest. The long packed line streamed on along the roadway, then disappeared someplace in the vicinity of the brushy ridge at the end of the road. A few voices drifted back on the night breeze, then suddenly all was quiet again.

"Wonder if they all had horses the other side of that ridge?" Oscar said.

"Probably not," Lanky replied. "Most of 'em came afoot, I'll bet. . . . Yeah, I know, it's about fifteen miles back to their camp, but I'll put my money on a Yaquente to outlast a horse any time. Those hombres are plenty tough."

"It's a wonder to me," Lance said, "they don't leave guards at this temple."

"What for?" Lanky said. "They figure the Yaquentes and Fletcher are the only ones to know about it, it's so well hidden. And they know you couldn't escape from that pit——"

"They must be pretty dumb then?"

"Pretty full of mezcal buttons," Lanky contradicted. "At the same time, you couldn't have escaped without Horatio's help, could you?"

Lance said, "I sure couldn't have."

Oscar heaved a long sigh. There came the rattle of a paper sack, then a sucking sound. "You hombres want any nerve tonic?"

"I wouldn't mind some out of a bottle," Lanky grunted.

The three remained motionless in the brush for some time longer to make sure, as Lance expressed it, "that none of those snake worshipers come back." Finally he rose to his feet. "C'mon, waddies."

"Ready to head back to the Three-Cross?" Oscar asked.

Lance nodded. "But first I want to give a look-see around that temple and learn if they've taken all the ammunition."

They left the brush, stepped to the roadway with its double row of ancient stone slabs and entered the temple once more. There still lingered about the big chamber the odor of sweating bodies and smoking pine torches. Lance struck a match. Lanky found an extinguished torch and lighted it. The flame threw weird, uncanny shadows about the high walls. Lanky commented, "I still don't like it here." He looked uneasy.

"I reckon I know just how you feel," Lance said soberly.

Oscar called Lanky to hold the torch where he could see the altar better. Next they glanced down into the pit where Lance had been held prisoner. "Sufferin' hawse thieves!" Lanky exclaimed. "That hole looks like it's a hundred feet deep. You can't even see to the bottom——"

"It feels deeper than that when you're down there." Lance smiled thinly. "Let's give a look at this other room."

He led the way through the doorway back of the altar into the smaller chamber. Except in size it looked much like the big room they'd just left. Neither was there an altar nor pit. There weren't so many stone pillars. Lanky held the torch high. Frescoes and sculptured reliefs ran around the walls, with the plumed serpent furnishing the subject for the majority of the decorations. Lance glanced toward the spot where he had last seen the boxes of ammunition and powder stacked against the wall. The boxes were gone.

"Well," Lance observed, "the Yaquentes will have something to shoot in their guns now anyway."

"And I don't like that, either," Lanky stated. "Supposin' they got right keen for a human sacrifice? The Three-Cross ain't very far from their village."

"They left one box, anyway," Oscar noticed, pointing across the room. The three men crossed the floor and looked down at the pine box against the wall. There were small holes bored in the cover.

"That's the box the snake was in," Lanky said. "I wonder if——"

"I'm aiming to find out," Lance said. He stooped and flung back the box cover. "You'd better watch yourself!"

He leaped back from the box, as did Oscar and Lanky. All three men had their hands on gun butts now. Lanky held the torch high. For a moment nothing happened within the box, then from the dark interior there came a movement—a dry, scaly rustling. An evil triangular-shaped head appeared above the edge of the box. In the light from the torch its beady eyes burned with a strange yellow light. The ovate head of the reptile moved about inquiringly, then its long scaly length flowed over the edge of the box and to the floor.

"It's that feathered snake!" Oscar yelled. He started to draw his six-shooter.

"Don't shoot!" Lance exclaimed. "I want it alive. I still don't believe in those feathers."

The snake didn't appear to want to put up a fight. It moved rapidly across the stone floor, leaving a channeled path in the dusty surface, until it reached the far wall. Then it turned and slithered along close to the wall in the direction of the doorway, closely followed by the three men. Lance was moving along at its side, in a crouching position, examining it as closely as the movements would permit. Oscar and Lanky were more wary and stayed back farther, gazing in some awe at the feathered length.

"Bring that torch closer," Lance said.

Lanky moved cautiously nearer with the torch. Lance put out one booted foot to impede the reptile's progress. The snake rattled viciously but seemed reluctant to coil for striking. Then in a sort of half-hearted fashion it drew itself to an S shape. Suddenly with the speed of lightning the triangular head darted forward, striking Lance's boot. Then the snake fell back and once more tried to escape.

Lance looked at his boot. There should have been a few drops of venom there or some sort of mark showing where the rattler had struck. Only there wasn't. Lance frowned, then again shoved his foot in front of the snake. The rattler came to a stop. Lance suddenly reached down, seizing the rattler just back of the head, and lifted the writhing, twisting coils from the floor. The feathers along its back seemed to vibrate with futile rage.

Oscar yelled, "Look out, Lance. Don't be a damn fool!"

"I reckon if Fletcher can do it so can I." Lance smiled. "Look here."

Oscar and Lanky came closer while Lance held the snake firmly in both hands. Lance went on, "Take a good look, pards. This poor ol' diamondback couldn't do any more than bump his nose against my boot."

Lanky said suddenly, "Hell's bells! His mouth is sewed shut!"

It was true. The snake's jaws had been firmly drawn together with stout linen thread. Lance swore softly under his breath. "I'm damned if I like rattlers," he said grimly, "but only a fiend would do a thing like this. I wonder how long since it's had water or food. Damn that Fletcher!"

"Those feathers are fake," Oscar said suddenly.

"They're faked." Lance nodded. "Look close and you can see. They've been sewed to a narrow strip of cloth, then glued to the rattler's back. No wonder this poor diamondback wanted to escape."

"I reckon it's up to us to put it out of its misery," Lanky said. "It's probably suffered plenty."

"It won't suffer much longer," Lance replied, "but we're going to keep it alive for a spell yet. Get that box it was in, then we'll be leaving. I've got an idea we maybe can put this snake to work for us."

XXI
"Ride Like Hell!"

Dawn was streaking the eastern horizon by the time the three men arrived back at the Three-Cross. They dismounted, unsaddled and put their ponies into the corral. Lance said, "You fellers better grab a little shut-eye in the bunkhouse. That's what I intend to do, but I want to go up to the house first and see the professor. I'm still wondering how Fletcher knew I'd escaped. Lanky, look around and see if you can find a burlap sack to put that snake in. It will be easier to carry it that way than in the box."

"You figuring to carry it someplace?" Lanky asked in surprise.

"Yeah, you and I are going to make a trip to the Yaquente village and see can we find Horatio. Somehow, someway, we've got to bust up Fletcher's game. I'll tell you about it later."

He started toward the ranch house, leaving Lanky and Oscar standing open mouthed behind him.

As he neared the ranch house Lance saw the back door open. Katherine stood there. "Lance," she exclaimed worriedly, "wherever have you been? You just disappeared last night—you and Oscar and Lanky. It bothered all of us." The girl looked as though she'd spent a sleepless night. Her denim overalls were wrinkled. A stray lock of yellow hair fell low on her forehead.

She moved away from the door as Lance stepped inside. He glanced around. They were standing alone in the kitchen. He shut the door. His right arm went around her shoulders. He took her chin in his left hand and drew her face to his. Katherine gave a long sigh. After a time her voice came to him, muffled. "Lance, you do worry a girl like the devil. I don't know whether I'm going to love you or not."

After a time they drew apart. Lance told her briefly what had happened. Katherine's blue eyes went wide with sudden fright. "I—I was afraid you'd done something like that. Oh, Lance, you mustn't run such chances. I mentioned that I thought you might have gone back to that temple of the snake. I wanted the men to saddle and ride after you three. But Uncle Uly stopped that. He said you were probably all right. I know he was just trying to quiet my fears. Then Trunk-Strap Kelly said as long as Oscar and Lanky were with you you were probably all right and knew what you were doing. They went to their bunks in the bunkhouse. I went to bed. I couldn't sleep. I fixed a room for you. You'd better turn in and get a few winks. . . . And to think that it's Fletcher leading those Yaquentes! Lance, he was here last night."

They were walking toward the main room of the ranch house now. Lance's arm was about Katherine's waist. At the girl's words Lance's face went suddenly grim. "So Fletcher was here last night, was he? I wondered——"

Katherine cut in, "He said he came to learn if you had been found yet. Oh, what a liar that man turned out to be! He had some Indians with him and he told Uncle Uly that they were going to see if they could find any track of you——"

"And Uncle Uly told him, I suppose," Lance said coldly, "that there wasn't any need of him looking any longer."

"Why, yes, he did," Katherine said in some surprise. "Lance, what's the matter with you?"

"Where's Uncle Uly now?" Lance asked tersely. "I'm aiming to talk to him."

"He's out on the front gallery. He was up before daylight. He's potting. He's been worried about that plant——"

"He's what? Potting?"

Katherine nodded. "Yes, you know, that rare cactus he named after me. Last night he found a small wooden tub and he got some earth and he's putting that cactus in it. He's as tickled as a child with a new toy. He wants that plant to have the best of care——"

Lance crossed the room in quick strides, flung open the door leading to the front gallery and stepped outside. He looked both ways along the gallery, then about two thirds of the way to the end he saw Professor Jones just in the act of lifting a small wooden tub to set on one of the deeply recessed window sills of the adobe wall. On the flagged paving of the gallery lay a trowel and the burlap wrappings Jones had removed from the plant's roots. A bucket of earth stood near by.

Deeply engrossed, a beatific smile on his lean features, the professor stepped back to admire his handiwork. He wasn't aware of Lance's approach with Katherine just behind until Lance was almost on top of him.

Then Jones looked up. His smile broadened. "Ah,

Lance! Back again, I see. Knew there was no sense—worrying about you. All right, what? Been potting my *Echinopsis gregoriana*. Handsome plant, what? Lucky to find—that tub. Deuced hard job, though—cutting holes in bottom—for proper drainage. Been at it since—before dawn. No drills here, y'understand. Practically wore out—blade of my pocketknife——"

"Uncle Uly," Katherine broke in, "will you please explain to Lance just what you told Fletcher last night?"

"That's what I'm waiting to hear," Lance said grimly.

"Right, quite right," Jones said. "But first—I insist you admire—*Echinopsis gregoriana*. Did you ever see—such blue blossoms? Perfect, what? That tub, just right. Suitable place to put it—until we leave. Right amount shade and sun——"

"Blast your plant!" Lance said angrily. "I want to know what you told Fletcher. This is important, Jones."

The professor raised his eyebrows in surprise. "Upset about something, what? Deuced sorry. Hope nothing I've said—accountable."

"What did you tell Fletcher?" Lance almost shouted. Katherine looked uneasily from Lance to her uncle and back again.

"Oh, Fletcher." Jones nodded. "Fletcher, quite so. Simply told him you'd returned. What else to say?"

"Uncle," Katherine put in, "take your mind off that cactus and tell Lance what happened. He's getting the wrong impression." She turned to Lance. "It was just as I told you. Fletcher came here last night. I don't think it was more than nine o'clock. He wanted to know if you'd been found yet. I was in my room but I heard Uncle talking to him. Our men were all down in the bunkhouse. Fletcher said he'd rounded up the Indians he had with him to help hunt for you. Uncle Uly told him there was no use looking farther. Uncle, tell Lance what you told Fletcher."

Jones colored. "Awkward situation. Didn't know what to say, 'pon my word. Had a feeling you might have returned to that snake temple. At the same time, you'd warned us all not to tell Fletcher about that place or how you escaped. If I had told him he might have gone there looking for you. I was in a stew. Fact! Then—sudden inspiration. Told Fletcher you had returned but that we'd found you unconscious—outside the door. Swore I didn't know where you'd been or what happened. Told him you were still unconscious—y'understand?"

Katherine said, "Fletcher insisted on seeing you. Uncle told him it was impossible and that you couldn't be disturbed—that you appeared to be in a highly dangerous condition."

Jones smiled shyly. "Embellished my story somewhat. Told him your hands—raw and bleeding—as though you'd been climbing for hours—up steep rock precipice. Gave him impression you'd had—nasty fall, what? Damn lie—of course. Awkward as the deuce—if I have to explain to Fletcher. Sorry if I said wrong thing, Lance. Now that I consider my words—silly thing to tell Fletcher. But couldn't think—anything else—spur of the moment. Fletcher looked startled——'pon my word!"

"What?" Lance fairly yelled. "You told him that? Professor, you couldn't have said anything better. Fletcher will think I escaped from his pit by crawling up the wall. No wonder he looked startled. This is the best yet! You've got my thanks."

Jones beamed. "Appreciate your attitude. Feared I'd upset plans or something———" He blinked suddenly. "What was that? Did you say 'his pit'? Fletcher's pit?"

Lance was shaking with laughter. "Jeepers! This is perfect. Professor, I owe you an apology. Will you shake hands?"

"No reason not to—but don't understand. Glad no harm done. Did my best—under circumstances. But— you should have told us where you were going—last night."

"Sometimes," Lance said, "a man has to keep his ideas to himself. Maybe you understand how it is, Professor."

Jones's angular features flushed embarrassedly. "Quite so, quite. Every man has his own ideas. Mine—strictly cacti. For instance, this *Echinopsis gregoriana*—create sensation someday. I———"

Katherine said, "Sensation? Wait until you hear about Fletcher."

"You've heard something new about Fletcher?" Jones asked, lifting his gaze from the beloved cactus. "I'll be glad—learn what it is."

Lance related the story of the night's happenings. About the time he had finished Cal Braun stuck his face through the doorway. "Breakfast's on, folks. Better come get it before I throw it away."

"It's this way, Lanky," Lance was saying, "if we can find Horatio and make him see what a fake Fletcher is I figure we can bust up this game. Once he sees the snake it should convince him that Fletcher is just using the Yaquentes for some motive of his own— though I don't know just yet what it is."

The two were loping their ponies along the trail

that led to Muletero. It wasn't more than an hour past breakfast. The sun was climbing rapidly above the rim of the eastern mountains. Brush and cholla and prickly pear flanked either side of the dimly defined roadway they were following.

Lanky nodded moodily. "I don't know just how much luck we'll have. I can take you down through that Yaquente village, but if we have any luck finding this Yaquente friend of yours I can't say. You say his name sounds like Horatio?"

"Horatio." Lance tried to pronounce the name as nearly like he had heard it as possible.

"Oh"—Lanky's frown cleared—"you mean Huareztjio. That's quite a common name among Yaquentes. Well, we'll see what happens when he looks into this burlap sack—if we find him." Lanky motioned toward the bulky burlap sack he carried on his saddle. From the sack came an occasional movement.

The horses pounded on. The houses of Muletero came into view. The town proved to be a typical Mexican settlement with adobe huts placed helter-skelter along either side of a dusty roadway. There were a couple of shops and a cantina. A few chickens and dirty-nosed, nearly naked children moved in the dusty roadway. In the shadows between buildings sat a number of seraped Mexicans who paid no particular attention to the *Americanos* riding through their village.

The dust settled behind as the two riders moved swiftly through the town, then turned right along a descending, rock-cluttered way that led for half a mile down into a canyon running between high granite walls.

Lanky said, "There's your village. Now to see if we can locate this hombre named Huareztjio."

Lance looked ahead and saw a string of shabby huts built along each side of the canyon. Some were of adobe and rock construction. A few had corrugated iron roofs; the skins of animals were stretched across the roof beams of other dwellings. A pair of goats was tethered before one house. There weren't many Yaquentes in sight. A few men, in their loose cotton clothing, were seen here and there. Several women, bearing firewood on their backs and wearing flopping, shapeless print dresses, scuffed through the dust in their bare feet. Their faces were brown and wrinkled; their straight black hair was gathered in an odd double knot at the backs of their heads. There were a large number of mangy-looking curs running about; these, at the sight of the riders, immediately set up a shrill yapping and barking.

"If you value your legs," Lanky advised, "don't get down from your horse. Them dogs just love calf meat."

The riders pulled rein at the first house before which they saw a Yaquente man sitting. The Indian glared at them but relaxed somewhat when Lanky spoke in the Yaquente tongue. After a moment of listening the Indian shook his head, rose and turned into his house.

"Nothing to be got from that hombre," Lanky told Lance.

They walked the horses until they came to the next man. This one was sprawled in the shadow of a big adobe oven built in the form of a half-sphere. The horses stopped. The Indian eyed them listlessly from his position on the earth. Lanky spoke to him but received no answer. Lanky said disgustedly, "C'mon, that Injun is still hopped up on peyote. You notice, Lance, all these Yaquentes is wearing guns?"

"I noticed it," Lance said grimly.

They went on through the village, Lanky asking questions here and there while the pack of mangy curs yelped at the horses' heels. Now and then Lanky found an Indian who would talk, but even those who talked denied they knew anyone named Huareztjio. Finally they had arrived at the end of the village street with no success. "Damn pack of liars," Lanky grumbled. "Right now your Horatio knows we're looking for him. But we can't make 'em talk. Oh yes, Horatio knows by this time. The Indians have a grapevine system that carries the news along faster than we moved. From now on it's up to Huareztjio. If he wants to see you he will. Otherwise we're out of luck."

They turned the horses and started back, Lance feeling extremely disappointed at the failure. They were more than halfway through the village when a Yaquente emerged from the house before which the pair of goats was tethered.

"There's Horatio now," Lance exclaimed.

"That's him, eh? And he owns goats. Must be he's a sort of chief of the tribe. All right, we'll give him a try."

The horses were pulled up when they reached Huareztjio's dwelling. Lance smiled. "Howdy, Horatio."

The Indian eyed him warily, no sign of recognition in his beady eyes. "What want?" he grunted. "Better go 'way—queeck!"

Lanky spoke a few words of Yaquente greeting. The Indian eyed him in stony silence. Lance and

Lanky didn't seem to be getting anywhere. Lance said, "Better give him the whole story, Lanky. Tell him we saw what happened in the temple last night. Tell him what a fake Fletcher is. Tell him Fletcher is bad clear through and that he's just using the Yaquentes for his own purposes. Then show him that feathered snake with its mouth sewed shut. That should convince Horatio if nothing else does."

Lanky started to speak. Now and then he was forced to use a word of Spanish or English but he was getting the idea across to Huareztjio. For a time the Indian listened in stony silence. Abruptly his eyes flashed, and an angry look passed across his flat brown features. Lance couldn't decide whether he was angry because of Fletcher's duplicity or because the scene in the temple had been spied on the previous night. Abruptly the stolid mask reappeared on the Yaquente's face.

Suddenly with a quick dramatic movement Lanky seized the burlap sack on his saddle, opened it and spilled the contents onto the earth at the Indian's feet. The feathered snake writhed, coiled, then straightened out to attempt escape. Huareztjio jumped back in alarm, then approached the reptile. Cautiously he stooped and seized the diamondback in both hands. His sharp, beady eyes took in the cruelly sewed mouth and the fake ridge of feathers along its back. The expression about the Yaquente's lips tightened, then suddenly he opened them in a wild, eerie cry that echoed along the village street.

The call brought an instant response. From every house along the way Yaquente heads appeared. Indians came leaping from all directions.

"What do we do now?" Lance asked.

"We ride like hell!" Lanky snapped. "They may

not like the idea of us being in their temple last night when your Horatio explains matters. Me, I'm not aiming to stay and learn what their attitude is. C'mon!"

Wheeling their ponies, they jabbed in spurs and went dashing out of the Yaquente village.

XXII
Action in Muletero

Once Lance glanced back over his shoulders. There weren't any Yaquentes following him, though back in the canyon village he could see the street filled with a packed mass of gesticulating white-clad forms. At the end of a quarter of a mile, when they were drawing near to Muletero, Lanky signaled for Lance to slow down.

They pulled the ponies to a walk. Lanky said, "Maybe we're lucky. Maybe their intentions would have been all right. Me, I wasn't taking any chances."

"I got your idea," Lance said dryly, "but I'd sure like to know what those Yaquentes will do next. I'd figured to stay long enough to learn from Horatio where Fletcher was."

"Everything seems to be up to your Horatio from now on," Lanky replied. "We'll just have to wait until he makes the next move."

"You mean," Lance asked, "that maybe we can go back and talk to Horatio later? Tomorrow, say?"

"You can if you like," Lanky drawled, "and I'll go with you—providing we got a troop of U.S. cavalry to lead the way."

"Otherwise," Lance said, "you're staying away?"

"I'm staying away," Lanky said promptly. "We've tipped our hand to those Indians. They know we're in on their secret. How they'll take it I don't know, and I'm going to take good care of my carcass until I find out."

They were approaching Muletero now. The hot morning sun reflected a brilliant white glare from the plastered adobe houses. They turned their horses into the hoof-chopped roadway that ran through the town. Muletero looked about as it had when they'd passed through an hour or so earlier. There may have been a few more Mexicans in sight hugging the shadows. Even the naked children who'd been playing in the dusty road earlier had retreated to the backs of the houses where more shade was to be found. Lance and Lanky were drawing abreast of the town cantina now.

Lanky said, "If I thought they had any cold beer in that joint I'd stop and wash out some dust."

"They'd have tequila and beer," Lance observed, "but I'm betting plenty it wouldn't be cold."

"Then we won't stop," Lanky said. They rode on.

The horses had passed the cantina at an easy walk, when Chiricahua Herrick emerged from the doorway of the building. He stiffened suddenly at sight of Lance and Lanky riding through the town. An angry scowl contorted Herrick's face. His hand swept swiftly toward his holster. The gun came up, spitting flame and leaden death. At the same instant Herrick yelled, "Bert! Anvil! Come a-runnin'!"

Lance's pony jumped suddenly even before Lance caught the report of the bullet. Then he noticed blood on his pony's left ear. The flying slug had just removed the tip. Lance whirled in his saddle even as his pony went to bucking, drew his gun and thumbed one swift shot. He saw a spurt of plaster and dust leap from the cantina wall at Herrick's back.

From the interior of the cantina Bert Ridge and Anvil Wheeler appeared, guns in hand. Lance heard Lanky swear, then from Lanky's six-shooter there came a heavy booming report. Wheeler grabbed at one of the uprights of the cantina porch to keep from going down.

Lance's horse was bucking madly by this time. Lance threw one leg across its back and dropped to the dusty roadway. A bullet fanned his cheek as he struck the earth. Again he fired and had the satisfaction of seeing Herrick stumble in mid-stride as he plunged toward the center of the road. Lance's pony went leaping and sun-fishing crazily off to one side.

Again Lanky fired. Bullets from Bert Ridge's gun were kicking up dust near Lanky's feet. Ridge suddenly gave a wild scream and pitched forward on his face. Herrick was still approaching Lance, limping slightly and cursing as he moved. His gun was swinging in a wide arc to bear on Lance.

Lanky swung his gun toward Herrick, fired, missed. Herrick fired once at Lanky, then turned back to Lance. Anvil Wheeler, supporting himself with one hand gripping the cantina upright, fired two swift shots at Lanky.

Lance's forty-five barrel tilted slightly. Smoke and fire mushroomed from the muzzle. Wheeler wilted suddenly, turned half around and stumbled to the earth. Bracing himself on one hand, he again shifted his aim toward Lanky.

Herrick was bearing in, planning to get close before he drew his bead on Lance. Lance waited coolly, then fired just a split instant before Herrick started to pull trigger.

Herrick's shot flew high in the air as he clutched at his breast, then he staggered back to a sitting position on the earth, the gun falling from his weakening grasp.

Even as Lance fired he heard Lanky's forty-five roar savagely. Wheeler groaned and slumped flat in the roadway.

Powder smoke drifted in the bright, dusty air. Lance's pony had bucked itself out by this time and stood docilely at one side of the road. Three men were down in the roadway, two of them motionless. Only Chiricahua Herrick showed any sign of life, though he was on his back now rolling from side to side in agony. Wild, excited Mexican yells sounded through the town, though none of the Mexicans put in an appearance.

The dust was commencing to settle. Lance swung toward Lanky. "You all right, pard?"

"Not a one touched me," Lanky said grimly. "Reckon I'm lucky. You?"

"Not even a scratch. Some of those slugs were coming close though."

"*You're* not telling *me* about 'em?" Lanky drawled. "Things was plenty hot for a minute. It looks like two of them hombres is finished."

"I'm figuring the third, Herrick, won't last long," Lance said tersely. "Slip into that cantina, will you, and see if there's any more of this breed looking for trouble?"

Lanky started across the road. Lance walked to Chiricahua Herrick who was quiet by this time. He knelt by Herrick's side. Herrick's eyes were open, but he hadn't much longer to live. He forced a wan, defiant grin as his fading gaze focused on Lance.

"Some hombres have all the luck," he muttered. "I

muffed . . . my chance. Fletcher . . . will have . . . better luck. . . ."

"Herrick," Lance broke in, "Fletcher's game is just about up. We know about his plans for a revolution. Where is Fletcher now?"

Something of surprise entered the dying man's glazing eyes. "Know about . . . revolution, eh? You won't stop it . . . though. Even if you . . . get Fletcher. Somebody . . . bigger 'n Fletcher . . . running things——"

"Who?" Lance interrupted quickly.

Herrick smiled through his pain. "Think I'm . . . going to tell you? I ain't . . . no damned snitch. Go 'way. I'm tired. Want to sleep . . . long sleep——" His eyes closed.

"Herrick"—Lance spoke sharply to cut through the man's rapidly fading consciousness—"where is Fletcher now?"

Herrick's eyes opened slightly. "Fletcher . . . took Ordway and Johnson," he said drowsily, "rode to . . . Apache Injun village . . . fifteen miles to the east. Going to get . . . more recruits . . . for revolutionary army. . . ."

The man was going fast. His eyes had again closed. His breathing was shallow. Lanky's shadow fell suddenly across Herrick's body. Lance looked up. Lanky said, "Looks like he won't last much longer." He held out a bottle of tequila. "Give him a shot of this. You may learn something." Lance took the bottle. Lanky went on, "Nothing but a bunch of frightened Mexes in that cantina. They don't want no part of this scrap. I reckon they're glad we downed the coyotes. Fletcher and his crew have been making things tough for Muletero. They've been living in one of the houses here. Put the rightful owners out. I looked at Wheeler and Ridge. They're both dead."

Lance scarcely heard what Lanky was saying, he was so busily engaged in trying to force some of the fiery tequila between Herrick's lips. Herrick opened his eyes again. "By Gawd!" he murmured, "that's good, Tolliver. Give me another swig." Again Lance held the bottle to the man's lips. Herrick drank with deep satisfaction. A trifle more life came momentarily back to his eyes. "Now—if I had a cigarette."

Lanky rolled and lighted a cigarette, placed it between Herrick's lips. Herrick inhaled, then coughed. Blood appeared on his pallid lips. Lance wiped the blood away with the man's neckerchief and gave him another swallow from the bottle.

Herrick commenced to talk again. "You ain't a bad hombre, after all, Tolliver. White, I call it. I suppose . . . Ridge and Anvil is dead. You two . . . was too fast for us. Mebbe I should go out clean, eh? Tell you what you want to know? You're . . . treating me . . . like a white . . . man. . . ." Again his eyes closed. He was beyond help from the bottle now. Lance spoke to the dying man, trying to hold him to consciousness.

Lance said, "Who killed Katherine Gregory's father?"

For a moment there was no reply, then Herrick's lips moved slightly to frame one word, "Fletcher." A shudder went through his frame, then he started to speak feebly again. The words were so low Lance could just distinguish them. "Fletcher . . . mean killer. Gregory wa'n't . . . the first. Fletcher killed Kilby that day to keep him from telling you . . . what he knew. Fired rifle . . . from hotel window, then ran down back stairs . . . hid rifle. Met you later . . . hotel lobby. Made a fool of you that day, Tolliver. It was Fletcher . . . damn nigh got you and the girl . . . out in the Pozo Verde hills . . . that day. Back East . . . he killed a couple of hombres. . . ."

"Herrick," Lance interrupted, "who's the man back of Fletcher? Tell me quick. You haven't much more time."

"I'll tell . . . you . . . whole story . . . Tolliver. Got to have . . . 'nother drink . . . first. . . ."

Lance started to hold the bottle to the man's lips. Lanky stood near, ready with Herrick's cigarette in case he called for another drag. Then Lance paused. Herrick's eyes were wide open now. They were like glass. Blood was welling from his open mouth. Slowly Lance got to his feet. "Lord, how I hate to have to kill a man," he said grimly.

"Gone?" Lanky asked.

"Gone." Lance nodded.

A few Mexicans had moved timidly out to the road by this time and were looking in awe-struck silence at the bodies of the dead gun fighters. Lance dropped the bottle of tequila to the road. "C'mon, Lanky, we'll get back to the Three-Cross. These Mexicans will take over the burying end of the business, I reckon."

Lanky climbed into his saddle. Lance caught up his pony and examined the animal's wounded ear. Herrick's bullet had done little more than remove the tip, and the injury had already ceased bleeding. The animal was quiet now. Lance put his left foot in the stirrup and swung up. The two men started for the Three-Cross at an easy lope. Both were thinking deeply of the events of the past hour and wondering grimly what still lay in store for them.

XXIII
Surrender or Fight!

As they neared the Three-Cross Lance noticed a saddled gray horse standing near the gallery of the house. The horse stood, head drooping and weary, as though it had covered a lot of miles in a short time. Lance said, "Damned if that doesn't look like Ethan Lockwood's big gray."

Lanky nodded. "If that ain't the sheriff's horse I'm a jug-headed sheep thief."

Even while they were talking about the matter Trunk-Strap Kelly rounded the corner of the house and led the beast away—probably to be watered and rubbed down. Lance yelled, "Hey, Trunk-Strap, wait and take our broncs with you."

Kelly turned and saw the approaching riders. He waited until they came up, dismounted, then grasped the reins of the ponies. "Have any luck in that Yaquente camp?" he asked.

"Yeah," Lanky drawled. "We escaped with our scalps. Had some more luck comin' through Muletero. I'll tell it later."

"That's Sheriff Lockwood's gray, isn't it?" Lance asked.

Trunk-Strap nodded. "He got here just a spell ago—been riding all night, I reckon, from the looks of the horse. Something's in the wind; I could tell it from his face. He's in the house."

"Must have come through Muletero just before we staged our shindig," Lanky commented.

Then from the doorway came a sudden hail. "Hi yuh, Lance! How they going, Lanky?" Ethan Lockwood was standing there.

Lance and Lanky stepped up on the gallery and shook hands. "What you doing here?" Lance asked.

"Ran across something I thought you should know," Lockwood replied. "Got a deputy from Saddleville to substitute for me, got on my horse and pushed hard. I even remembered to bring Oscar a fresh supply of lemon drops." They entered the house. Katherine, the professor and Oscar were just beyond the door. The sheriff continued, "I've been hearing about the lively time you're having down here, what with snake temples and Aztec gods and that damned—excuse me, Miss Gregory—that damned Fletcher. If he ain't a dyed-in-the-wool blackguard I never seen one. Coming through Muletero a spell back I thought I caught a glimpse of Chiricahua Herrick going into a cantina, but I couldn't be sure. I was riding fast and didn't want to stop."

"Ten to one it was Herrick." Lance nodded. "Lanky and I had a fuss with 'em when we came through. Herrick, Wheeler and Ridge."

"Lance!" Katherine exclaimed. "More trouble! What happened?"

"We won't be bothered with those three any more," Lance said meaningly. "I'll give you the details later." Everyone was silent for a minute. Lance went on, "What's on your mind, Ethan?"

"Quite a bit," the sheriff said. "I've been saving it

until you get here so I wouldn't have to tell it twice. There's so much to tell I don't just know where to start. In the first place, Lance, that feller you were trailing is——" He broke off, then: "Is it all right to tell what brought you to Pozo Verde, Lance?"

"I'll tell it myself," Lance said, and turned to the others. "You see, I'm an operative of the Special Agency Service, U.S. Treasury Department. I came to——"

"Lance," Katherine exclaimed, her violet-blue eyes widening, "you mean that you're a secret-- service man?"

"Something of the sort." Lance smiled.

"Great Godfrey!" the professor burst out. "Why didn't you tell us?"

"You never asked me." Lance grinned. "How-somever, I'm asking you something right now. Just where do you fit into the scheme? There isn't any Jonesian Institute in Washington, D.C., you know. I've already checked on that."

Jones colored. "I suspected—as much. Deuced awkward. Made a fool—myself—no doubt. Posed as cactus expert. Bah! Should have known better. Just a rank amateur. Small knowledge of cacti. Embarrassing, what? Didn't intend—deceive you—Lance. 'Pon my word. I—I——" He paused, his face crimson.

Katherine came to his rescue. "It's all right, Uncle Uly. Lance, Uncle may say he's not an expert on cacti but he's pretty close to it. It's been his hobby, his ruling passion for years—more years than I can remember. But in addition to that Uncle Uly is one of the finest criminal investigators in the country. Out in California it's that phase of his career, rather than for his collection of cacti, for which he is best known."

Jones looked embarrassed. "Katherine laying it on—too thick," he said disparagingly. "Had—great deal—luck—one or two criminal problems. Reputation overrated—assure you."

"Don't take his word for it," Katherine said earnestly. "Anyway, I wanted to come down here and see if anything could be learned regarding Father's death. Uncle Uly consented to lend me his assistance. We decided it was best for him to pose as being sent on a cactus-hunting expedition by some big institute, so as not to arouse suspicions. From the first Uncle suspected Fletcher of a hand in Father's death but couldn't get the necessary proof. He also guessed that Frank Bowman was on Fletcher's trail, though for what purpose he didn't know. Fletcher kept trying to dissuade us from the trip down here. Later, when Bowman had been killed, Uncle Uly wanted a man he could count on in a pinch rather than a guide. He liked Lance's looks in that capacity. Uncle has also wondered if Lance wasn't a law officer of some sort."

Lance crossed the room, hand outstretched. "I reckon I owe you a heap of apologies, Professor."

"Not at all." Jones smiled. "Natural mistake, what?"

Katherine added, "He really was a professor of botany once too. But the search for cacti was secondary. It was a desire for news regarding Dad's death that really brought us down here."

"I can help out there," Lance said. "Fletcher killed your father, Katherine. Herrick confessed that much——"

"That's one of the things I had to tell," Lockwood broke in. "You'll be telling me next that you know where Matt Foster is and——"

"At least I know who he is," Lance interrupted.

"Wait a minute, Ethan." He turned to the others. "I was sent on the track of a man named Matt Foster. Foster had robbed a Treasury Department messenger of thirty thousand dollars. A record of the numbers on the bills had been kept, and they were traced to Pozo Verde. Last night I recognized Matt Foster."

Lance took from his pocket a photograph. "Here's a picture of Matt Foster and his gang—the gang he had at the time they held up the Treasury Department messenger. Lanky—Oscar, take a look at this photo. This one at the back of the group is Matt Foster—the one with the heavy growth of black whiskers."

Oscar said, "You showed that picture to Ethan and me once."

Lanky said slowly, "There's something looks familiar about that Foster hombre, but I can't just place him."

"I'll help you," Lance said. "Just pretend that derby hat is a helmet and those black whiskers are black feathers. Remember, last night in the Temple of the Plumed Serpent?"

"Fletcher, by Gawd!" Lanky exclaimed.

Oscar said, "Sure it's Fletcher. Well, I'll be danged!"

Lance nodded. "Malcolm Fletcher is Matt Foster. I recognized him last night. Remember, I told you to remember that face?"

"By cripes," Lockwood said disappointedly, "that's another of the things I came down here to tell you, Lance. Don't tell me you already know that we found Elmer Manley——"

"Dead or alive?" Lance asked quickly.

"Alive—plenty alive."

"Tell it," Lance said. "You've been interrupted enough, Ethan. Where did you find him?"

Ethan laughed. "You can credit Johnny Quinn and his hemoglobinuria scare with the discovery of Elmer. Old Johnny saw Banker Gill Addison taking some stomach pills one day and he got to wondering if Gill had hemoglobinuria. The more he thought about it the more he became convinced he should tell Addison to drink bourbon for the disease. So he went to Addison's house. Addison wasn't home. The house was dark. But Johnny Quinn thought he heard someone inside making strangling noises. Johnny came running to me, all in a dither, saying that Gill Addison was dying of hemoglobinuria and that I'd better enter the house and call a doctor. To cut a long story short, I went to the Addison home—he lives alone, you know—broke down the door after I'd heard those same strangling noises and discovered Elmer Manley, roped and gagged. Elmer had been trying to call for help through his gag. About the time I untied Elmer and got him on his feet, Gill Addison came home. I put him under arrest pronto."

Lanky growled, "Don't tell me Banker Addison was mixed up with Fletcher?"

"He was mixed up plenty." Lockwood nodded. "Once I got him in a cell and worked on him a mite he broke down. Addison never did have much nerve, so it wa'n't hard to make him talk. It seems that Matt Foster—or call him Fletcher—had known Addison some years back, just about the time Addison got out of prison after serving a forgery sentence. Fletcher had that stolen money, but the bills' numbers having been recorded, they were risky to get rid of. Addison took them over at a discount and from time to time slipped them in with the bills that Manley passed through his cashier's cage. Addison got rid of quite a few of the bills himself when he handled the cage while Manley was out to dinner."

"Being a banker," Lance put in, "Addison could pass such stolen money without being suspected, of course."

"It was a cinch," Lockwood said. "Addison, like other bankers throughout the country, had a list of the numbered bills. By accident Elmer Manley had a short look at that list and remembered some of the numbers. Thus he recognized some of the bills Addison had slipped into his cash drawer. He didn't know how they'd come there. When he reported the matter to Addison, Addison insisted he was mistaken in the numbers. However, he refused to let Elmer see the list of missing bills. In short, he told Elmer to stick to his cashier's cage and forget about stolen money. That aroused Elmer's suspicions."

Lockwood paused to assemble his facts, then continued, "Meanwhile, Jared Gregory had been looking for a partner to take a half-share in his ranch and buy some blooded stock to raise the quality of his cows. He asked Addison to suggest someplace where he could find a partner. It looked like a good proposition. Fletcher was looking for an investment. He bought a half-interest in the ranch. A few days later Jared Gregory discovered on the property an ancient Aztec temple. Well, gold and jewels are usually found in such places. Fletcher and Addison decided they wanted the temple all to themselves, so it was planned for Fletcher to kill Jared Gregory and——" Lockwood broke off in some embarrassment. "Gosh, Miss Gregory, I hate to be reminding you——"

"Go on," Katherine urged. Her eyes were a trifle

moist. "After all, we've got to know the facts so we can—can——"

Her voice broke. Lance moved closer and took one of her hands in both his own. Lockwood went on, a trifle hurriedly, "Anyway, they were mistaken about the gold and jewels. They never did find any treasure beyond a few silver trinkets that weren't worth much. Meanwhile, an Indian—half Yaquente, half Apache—had witnessed the killing of Jared Gregory. This Indian decided to blackmail Fletcher. Fletcher was in a tight. He asked Addison's advice. Addison advised him to hire Chiricahua Herrick to kill the Indian. Instead, Herrick made friends with the hombre who had certain ideas about cooking up a revolution in Mexico."

"He was probably that interpreter Fletcher used last night," Lanky put in, "at the temple of the snake."

"Might be," Lockwood agreed. "Anyway, this Indian knew about the Yaquente ceremonies that were being carried on in the temple. He also knew that anyone who would furnish mezcal buttons to the Yaquentes could get a lot out of them and make it an easy matter to work them into fomenting a religious war. They talked it over with Addison and Fletcher. It looked good. Once the revolutionists had conquered a few towns and picked up strength they planned to attack Chihuahua City. Thereafter Herrick, Addison and Fletcher had plans of their own. The government mint is located at Chihuahua City, you know. Once the mint was in their hands they planned to seize the gold and silver bullion, transport the loot to the States, double-cross the Indians and forget the revolution."

"Jeepers!" Lance exclaimed. "They reckoned to

work on a big scale, didn't they? What a plot! Going to raid the Chihuahua mint, eh? The nerve of the skunks!"

"There isn't much more to tell," Lockwood resumed. "Frank Bowman had arrived in Pozo Verde on the trail of those stolen bills. He worked himself in with the Herrick gang. Some of them talked too much—as they later admitted, Addison told me. Addison thinks that Bowman must have commenced to grow suspicious of Fletcher. Fletcher was friendly with Professor Jones. Probably Bowman didn't know what the tie-up was but by that time he must have begun to suspect the game was bigger than he had at first thought. Anyway, when the professor stated he was going to make a trip down into Mexico Bowman got the job as his guide. Then Bowman made his bad mistake."

"What was that?" Lance asked.

Lockwood said, "Apparently he wasn't making much headway on finding the stolen money. Thinking he'd be dealing with an honest banker, he went to Addison, told Addison he was a government agent and asked for cooperation in watching for the missing bills. Addison passed the news to Fletcher, of course, and that sealed Bowman's fate. He was put out of the way. By this time, though, Addison was getting scary about so much killing and he balked on Elmer being rubbed out."

"What happened to Elmer, anyway?" Lance asked.

Lockwood explained, "That day you talked to Elmer in the bank and he promised to meet you that night he gave you two of the missing bills, didn't he?" Lance nodded. Lockwood continued, "Addison saw the bills in your hand and became suspicious of Elmer's actions. That afternoon he told Fletcher what he had seen. Fletcher said Elmer would have to die. Addison bucked on the proposition. He promised to keep Elmer a prisoner until such time as their plot had been pulled off. That afternoon he sent Elmer to hire a horse and buggy for him with the excuse that he had to drive to Saddleville with a satchel of money to deliver to a bank there. Elmer drove the rig to Addison's bank. Addison came out with a grip packed with old newspapers which he pretended was money. Then he said he had to stop at his home to get some ledgers to take to the Saddleville bank. He asked Elmer to drive the rig that far. At Addison's home Addison asked Elmer to come in and help him carry out the ledgers. Once Elmer was in the house Addison hit him on the head, knocked him unconscious and tied and gagged him. Later Addison drove the horse and buggy out to the edge of town and turned it loose. Elmer was kept a prisoner at Addison's home until old Johnny Quinn and I released him. Incident'ly, the State Banking Board has put Elmer in charge of the Pozo Verde bank."

"Ethan," Lance said, "your story has sure cleared up a heap of details that had my brain whirling dizzily. All I've got to do now is find Fletcher and arrest him, and the case is cleared up."

Katherine said, "Before you talk about arresting anybody, Lance, you'd better get some sleep. You look dead tired. First, however, will you please tell me what hemoglobinuria means? I'm feeling sorry for old Johnny Quinn without knowing what kind of a disease he has."

Lance laughed and told her the story. Professor

Jones smiled and said, "Hemoglobinuria, eh? Excellent word, what? Reminds me—botanical nomenclature—various cacti. By the way, Sheriff, you haven't seen my *Echinopsis gregoriana*. Startling discovery, y'understand. Come out on the gallery." He seized the reluctant sheriff and started him toward the door.

Lockwood spoke over his shoulder. "Oh yes, Miss Gregory, there's quite a sizable balance of your father's money on deposit in the Pozo Verde bank. Addison had figured to do some forging and grab that money for himself, but now that Elmer is running the bank it will be safe until you want it."

"But—but," Katherine said, "it was stolen money Fletcher paid Father for the share in the Three-Cross."

Lance shook his head. "No, it was Addison who accepted that stolen money from Fletcher. That's Addison's responsibility. The money credited to your father's account, Katherine, is backed by the Pozo Verde bank.

The girl turned on Lance and spoke with pretended severity. "Lance, are you still here? I told you to go get some sleep."

"Yes, Katy, my dear," Lance said meekly, and left the room.

It was late afternoon when Lance awakened to find Oscar shaking his shoulder. "Sorry to spoil your snooze," Oscar was saying, "but a Mex from Muletero just arrived with a note for you. He claims Fletcher made him bring it here. Maybe it's important."

Lance swung his feet off the bed and sat up, rubbing sleep from his eyes. He took the sealed envelope and broke the flap. Inside was a single sheet of paper, written in lead pencil:

TOLLIVER:

The discovery of my feathered rattler won't help you any. I have plans that can't be interfered with, so this country isn't big enough to hold both of us. If you and your friends will surrender to me I promise you safe conduct out of Mexico after my plans have been fulfilled within a few months. Otherwise my Indians will wipe you out. I'll give you until dawn to make up your mind, but think fast. Surrender or fight! But you won't have a chance if you fight.

FLETCHER.

Lance rose to his feet. "This," he said grimly, "is the worst yet. Read this, Oscar. There's hell to pay, and no pitch hot!"

XXIV
"Fighting Is a Yaquente's Life"

Oscar's face blanched as he read the note. Lance said, "Fletcher's mention of that feathered snake proves he's seen Horatio, I reckon. Is the messenger who brought the note waiting for an answer now?"

Oscar shook his head. "He ducked out as soon as he delivered it. I reckon he didn't want any part of either game and only came here on protest because he was afraid of Fletcher."

Lance nodded. "Probably so. Oscar, while I'm getting dressed you go out and round up our crew. Show 'em the note. Bring 'em into the main room of the ranch house, and we'll hold a council of war and see what's to be done."

Oscar said, "I'll do that," and hurried away.

When Lance entered the big room a few minutes later everybody was there waiting for him. All eyes turned his way as he came in, and he realized they were looking to him for leadership. His heart sunk a little at the thought. It was going to be difficult to decide the best course to pursue. All had seen Fletcher's note by this time, and the seriousness of the situation was fully realized. Katherine was the first to speak when Lance entered.

She said, "At the start, Lance, I want it understood that I'm not to be treated as a woman. I can handle a gun and do my part. And there mustn't be any talk of surrendering because of me."

"Frankly," Sheriff Lockwood said, "I think we'd be fools to surrender. We couldn't trust to Fletcher's word——"

"Certainly not," Jones put in. "The man's a mad dog. We've got to fight. Our case may not be hopeless. There are"—he counted rapidly—"Lance and the sheriff and Oscar are three; Lanky, Tom Piper and Trunk-Strap makes six. Then there's Hub, Cal Braun, Luke Homer and myself. That's ten. And Katherine. I wonder how much of a force Fletcher will have? Himself, Ordway and Johnson. Jehovah only knows how many Yaquentes, though——"

"I wish there was some way we could get Miss Gregory away." Oscar frowned, absent-mindedly crunching a lemon drop.

"I've been thinking of that." Lance nodded moodily. "We might make some sort of deal with Fletcher——"

"Lance," Katherine protested, "I won't hear of that. I'd sooner stay than trust myself to that beast."

Lance nodded. "I think you're right at that, Katherine, much as I hate to say it."

"Do you reckon," Lanky drawled, "that we could slip Miss Gregory away after sundown——?"

"Fiddlesticks!" Katherine snapped. "Don't you suppose Fletcher will think of that and have men out watching for just such a move?"

The men in the room remained silent, realizing the girl spoke the truth. Katherine went on, "I'm staying here and fighting with you. That's settled. The sooner you men realize that the sooner you can get down to business and prepare a defense for this house. We've only got until daylight, remember. It's suppertime now. I'll take over the cooking of food so Cal can help the rest of you. Just forget about me."

Lance had to face the facts. He knew Katherine spoke the truth and that there was nothing else to do except as she pointed out. Reluctantly he conceded the point. "Right." He nodded tersely, though his heart warmed to the girl's courage. "It's decided then that there's to be no question of surrendering?"

"No-o-o!" the room roared collectively. "We fight!"

Lance smiled thinly and gave a sigh of relief. "Thank heaven you folks settled the question for me. I sure didn't want that responsibility." His manner stiffened. "All right, we fight. Get all the guns and ammunition together and see what we have."

"By the way," Lanky said, "when I was hunting a burlap sack to put that snake in I found a whole pile of sacks in that shed beyond the corral. Suppose we fill 'em with sand and stack 'em along the outside edge of the gallery. It would make a dang good shelter to fire from."

"That's an idea," Lance said enthusiastically. "Lanky, you got a head on you. Get some picks and shovels, and we'll get busy. The yard out in front of the house is sandy, gravelly stuff. Take it from there. Dig in the shape of a wide trench. We won't have time to make it deep, but any obstruction should slow up the Fletcher gang when they come raiding. Maybe we're not so bad off after all. The walls of this old house are fully two feet thick. We can do our fighting from the gallery; that will leave us the house to retreat to if things get tough. All the doors are stout, and we can bar them. We want to be sure and bring plenty of water into the house tonight and stack our food where it will be handy. We might be in for considerable siege."

It was dark now. Oil lamps were lighted. Katherine started to prepare supper. Blankets were hung at the windows around the house. Guards were set to be on the watch for the first hostile move. Lanterns were lighted, and the men toiled to fill sandbags which were placed in the form of a breastwork around the edge of the long gallery. By twos and threes they dropped in to eat the food and drink the coffee Katherine had prepared. They all worked like beavers to get ready for the coming fight. The professor proved he could work with the best of them. For the present he seemed to forget his beloved cactus.

By midnight practically all was done that could be done. The two wagons of the expedition, in addition to a couple of Mexican carretas that were found on the place, had been placed at strategic points about the house to furnish further barriers against the raiders. Lance had had the horses brought from the corral and tethered along the back of the house near the doors. Not that they'd help a great deal, but every possible obstacle against a charging army was considered good tactics.

By this time all but the guards Lance had posted were in the big main room of the house oiling guns and in other ways preparing for the fight. Back of the house the earth had been cleared for some distance. It was probably from the front the attack would come, Lance decided. Not more than seventy-five feet from the gallery grew thick brush and trees, except for the opening that pointed the road to Muletero. "And it's a cinch," Lance mused, "Fletcher won't be fool enough to come riding along that road. No, he'll have his Yaquentes scattered through the brush, I'm betting."

Katherine was seated at a long table tearing into strips a bolt of cotton she had found in the house. She smiled at Lance.

Lance said, "Bandages?" The girl nodded. Lance forced a smile in return. He didn't say anything. The door to the gallery opened suddenly and Trunk-Strap Kelly entered. Kelly and Lanky were standing guard at the front of the house. Trunk-Strap said, "Lance, Lanky wants to see you. There's a Yaquente outside making some sort of palaver. This Injun's got the skin of a freshly killed rattler for a hatband on his sombrero—and the skin's got feathers on it."

Lance hurried outside. In the dim starlight beyond the sandbag barricade he saw Lanky conversing with Huareztjio. Lance leaped the barricade and approached. "What is it, Lanky? Howdy, Horatio."

Huareztjio's white teeth showed in a grin. "I'm t'ink fight weeth you, señor. Fletcher, him *malo*. How you say—bad, no?"

"Fletcher is damned bad," Lance said grimly.

"Here's the setup, Lance," Lanky explained. "We're getting a break. Huareztjio and his gang confronted Fletcher with that phony snake and asked questions. Fletcher tried to talk himself out of the fix but he didn't convince all the Yaquentes by a long shot. Huareztjio and some of his buddies have come to fight for us if we'll let 'em. They're spoiling for a fight, anyhow——"

"This isn't some sort of trick?" Lance asked sharply.

"I don't reckon so. You saved Huareztjio from a beating one time and you showed him how Fletcher was pulling the wool over the eyes of the tribe. He and the cooler heads from his village want to show their gratitude. They've brought their guns and ca'tridges. Lance, we're in luck. They're fighting fools."

"How many men can Horatio produce?"

"He claims to have seventy-five, but I ain't seen one yet. Didn't see Huareztjio until he was almost on top of me."

"Ask him if he knows how big a force Fletcher has."

Lanky put the question to Huareztjio. The Yaquente made quick reply. Lanky turned back to Lance. "He says Fletcher has gathered around a hundred and fifty men—Yaquentes and Apaches and breeds of various descriptions. Some of 'em are carrying pretty old guns too. Only the Yaquentes have modern arms."

Lance frowned. "And will Horatio and his men fight against Indians of his own tribe?"

Lanky nodded. "A lot of the tribe wouldn't have anything to do with either side. The Yaquentes who went with Fletcher are just young bucks with no sense, Huareztjio claims. Huareztjio and his pals are just spoiling to teach the young bucks a lesson, and—like I say, after all, fighting is a Yaquente's whole life. Shall we take him up on the offer?"

"I figure we'd be fools not to. But where are these seventy-five men he claims he has with him?"

Lanky spoke to Huareztjio. The Indian gave a quick, short call. Instantly from all sides white-clad forms, carrying guns, came leaping from the brush. In a moment they were gathered all around Lance and Lanky. Lanky gasped with surprise, then spoke quick words to Huareztjio.

"My gosh!" Lance exclaimed. "We were surrounded and didn't know it. Lanky, I reckon it would be a good idea to put a couple of these Yaquentes on guard."

"Sufferin' sheep thieves!" Lanky said. "What do you think I just told Huareztjio? I got that idea as quick as you. Better take these hombres inside, Lance, and throw some coffee and food into 'em. You'll make yourself solid. Trunk-Strap can stay out here with a couple of Yaquentes. I'll go along to make talk if anything comes up."

They herded the Yaquentes into the house, much to the surprise of those inside. Lance explained briefly, "Horatio and his friends have come to fight for us. Our luck's not all bad." He told Katherine he could use some help fixing coffee and food for the Indians. The girl rose to go to the kitchen.

A sudden clamor lifted among the Yaquentes. They were all staring at Katherine and talking excitedly. Lanky listened, then started to laugh. "It's Miss Gregory's yellow hair that gets 'em," Lanky exclaimed. "There's some old legend in their tribe about a white maiden with yellow hair coming to lead them to a great victory someday."

Katherine smiled up at the Indians crowded around her. More talking followed and the flash of even white teeth. Huareztjio grinned and pointed to Katherine, then said to Lance, "Your woman?"

Lance flushed and stood tongue-tied. Katherine smiled. "His woman"—pointing to herself and then Lance.

"My woman," Lance answered Huareztjio. The Indians commenced to talk louder. They were fast making themselves at home.

"If I'm your woman," Katherine told Lance, "you can prove it by coming with me to the kitchen. There's food and coffee to fix."

By the time they returned, bearing steaming pots and dishes, the big room in the ranch house was in an uproar of excitement. Oscar had brought out his stock of lemon drops and passed them around. Lanky laughed. "Those Yaquentes sure go for leming drops."

"Never made so many converts so fast in my life." Oscar chuckled. "Maybe this is the way to wean 'em from that peyote habit."

"One thing's certain," Lanky said. "We're solid with these Yaquentes now. They'll fight for us until they drop."

About two o'clock in the morning Lance ordered all the lamps extinguished, saying, "Fletcher may not wait until dawn to attack." A number of the Yaquentes spoke some Spanish and a smattering of English. These Lance delegated to key positions subordinate to white men. At the back of the house Lockwood and Cal Braun commanded five Yaquentes; on the east end of the building five more Yaquentes waited, with Trunk-Strap and Tom Piper near slightly opened windows; at the west end Hub Owen and Luke Homer performed a similar job. Ranged along the front gallery, shielded behind the sandbag barricade, were Lance, Jones, Lanky, Oscar and Huareztjio with the remainder of the Yaquentes. It was at the front of the building Lance expected the attack to strike, as the brush and trees grew much closer in that direction. Lance had asked Katherine to stay within, out of gun range, and act as a messenger working between the gallery and other sections of the house.

The minutes dragged slowly for the men awaiting the attack. They talked in hushed voices, smoked cigarettes or pipes, always shielding the glow of the burning tobacco from any enemy who might be concealed in the brush beyond the house. Three o'clock came, and then three-thirty. Huareztjio had three spies out in the brush. Now these three returned with word that the thickets were alive with men. Lance and his companions drew deep breaths and waited, their fingers itching to pull triggers.

Time passed. It wasn't more than an hour to dawn now. False dawn had already come and faded in the east, but along the distant horizon a faint streak of silvery gray, almost like a mist, was commencing to rise. Now, Lance noticed, the usual calling of night birds was missing from the vicinity of the house. He spoke, low voiced, to the professor crouched at his side behind the sandbags. "It can't be much longer now."

"Quite so, quite," Jones replied calmly. "Terrific wear on nerves, though, what? Strong desire—for action, y'understand."

"You'll get your fill of action," Lance stated grimly.

A few feet away Oscar crunched lemon drops. He wasn't talking. Lanky spoke to Huareztjio. Certain guttural words of Yaquente passed swiftly along the gallery. Lance wondered if Fletcher would send somebody to learn if the Three-Cross had decided to surrender or fight. Fifteen minutes more brought the dawn nearer.

XXV
The Battle at Three-Cross

The attack came with savage suddenness! The brush on four sides of the house erupted violently with orange fire. Shattering explosions rent the early-morning air. As Lance had expected, the bulk of the attack was concentrated at the front. Bullets thudded into the adobe house walls and ripped into sand-bags. Lance caught one low, suppressed moan; that was the only sound uttered. True to Lance's instructions, the men were holding their fire, awaiting the attackers' closer approach. A second furious volley came from points nearer the front of the house.

Lance yelled as loud as he could, "Let 'em have it!"

Four sides of the building suddenly roared with gunfire. Cries of pain rose from the neighboring brush. Lance yelled exultantly: "We scored that time, fellers!" Rifles and six-shooters cracked madly. The battle was on. Lance sent another shot crashing from his gun. On both sides men were firing and reloading as fast as possible. From time to time Lance caught the booming of six-shooters from the rear of the house, though the attack from that direction was more or less desultory. Lance emptied his gun, loaded and reemptied it he didn't know how many times. He only realized the weapon was growing hot in his hand. He felt a touch on his arm. Turning, he saw Katherine offering him a loaded Winchester in exchange for the depleted six-gun in his hand. "Good girl," he grunted. "Better get back in the house though."

Even while he jerked the Winchester to his shoulder and levered shot after shot from the barrel in the direction of flashes of fire from the brush he felt her fingers tugging at the cartridges in his belt as she reloaded the hand gun. He heard her cool voice saying something about "angry, droning hornets." He remembered taking his six-shooter from her, and that was all at the time. She had passed on to her uncle.

Again and again Lance fired. Every time he glanced along the rim of the sandbags they seemed to be fringed with living flame. It was hot, sweaty work. Powder smoke hung low along the length of the gallery, stinging eyes and throats and nostrils with its acrid fumes. Sharp lances of flame stabbed viciously from the brush and trees. Now and then a man screamed in agony or yelped with sudden pain. By now the attackers were concentrating on the front of the house. Those within emerged to squeeze down among the men lined behind the barrier of sandbags.

Lance didn't know how long they'd been fighting, but suddenly he saw that the flashes of gunfire had changed from vivid orange to white and he realized it was daylight. He glanced along the gallery and saw several wounded and dead Yaquentes. Oscar had a bloody gash across the back of one hand; his left cheek bulged with lemon drops. Lanky's shirt sleeve had been slashed with flying slugs at two places. The building wall behind the fighters was pockmarked as though it had withstood a storm of hailstones. Katherine was moving along the gallery, crouched low, lending such aid as she could to the wounded. Lance yelled at her to get back into the house. He didn't know what she said in reply. He didn't have time to listen just then.

A group of about thirty white-clothed forms under big straw sombreros, with bandoleers around their shoulders, came charging out of the brush, their gun muzzles spurting flame and smoke. Lance yelled, "Don't give an inch, hombres! Pour it on 'em!"

His men responded with a crashing torrent of lead that all but cut the attackers in two. For a brief instant all motion seemed to stand transfixed in the hideous din, and in that instant Lance caught a picture he never forgot. The attackers appeared to hesitate momentarily, then more than two thirds of them bent suddenly at the middle and pitched forward. Others turned and ran back for the brush. Several were limping frantically from the scene. The Yaquentes along the gallery gave a high-pitched yell and renewed their fire. Only a few of the attackers regained the shelter they had left less than a minute before.

Powder smoke hung like a gray blanket between the house and the brush. For a minute the firing of the attackers ceased, then burst forth with a renewed fury that caused the men behind the sandbags to crouch low. A steady, unceasing tattoo of flying lead drummed against the house wall. It seemed it would never stop.

Lance heard the professor's voice. "Like rain on a tin roof, what?"

"Some storm," Lance grunted. He lifted his head a trifle to peer above the sandbags. Three bullets instantly drilled holes into his sombrero crown. Lance dropped down with the maximum of haste but he had seen enough to puzzle him.

"That one wagon we placed out there"—he frowned—"it's only about thirty feet away. I figured it might help slow up a rush. I just saw several men break cover from the brush and run to get behind it. I wonder what they're up to. If they're figuring on charging us from there they'll get a surprise——"

He stopped. An object had been thrown from behind the wagon. Lance saw it skim the top of the sandbags and land among a group of Yaquentes. It looked like a tin can, but . . .

And then Lance didn't see the tin can any more. It abruptly disappeared in a burst of white fire and a deafening detonation. A cloud of thick, yellowish smoke enveloped the gallery. Small chunks of rock exploded viciously in all directions.

Lance exclaimed, "My God! They've made bombs and——"

He had no time to say more. A tomato can came hurtling through the air to land on the gallery. All in a split instant Lance saw the top had been tied down with hemp cord. From the opening where the can had been cut a length of fuse burned with a fierce sputtering sound. Lance pounced on the can, seized it, hurled it with all his might in the direction of the wagon behind which the bomb throwers were sheltered. He saw it land beneath the wagon. BOOM! Smoke and flame enveloped the wagon. Men rolled on the earth. Several scrambled frantically for the shielding brush.

A cheer ran along the gallery. By now the smoke had cleared. Several forms lay silent and bleeding behind the sandbags. "That's the game!" Lance yelled. "Throw those cans back when they come over!" He glanced toward the wagon. It was tilted crazily on one side. One wheel was missing. Lance saw a movement up near the front of the vehicle. He thumbed one swift shot, not knowing whether or not he scored. He heard a sudden exclamation from the professor. Jones had gone the color of ashes. One hand was clapped to his forehead in sudden dismay.

"What's the matter?" Lance yelled through the din of gunfire. "Are you hit?"

The professor shook his head. He lowered the hand from his forehead, and Lance saw that his brow was beaded with tiny beads of perspiration. Jones looked sick. He gulped and stammered, "My—my *Echinopsis gregoriana*. Forgot all about it—all this excitement. If anything—should happen—great loss—to the world."

He glanced fearfully over his shoulder, then a look of relief passed over his face as he saw the small wooden tub still intact on the recessed window sill. Heedless of the flying lead spattering against the adobe wall, the professor started for his beloved plant with the intention of removing it to the interior of the house.

"Professor!" Lance warned. "Stay down. You'll be hit!"

The warning came too late. Another tomato can came sailing in behind the sandbags. It bounced once on the gallery floor, then disappeared in a thunderous roar. Even as the smoke spread and billowed along the gallery Lance saw Jones stagger back and fall flat. Bits of rock rattled along the gallery floor and walls. Two Yaquentes were down. Tom Piper had been picked up as though hurled by some giant hand and dashed against the adobe wall to fall in a crumpled heap.

Lance moved swiftly through the drifting powder smoke and reached the professor's side. Jones was already staggering up. "Not hit," he gasped. "Force of—explosion—floored me—that's all. Must get my *Echinopsis gregoriana*—place of safety."

He broke away from Lance's restraining hands and started toward the window sill for his plant. Then he stopped short. An anguished moan left his lips. Bullets were whining all around him, but he didn't seem to notice them. He was speechless now. There wasn't any window sill there. The whole window was gone. Left only was a gaping hole in the adobe wall. The professor's plant had been blown to bits. Not even the slightest bit of earth in which it had been planted remained in sight though a few slivers of splintered wooden tub lay on the gallery floor.

For a brief moment the professor swayed unsteadily like one who has received a death blow. Suddenly his face reddened; his features became contorted with rage; his whole body stiffened. "The dirty blackguard scoundrels!" he stormed furiously, shaking a menacing fist toward the brush and trees. "They should be taught a lesson, what? By Christopher! I'll show them a thing or two! Destroy the greatest discovery of the century, will they? Not and escape unscathed, the low-lifed, hell-hound mongrels! Not while my name is Ulysses Zarathustra Jones!"

And in that minute the professor went thoroughly berserk. Seizing his gun from the gallery floor, he leaped over the sandbags and charged the enemy single-handed! Lance leaped to catch him but missed. "Professor!" he yelled. "Come back! You'll be killed! Oh, you fool, you!"

Behind him he heard Katherine's wailing. "Uncle Uly, come back!"

But their pleas accomplished nothing. Deaf to all entreaty, with but a single thought dominating his movements—that of annihilating the enemy—Jones dashed recklessly into the very teeth of the flame-spitting brush, bullets kicking up sand and gravel all around him as he plunged on!

XXVI
The Dust Settles

Lance glanced in sudden dismay at the white men on the gallery. Their faces reflected the hopeless thought in his own mind. He snapped grimly, "Get ready for a lot of hell, fellers! We can't let him go it alone."

But the Yaquentes on the gallery had already reached that decision. Wild, joyful, bloodcurdling yells left their throats as they leaped erect and vaulted over the sandbags, eager to catch up with the professor, in the belief that Jones was leading them in a charge against the enemy!

This was what Lance's Yaquentes wanted, the sort of action for which they had been impatiently waiting. Straight into a hailstone of fire they moved like some relentless, avenging juggernaut. For just an instant Lance stood as one paralyzed by the sight of the white-clothed forms, their guns spurting lances of flame as they shouted wild battle cries and closed in toward the enemy. Then Lance moved. "C'mon, waddies," he yelled, "we can't let the Yaquentes get there first!"

Wild cowboy yells sounded above the rattle of gunfire as the men followed Lance from the gallery.

Bullets were whining like angry bees through the air, but the enemy was momentarily unsettled by the unexpected charge, and its aim was none too good. Lance and his men fanned out to cover a wide area, shooting as they ran. Here and there Lance saw a Yaquente drop, but the majority charged on in the direction taken by the professor who had, by this time, disappeared among the brush and trees.

Lance sprinted swiftly in the direction of the wagon from which the tin-can bombs had been hurled. Two men crouched in its shelter. One of them was lifting a can to throw in the midst of the Yaquentes who had just charged past. Lance flipped his six-shooter to one side, shooting by instinct rather than aim. He saw the man drop the can and pitch to the earth. A moment later, as he ran on, he heard a tremendous explosion from the direction of the wagon.

"Good work, Lance!" Oscar shouted, running a few feet from Lance's side.

They plunged into the brush together. All around them guns were cracking and roaring. Once or twice, through the trees, Lance caught glimpses of fleeing forms. The enemy was retreating toward a nest of rocks some distance farther on. Some of them were already there, shaking lead out of their gun muzzles.

Lance shouted to Oscar, "We've got 'em on the run anyway!"

The fighting raged in and out among the trees. Lockwood and Lanky weren't far from Lance and Oscar now. They were making every shot count. Abruptly Lance and Oscar rounded a high clump of prickly pear and nearly ran into the professor. Lance heaved a long sigh of relief. Miraculously he was so far unwounded.

"Well, don't stand there gaping at me like a dummy," Jones yelled angrily. "Can't you see I'm out of ammunition? Give me some cartridges!"

Lance handed him some cartridges from a pocket. Jones feverishly commenced to shove loads into his cylinder. "Took you long enough to get here," he grunted, "but we've sure forced 'em back. Took 'em—by surprise—y'understand." He gestured toward a low, rock-covered ridge lifting above the brush. "Most of 'em—retreated up there. If we can—only dislodge 'em—we got 'em—licked, by Christopher! Come on!"

They hadn't taken more than a half a dozen steps when Lance stumbled and plunged into a small ditch cut by the runoff of the rainy season. He started to rise, then, warned by a sudden noise, glanced around. Two of the enemy were cowering there, swarthy-faced, brutal-looking men who had been taken by surprise when the Three-Cross attacked. Then Lance's eyes opened wider. The two men had already thrown down their guns and were holding their hands in the air. But that wasn't what caught and held Lance's attention. He raised his voice in a sudden yell to Oscar and the professor who hadn't stopped to wait for Lance. "Hey, Oscar! Professor! Wait! Look what I found!"

Oscar and the professor turned and came running back. Lance pointed. The professor gave one wild shout of unholy glee. He took in the supply of powder, chunks of rock, fuses, tin cans, with which the two men had been manufacturing bombs. At one side was a stacked pile of bombs ready for lighting.

"Now we've got 'em!" Lance yelled. He thrust matches into the hands of the two prisoners. "You light 'em; we throw 'em," he ordered. "Otherwise we'll be plugging you—savvy?"

Whether the two Indians understood the words or not, they at least caught the idea—and they obeyed.

That was really the beginning of the end. The Indians struck matches. Lance, Oscar and the professor held fuses to the flame and then exercised their throwing arms. Tin-can bombs went hurtling through the air to land in the nest of rocks on the ridge.

Kr-umph! Kr-ummph! Krump! Krump! Kr-r-ummph! The very earth shook as the bombs exploded, hurling broken rock in all directions. Leaves and branches went shooting into the air. Yellowish smoke rose in dense clouds. *Kr-umpkr-umph-krumph—h-h!* Three bombs had landed at the same instant.

Abruptly the ridge commenced to erupt men. They scattered in all directions, voicing wild, frantic cries. Lockwood and Lanky came plunging through the brush, eyes wide with astonishment.

"What's going on here?" Lockwood demanded. Then as he saw the depleted pile of bombs he caught the idea, and he and Lanky went into action. By this time the gunfire had fallen off considerably.

"We've got 'em licked!" Lance yelled triumphantly. "Get Horatio and his men to round up the prisoners—what's left of 'em——"

He paused suddenly. Through the trees he had caught sight of a man making a getaway on horseback. Fletcher! Without stopping to explain, Lance leaped in swift pursuit. He fought his way through a tangle of brush to a small clearing. Several horses were tethered there Lance picked out a likely-looking buckskin, gathered up its reins and vaulted to the saddle. Plunging in his spurs, he got under way.

It was slow going for a few minutes, dodging mesquite and prickly-pear clumps. Then suddenly the way opened. He was on the road that led to Muletero. Of Fletcher there was no sign.

Lance gave the buckskin the spurs again. The horse responded nobly, leaping out in great space-devouring strides. The wind whipped into Lance's face. Prickly pear, mesquite, yucca flowed past on either side with a panoramic monotony. The buckskin was giving all it had now. Lance patted its neck in admiration. "By cripes, horse! You're a goer!" They speeded on, mile after mile.

Suddenly Lance saw the houses of Muletero. A cloud of dust moving swiftly through the town caught his eye. Fletcher! The man was riding hard in a final desperate attempt to escape. Once he glanced back and saw Lance in speedy pursuit. Lance saw Fletcher's arm rise and fall as he beat his horse over the head in an effort to draw more speed from the beast.

"Damn skunk," Lance muttered. "That's no way to treat a horse that's trying to help you."

He caught a glimpse of houses and open-mouthed Mexicans as he flashed through Muletero. That was about all he saw of the town, then he was in open country again. That dust cloud being kicked up ahead wasn't so far away now.

Suddenly Fletcher turned in his saddle. Lance crouched low. He heard the sharp whine of a bullet past his ears, saw the white flash of fire. Again Fletcher unleashed his lead and again he missed. Lance was rapidly closing the distance between them now. He saw Fletcher reach to his cartridge belt and judged the man was reloading.

"I'd sure like to take you alive, mister," Lance grunted. He glanced down at the lariat on his saddle. It was of rawhide. Lance preferred Manila hemp, but rawhide would have to do. He grasped the lariat and commenced to shake out a loop, meanwhile urging his pony to greater efforts as he swiftly closed in on the fleeing rider.

Twice the loop circled about Lance's head, each time widening in size. Abruptly he released his cast, made his dally about the saddle horn and watched the rope sail through the air. "Straight and true for Fletcher's head," Lance thought. "It will probably get him around the shoulders." At the same instant, turning to throw another shot at Lance, Fletcher saw the rope dropping swiftly through the air. He twisted to one side in an effort to dodge it. The loop settled and tightened about the neck of Fletcher's horse.

Instantly, true to its training, the buckskin pony stiffened its legs, dug in its hoofs in a long, sliding halt that sent sand and gravel flying in all directions. The rope went taut, tightening about the neck of Fletcher's horse and stopping the beast so suddenly all four hoofs left the earth as it crashed down. Fletcher had already loosened his feet from stirrups and landed, catlike, running toward Lance, his right hand spitting smoke and flame.

Lance swung down from the saddle. He fired. Missed. Two bullets from Fletcher's gun came dangerously close, the second one cutting the neckerchief below Lance's left ear.

Even as Lance thumbed a second shot from his

six-shooter he was thinking, "My God! The man's fast!" He saw dust spurt from Fletcher's vest, saw the amazed look that crossed Fletcher's features. Fletcher's next shot blended with Lance's. Lance felt the sombrero jerk on his head and knew that one had been close too. Through the haze of smoke from the guns he saw Fletcher's body go rigid, pulling him up on his boot toes. Fletcher half turned, one hand clawing at his breast, then he crumpled in a lifeless heap.

Methodically Lance plugged out empty shells and replaced them in his gun cylinder as he moved toward the body. "Lord knows," he said grimly, "I tried to take you alive, Fletcher, but you wouldn't have it that way. I reckon it wasn't meant to be."

It was nearing noon when Lance again came within sight of the ranch house. Considerable clearing up had already been done. Oscar and Trunk-Strap Kelly, aided by Lanky, Huareztjio and a bunch of Yaquentes were working at the edge of the brush clearing away the last remnants of battle. Oscar looked up as Lance approached. He said solemnly, "Have a lemon drop? They're good for that shaky feeling."

Lance took a lemon drop. He said, "Where's the rest?"

"The professor and Miss Gregory are in the house. She's bathing a scratch he got on one hand. Lockwood is down in the bunkhouse, which same we've turned into a hospital. Ethan is right good at treatin' wounds, you know, and there's a first-aid kit. No—none of our men were hurt bad. Tom Piper's got a couple of ribs and an arm broken. Hub Owen got his hair parted with a bullet. Most of the losses were on the other side. Horatio's got some of his gang doing a job of burying back in the hills. The

Yaquentes took some prisoners back to their village. We found both Larry Johnson and Luke Ordway dead. That's Ordway's buckskin you're riding."

"It's one sweet pony," Lance said.

"I don't see Fletcher's horse."

"I tried to take him alive. Only succeeded in breaking his bronc's neck."

"We knew you'd be back right soon," Oscar said gravely. "It was nice going, Lance, all of it."

Huareztjio pushed up, grinning, and took Lance's hand. Lance returned the friendly clasp, touched spurs to his pony and moved on.

The professor was waiting for Lance at the edge of the gallery. One hand was bandaged. He held out his right hand as Lance climbed stiffly down from the saddle. "Back safe—thank God," he said jerkily. "Made a fool of myself—lost my head, what?"

Lance said, "It's a damn good thing you did. You started the ball rolling. It was you that turned the tide our way."

Jones smiled shyly. "Good ruckus, what? Enjoyed it—fact."

"Only thing I'm sorry for," Lance said awkwardly, "is the loss of your cactus plant. That was really tough."

"Regrettable," Jones said philosophically, though his eyes looked a trifle moist, "but not vital, y'understand. Now I know it exists—search for another *Echinopsis gregoriana*. Katherine wants to—spend honeymoon here. Hope you won't mind—having an old fool about cacti—around the house. She's waiting for you, Lance. Better go in. Now that the dust has settled—peaceful days ahead, what?"

Lance passed through the doorway into the big room. It was cool and dim within. He saw movement and her hair like yellow pollen dust. The girl's face was luminous in the purple shadows. He felt her heart beating against his own, and her arms were warm about his neck. After a time he said unsteadily, "Now that the dust has settled . . ."

"When you think of the West, you think of Zane Grey." —*American Cowboy*

ZANE GREY

THE RESTORED, FULL-LENGTH NOVEL, IN PAPERBACK FOR THE FIRST TIME!

The Great Trek

Sterl Hazelton is no stranger to trouble. But the shooting that made him an outlaw was one he didn't do. Though it was his cousin who pulled the trigger, Sterl took the blame, and now he has to leave the country if he wants to stay healthy. Sterl and his loyal friend, Red Krehl, set out for the greatest adventure of their lives, signing on for a cattle drive across the vast northern desert of Australia to the gold fields of the Kimberley Mountains. But it seems no matter where Sterl goes, trouble is bound to follow!

"Grey stands alone in a class untouched by others." —*Tombstone Epitaph*

ISBN 13: 978-0-8439-6062-4

COTTON SMITH

"Cotton Smith is one of the finest of a new breed of writers of the American West."

—Don Coldsmith

Return of the Spirit Rider

In the booming town of Denver, saloon owner Vin Lockhart is known as a savvy businessman with a quick gun. But he will never forget that he was raised an Oglala Sioux. So when Vin's Oglala friends needed help dealing with untruthful, encroaching white men, he swore he would do what he could. His dramatic journey will include encounters with Wild Bill Hickok and Buffalo Bill Cody. But when an ambush leaves him on the brink of death, his only hope is what an old Oglala shaman taught him long ago.

"Cotton Smith is one of the best new authors out there."

—Steven Law, Read West

ISBN 13: 978-0-8439-5854-6

# ☐ YES!

Sign me up for the Leisure Western Book Club and send my FREE BOOKS! If I choose to stay in the club, I will pay only $14.00* each month, a savings of $9.96!

NAME: _____

ADDRESS: _____

TELEPHONE: _____

EMAIL: _____

☐ I want to pay by credit card.

☐ **VISA**   ☐ MasterCard   ☐ DISCOVER

ACCOUNT #: _____

EXPIRATION DATE: _____

SIGNATURE: _____

Mail this page along with $2.00 shipping and handling to:
Leisure Western Book Club
PO Box 6640
Wayne, PA 19087
Or fax (must include credit card information) to:
610-995-9274

You can also sign up online at **www.dorchesterpub.com.**
*Plus $2.00 for shipping. Offer open to residents of the U.S. and Canada only. Canadian residents please call 1-800-481-9191 for pricing information.
If under 18, a parent or guardian must sign. Terms, prices and conditions subject to change. Subscription subject to acceptance. Dorchester Publishing reserves the right to reject any order or cancel any subscription.